This
Holiday
Magic

This Holiday Magic

CELESTE O. NORFLEET
JANICE SIMS
FELICIA MASON

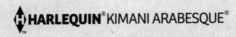

HARLEQUIN® KIMANI ARABESQUE®

This Holiday Magic
ISBN-13: 978-0-373-09162-1

Copyright © 2014 by Harlequin Books S.A.

The publisher acknowledges the copyright holders of the individual works as follows:

A Gift from the Heart
Copyright © 2014 by Celeste O. Norfleet

Mine by Christmas
Copyright © 2014 by Janice Sims

A Family for Christmas
Copyright © 2014 by Felicia Mason

Recycling programs for this product may not exist in your area.

Printed in U.S.A.

www.Harlequin.com

CONTENTS

To Fate & Fortune

A GIFT FROM THE HEART
Celeste O. Norfleet

Chapter 1

"Hey, girl, you were supposed to call me when you got home."

"I didn't call because I'm not home yet."

"What? Where are you?"

Janelle Truman shifted her cell phone to her other ear as she tugged and pulled the collar of her cashmere coat up around her neck. "I'm in a cab. I just left the airport."

"Are you kidding me? Your flight landed almost three and a half hours ago. Why are you just now leaving the airport?"

"Nya, it's Sunday night, three days before Christmas. The security lines are outrageous and Customs took way longer than I expected."

"See, none of this would have happened if you'd just listened to me. I told you I had a friend headed this way from Dubai. He could have easily picked you up in Tanzania, no problem. You would have cleared Customs while sitting on his private plane, sipping champagne and singing Christmas carols. All you had to do was…"

Janelle sighed and rolled her eyes. This was the last thing she needed right now. After an eighteen-hour double shift at the small medical center just outside of Dodoma and then traveling for the past twenty-six hours in every kind of vehicle imaginable, she didn't need a lecture from her stepsister.

Granted, Nya Kent, with her father's money and infinite resources and her own vast connections, was Janelle's go-to person for any problem that needed to be solved, but right now she was a nagging pain.

"…and that would be it. But you never listen to me."

"There's a reason for that, Nya, but right now I'm way too tired to argue with you."

"You're right—get some rest. We'll talk over lunch tomorrow. You can tell me everything."

"Lunch tomorrow," Janelle repeated.

"Well, of course. You didn't think I'd forget our annual pre-Christmas lunch, did you? Unfortunately, Mia can't make it this year with the baby, but I'm flying down in the morning. You don't seriously think I'm not gonna see my big sister after she's been hiding in Africa for the past two and a half years? We have a lunch reservation at the Chesterfield for twelve o'clock."

"I didn't know they were open for lunch."

"They're not," Nya said nonchalantly. "You see, I have this friend who…"

Janelle shook her head. She'd learned long ago that Nya had an uncanny ability to make things happen that others would find nearly impossible. "I'm too tired to ask how you got them to open for lunch. And, for your information, I haven't been hiding in Africa. I've been opening and working in a children's relief clinic. Medics International is an extremely important organization. Their work is vital and I was lucky to help them."

"Like I said, we'll talk about it tomorrow over lunch. It's just a shame Mia won't be able to join us. Apparently our darling little nephew has been keeping her awake day and night. Hey, you're a pediatrician. Can't you do something to help?"

"No, Nya, I can't. He's a baby. That's what they do." She shivered and tugged at her collar again. "Man, I'm freezing."

"Of course you're freezing—it's winter in Baltimore. You have to reacclimatize your body to this weather. You've been hiding in the middle of the Serengeti desert for too long."

"I was not hiding," Janelle insisted.

"Two words. *Tyson Croft.*"

Janelle stilled at Nya's words. Two words, one name—that was all it took to spin her world around all over again. She gripped her collar tighter and tensed as her heart trembled. Then she released a long-held breath. "For the last time, I was not hiding, and Tyson Croft had nothing to do with my going to Africa," Janelle emphasized.

Nya laughed. "Okay, okay, but remember, Janelle—I know you, and I was there. Two and a half years ago you and Tyson had the epic romance of the century. When he walked away, you went all the way to Africa to forget him. Tell me, did it work? Are you over him?"

"Yes," Janelle said too quickly.

"We'll see," Nya said. "And we'll talk about it…" she began.

"I know. I know." Janelle yawned loudly "We'll talk about it tomorrow."

Nya interrupted her yawning. "Girl, you really do sound tired."

"*Tired* isn't the word. I'm worn-out, beat-down, bone-weary exhausted, and on top of that, I'm already beginning to experience symptoms of jet lag from the multiple time-zone changes. My focus is near zero and all I can think about is crawling into my own bed and sleeping for the next few hours."

"Well, I'm just happy you're home. I missed you."

"I missed you, too."

"And you're really finished with Medics International?"

"Yeah, I'm pretty sure I'm done. Five months working all over Africa, five months in Tanzania, seven months in Kenya, six months in Ethiopia and another six months back in Tanzania is enough. The experience was invaluable. As a pediatrician there I learned more in the past few years than in all my years of medical school. But it's time to move on and come home. I just have to give my formal notice."

"Good. All right, get some rest. I'll see you tomorrow."

"Okay, good night."

Janelle ended the call and stifled another yawn as the cab continued through the downtown area. It was almost ten o'clock at night and, surprisingly, the streets were bustling with activity. The stores were still open and holiday shoppers were out and loaded down with bags of gifts. It was less than a week before Christmas and she hadn't done anything.

This used to be her favorite time of year, but that was a long time ago. Now the holidays just seemed to fade in and fade out. She told herself that she was always too busy with school or with work, but she knew that wasn't true. Her mother had died on Christmas Day. Nothing would ever change that.

She yawned again. Right now, the only thing keeping her awake were the too-often craterlike potholes littering the streets that kept her body rocking and rolling like a bobble-headed doll.

No, that wasn't the truth. Who was she kidding? It was Nya's two words that stayed with her. *Tyson Croft.* He had exploded into her life and swept her off her feet. She'd fallen in love with him the second she'd seen him. At one point he'd been everything to her. She'd even considered giving up being a doctor to be with him. But that was another lifetime ago.

She shook her head, as if to clear her thoughts, and then stared out the window, trying to focus on the sights as they passed. Twinkling Christmas lights sparkled down every street, and holiday decorations covered lawns and topped roofs. This was Baltimore, her hometown, a whole world away from the past two and a half years of her life. The city had been torn down, rebuilt, trashed, revitalized and torn down again so many times she'd lost count.

Now everything that was once familiar looked foreign to her. The asphalt streets and concrete sidewalks were a far cry from the arid Serengeti desert and the lush greenery surrounding Mount Kilimanjaro. The cab drove past a sign pointing to the massive Johns Hopkins Hospital complex. She smiled, remembering her years there in med school and during her residency. They had been the best years of her career. She made a mental note to stop by to visit with her friend and mentor, Dr. Richardson. But right now her body needed rest.

She closed her eyes and tried to relax in the tattered leather seat. The scents of the car's pine air freshener and the driver's musk and cheap aftershave assaulted her senses. Years ago the smell would have provoked stomach-wrenching nausea, but not anymore. She'd smelled worse—much worse. Her life was far different from when she'd grown up as the charmed daughter of a wealthy real-estate developer.

She hadn't spoken to her father in a few days, so he had no idea she was coming home. He didn't expect her until after the holidays. She smiled. This was going to be the perfect surprise holiday gift for him.

The cab turned the corner and drove down the quiet street. It stopped in front of her two-story town house, located just a few blocks from Inner Harbor. She smiled, looking up at her own private sanctuary. A gift from her father when she'd graduated medical school, it had been hers for five years, but she had yet to really live there.

Janelle paid the driver, giving him a generous tip. He immediately hopped out, helped gather her luggage from the trunk and placed it up the steps by the front door.

Now, barely half-awake, she unlocked the front door, turned off the security system and then immediately stopped. Her heart lurched as she slowly looked around. Something was very wrong.

She must have been too tired to realize it. This wasn't her town house. For one thing, this home had furniture. Hers didn't, except for a bedroom set. "Oh, my God," she whispered, realizing she'd just broken into some-one's home. She quietly stepped back and looked at the address number plate beneath the outside security light, then checked the front-door key still in her hand. It had opened the door with ease and her coded number had turned off the security alarm, so this had to be her home. She continued into the small foyer. That was when she heard the laughter and realized that she wasn't alone. Her heart jumped.

There was only one logical conclusion—squatters.

The word leaped out at her like a snake from the bush. She tensed just thinking it. She was all too familiar with squatters. They were extremely common in many places in Africa. Mostly displaced refugees in fear of their lives, they moved into an area and took over completely. Some were compliant and assimilated with ease. Others were more fierce and forceful. They came. They usurped the resources. They stayed. Getting them to leave was nearly impossible. She continued looking around, knowing already that this was going to be a nightmare.

She walked in and examined the living-room area more closely. There were no crates, wooden pallets, cushions or discarded debris on the floor. No empty alcohol bottles, no drug paraphernalia and no stomach-turning stench.

Instead there was a huge television, beautiful Oriental rugs, stunning accent tables with lamps and very-expensive-looking mahogany wood furniture. None of which was hers. Her once-rigid and antiseptic living environment, devoid of personal effects, was now a family setting ripped from the pages of *Architectural Digest*. So, unless squatters had upgraded their game a thousand percent, there was something else going on here.

She relaxed a bit, then took a few more steps into the room, noting a cartoon movie muted and frozen on the large flat-screen television. There was also a kid's puzzle and a few children's books scattered on the floor. The last thing she needed to deal with right now was a squatting family with children at Christmastime.

"Who are you?"

Janelle turned quickly and looked down, seeing a small child peeking around the corner at her. She was holding a doll and wearing pink pajamas with a sparkling little crown on her head.

"You're not s'posed to be here," the child added. "This is my daddy's castle."

"No, sweetheart," Janelle said slowly, "I am supposed to be here. This is my home."

"Aneka, who are you talking to, child?" asked a female voice.

"The lady with the bags," the little girl said.

"What lady with the bags?"

"Hello?" Janelle called out to whoever was with the child.

"Who the…?" There was a loud rush of movement and an older woman came hurrying out from the kitchen area. "Aneka, get over here now. Who are you? We don't have any money and we're not…" She stopped and looked more closely at Janelle.

An instant later she smiled joyfully. "Well, I'll be. Janelle, child, is that you?" The woman walked over, grinning from ear to ear, her arms wide-open. She grabbed Janelle in a huge bear hug. "Welcome home."

"Mrs. Ivers," Janelle said, finally recognizing the older woman as her neighbor from across the street.

"Well, of course it's me. Who else would it be? Child, you scared me half to death. You're a sight for sore eyes. It's been almost a year since you've been home."

"Mrs. Ivers, what are you doing here?"

"Me? Babysitting. What in the world are you doing coming in here this late at night?"

"I live here," she said with uncertainty as she looked around. "At least, I used to live here. It doesn't much look like I do anymore."

"Well, of course you live here." Mrs. Ivers's smile widened. "Where else would you live? It's so good to see you. You must be exhausted. But I thought you weren't coming home until after the first of the year. At least that's what your father told me."

"Mrs. Ivers, what's going on? Why are you here with this little girl? Who is she and where are all my things?"

"Oh, your father had everything moved out and put in storage about a month ago. I'm here babysitting Aneka while her father's at work. He should be home soon."

"I still don't understand. Who are these people, and why are they living in my house?"

"Your father said it would be okay for the time being."

"My father?" she questioned. "Why would he say that? Why wouldn't I mind my home being taken over while I'm away?" she added sarcastically as she pulled out her cell phone and called her father's home. There was no answer.

She called his cell phone. Again, no answer. She sighed. "He must be out to dinner or in a meeting."

"Things have changed, Janelle."

"What do you mean?" Janelle asked. Just then the microwave beeped. Mrs. Ivers turned and headed back into the kitchen. Seconds later the aroma of buttered popcorn filled the room. Janelle followed the scent and the little girl trailed after her.

"My name is Princess Aneka," she said as her tiny little fingers held tight to her doll.

Janelle looked down at the mass of dark curls and ringlets looping just below her shoulders. Her dark eyes shone brightly as she looked up. The child was adorable. "It's very nice to meet you, Princess Aneka," Janelle said as she continued into her kitchen. "Mrs. Ivers, I'm exhausted. Would you please just take Aneka to your house? We can straighten all this out tomorrow."

"Perhaps you should speak with your father first. My guess is that he's still at the office."

"No, he never works this late," Janelle said as she looked at her watch, realizing that it was still on Tanzania time.

"That was before."

"What do you mean? Before what?"

"You need to talk to your father," Mrs. Ivers reiterated.

Janelle shook her head with annoyance. All she wanted was to go to sleep, but that was clearly not going to happen anytime soon. "Fine."

She dialed her father's private office number, expecting no answer since the company should have been closed hours earlier. To her surprise someone picked up the phone.

"Truman Developers."

Janelle frowned. It was a man's voice, but not her father's. The voice seemed familiar, but that was impossible. It couldn't be. "Yes, I'd like to speak with Ben Truman, please."

"He's unavailable at the moment."

"Just tell him it's his daughter."

"Janelle?" he said.

"Yes. Who is this?"

There was a short pause as the man's voice softened. "I'm sorry. Your father's unavailable. You might want to call back tomorrow morning."

"No, I don't want to call back tomorrow morning. I need to speak with him tonight, right now."

"I'm sorry. I'll tell him you called."

"Fine," she snapped. Annoyed, she disconnected the call and looked across the kitchen. "What's going on, Mrs. Ivers?"

Mrs. Ivers shook her head. "Your father ran into some financial trouble a while back. He's working on fixing it."

"What do you mean 'financial trouble'? What's going on and who's the man answering my father's private line this late at night?"

"Go to the office, Janelle, and talk to your father. Here, take my car," Mrs. Ivers said as she grabbed her purse and began digging for her keys. She found them and handed them to Janelle.

Two minutes later Janelle was out the door and headed to the Truman Building. The usual thirty-minute drive took less than twenty.

As soon as Janelle drove up to the building, she looked up, seeing that the lights in her father's office were still on. She parked the car and hurried inside. The security guard she'd known for years greeted and welcomed her back. She signed in and took the elevator to the top floor.

Her thoughts raced as she hurried down the long hallway. Her father was unavailable and there was a strange man in his office. At this point she had no idea what to expect. She turned the corner and saw that her father's office door was cracked open. She could see a light shining from inside. She knocked once but didn't bother to wait for a reply, opening the door wider and peeking inside. "Dad…"

For the second time that night a shocking sight met her eyes.

Chapter 2

When Janelle had called, Tyson Croft had held on to the receiver, forgetting all about hanging it up. As soon as he picked up and she had spoken, his heart had faltered. There was no need to ask who was calling. He had known it was her even before she had said who was speaking. The sound of her sultry voice was unmistakable. He closed his eyes as a slow, easy smile pulled wide across his lips.

"Janelle," he had whispered softly and then shaken his head slowly. Hearing her voice again after two long years was like awakening from a long deep slumber. His body stirred just as it had done so many times before.

He remembered what it was like walking away from her years ago. It had nearly broken him, but he hadn't had a choice at the time. Now he *did* have a choice. And nothing—and no one—was going to stand in his way this time.

"All righty, then. This ought to just about do it."

Tyson quickly hung up the phone. Ben Truman bumped the office door wider as he walked through carrying another lidded cardboard box. Tyson nonchalantly cleared his throat and nodded, looking back at the computer monitor.

He had no idea how long he'd been holding the phone receiver. Thoughts of Janelle had clouded his mind again. It had been happening more and more lately.

"There're a couple more boxes in the storage room, but I doubt they have anything in them that will be useful. Was that my phone I heard ringing?" Ben asked.

"Uh, yes. It was Janelle."

Ben frowned as he set the container down on the small conference table in the center of his office with the other boxes. "Janelle, huh? That's surprising. I didn't expect her call."

"What do you mean?" Tyson asked, looking more interested.

"She usually calls me at home, and this isn't her usual day. She calls on Sundays. I hope everything's all right over there."

Tyson instantly tensed. "I thought you said she's safe where she is in Africa. Is there a possible problem where she's assigned?"

"Well, for the time being, she is safe. But you know as well as I do that my daughter is a dedicated physician. Wherever they need her, she'll go. She's almost eight thousand miles away in an unstable region…" Ben said, then stopped, seeing the horrified look on Tyson's face.

"But no, I'm sure she's fine. As you well know, Janelle is a brilliant doctor and a very levelheaded woman. She'd never intentionally put herself in danger. She's very capable and can certainly take care of herself, even in the middle of Africa. I'm sure she's fine. I'm just surprised she called me here at the office. She knows I don't work this late."

"When is she coming back stateside?"

"In a couple more months. She said February or March."

Tyson nodded, not feeling at all reassured. "Maybe you should call her back just to make sure everything's okay," he suggested eagerly, failing miserably to play down his uneasiness.

"Yeah, I think I will." Ben nodded and pulled out his cell phone, only to see that the signal was gone and the phone was turned off. "Damn, no signal. I forgot to charge the battery this afternoon. No wonder she called me here." He crossed the room to use the phone on the desk.

Tyson grabbed his cell phone off the desk, stood and quickly handed it to Ben. "Here, use my cell phone," he offered. "It's international. It'll reach anywhere in the world."

Ben nodded, took Tyson's phone and dialed Janelle's number. The call rang six times, then went to her voice mail. "No answer," Ben said, looking at his watch.

"Where exactly is Janelle in Africa?" Tyson asked as he continued working.

"Tanzania, but she moves around a lot. Three weeks ago she was in Dodoma. Last week she was in Dar es Salaam. But one thing for sure, she calls me every Sunday evening to let me know where she is and that she's okay."

"And is she—" Tyson paused to look up "—okay?"

"That's a matter of opinion. She's lost faith."

"Faith? How do you mean?"

"She lost faith in love, in her ability to love and be loved."

"Because of me," Tyson said flatly, laying his pen on the desk. He walked over to the window, glancing out.

"Because of a lot of things, son," Ben said, sitting with a stack of files at his side. "Truthfully, I'm right there with you. Since her mother died, I've had three different wives. She's seen me in and out of love dozens of times. For the past two and a half years she's thrown herself into work and had time for nothing else. You might have been the last straw, but I was right there, too. If there's one thing I want more than anything, more than cleaning this mess up, it is to help her love again."

Tyson's heart tightened from the pain that gripped it.

Janelle had lost faith in love and he was partially responsible. But at least she was physically safe. He nodded slowly, but he wasn't at all satisfied.

Sitting, he absently glanced at his notes and then back at the monitor. All of a sudden the program he had been using for years didn't make any sense. His notes were a confusing scramble of numbers and notations that made even less sense.

Tyson looked over at Ben, who had begun talking about his last trip to visit his daughter. The more Ben went on, the edgier Tyson got.

"I tell you, the moment I stepped off the plane I was amazed," Ben said. "The country is the perfect duality—both stunningly beautiful and horrendously terrifying. I tell you, every moment I was there I was…"

Tyson looked back at the monitor again. There was no use—his focus was shot. Everything he'd done in the past three hours meant absolutely nothing. All he could think about now was Janelle's safety.

Ben had moved on to a story about shopping in an African marketplace, but Tyson had long since stopped paying attention. Unlike her father, he wasn't as convinced that everything was all right with Janelle. He didn't want to alarm the man, but there'd been something in Janelle's voice that was definitely stressed. He hadn't liked the sound of it. But calling her back to make sure she was okay was out of the question. He was the last person she'd want to hear from. He was one of the reasons she'd joined Medics International and left for Africa in the first place—to get away from him.

Still, two and a half years was a long time. There was a good chance she would have gotten past their relationship's ending. The nerve in his neck tightened and his jaw tensed. Yeah, he had messed up. He'd let his ego and his ambition overrule his heart. Walking out on Janelle had been the biggest mistake of his life.

"Okay, here it is. I knew it was packed away in one of these old boxes someplace. This ought to do it." Ben sighed as he placed an accordion file on the desk. "I believe everything you're gonna need is in here. Hey, you okay, son?"

Tyson looked up and nodded. "Uh, yeah. I'm fine."

"Are you sure? You look a little distracted."

"No, I'm good," Tyson said, picking up his pen and turning back to the monitor. He didn't want to tell Ben the truth, that he'd been thinking about Janelle. "I'm just a little tired."

"I can certainly understand that. You work all day at your business and then you come here in the evenings and work on my mine. You've been a godsend. I really don't know how to thank you."

"How about getting us a cup of coffee?" Tyson suggested.

"Done," Ben responded, hurrying to the door. "I'll make a fresh pot. Cream and two sugars. I'll be right back."

"Thanks."

Tyson looked at the computer monitor. He was right back where he'd started; nowhere. Moments later he tossed the pen onto the desk and sat back in the chair. Coffee was a ruse. He'd just needed Ben out of the office.

Restless, edgy, he stood and walked over to the window again. He closed his eyes and shook his head. Hearing her voice had brought it all back.

"Damn," he whispered. This wasn't what he'd expected. But in truth, he didn't know what he had thought would happen. When he'd agreed to review Ben's finances and help pull him out of bankruptcy, he had been thinking only about getting Janelle back. It had been a long shot and probably wouldn't work, but he'd try.

He looked up at the night sky. He was tired. But that was not what was distracting him and he knew it. She was his own personal drug—just one spark was all it took to reignite his passion. "Janelle," he said softly, moving back to the desk to force himself to focus on the job.

The knock on the office door was soft. He didn't look up, assuming it was Ben coming back with the coffee. It wasn't until he heard her voice and her gasp that he looked up and saw her standing there. His eyes widened; then, just as quickly, a wave of emotional relief washed through him. She was back, she was safe and she was here with him again.

Chapter 3

"Dad! Ho, ho, ho! Merry Christmas. Surprise!" Janelle called out as she opened the door to her father's office.

She stopped, stunned, and shook her head. She could not believe what she was seeing. Her heart lurched. This was impossible. A small gasp escaped her lips.

As he looked up at her, his eyes narrowed, holding her still. He appeared just as stunned and confused as she was. She stood there for what seemed like forever, her questioning eyes cemented to a face she hadn't seen in more than two years.

He was still as handsome as ever. Surprisingly, he was clean-shaven now, without the always perfectly cut goatee he'd had years ago. He was casually attired, having removed his jacket, but even so, he was still perfectly styled. Impressively tall with broad shoulders and a narrow waist, he wore a dark dress shirt, unbuttoned at the neck, with a loosened tie. His sleeves were rolled up, baring the strong solid strength of his arms.

Seeing Tyson Croft sitting at her father's desk was like pouring salt into a healing wound. For her own sake, she had long ago released the anger and the pain she had felt when he'd left. She had moved on, was over him and had never been happier with her life than she was now.

But now, for some reason, a sudden rush of emotion she'd long ago set aside began to envelop her. The hurt was still there. Janelle realized that she had never quite sealed that door. She watched as his gaze eased down her body, then came up and steadied on her face.

"Janelle," he whispered softly.

The eerie misplaced feeling of seeing something or someone who didn't belong in a familiar location stunned her to silence. She swallowed hard, trying to dislodge the impossibly huge lump in her throat. How was this possible? How could the last man on earth she ever wanted to see again be sitting there, staring straight at her?

Then it hit her. The diagnosis was obvious. Among the plethora of symptoms for extreme exhaustion and jet lag was hallucinations. That had to be it. She smiled at the absurdity of her mind's twisted sense of humor. She had been thinking about Tyson a lot lately and her subconscious had tuned in, so of course, here he was.

Then the fabricated image slowly stood. "Hello, Janelle," it said, smiling cautiously.

Wow. This specter was amazing. It seemed so real, so much like Tyson, who was exactly the same as she remembered…same deep soul-stirring voice, same knee-buckling smile and same drop-dead-gorgeous body.

She gazed at the face she knew so well. He was still handsome with keen angular lines and dark sexy bedroom eyes framed with long curly lashes. High cheekbones added to his classic features and his mouth was bowed just right with perfect fullness, his lips soft, firm and always so damn kissable. He was a confident man who had wealth and power. In all respects he was everything any woman could ever want and then some. She shook her head again. Even when he appeared as an illusion, the lean perfection of his body made her stomach flutter. She stared, unable to look away. Why did this vision have to be of him? She watched as his lips moved.

Then he smiled and suddenly everything seemed all too real. A few seconds passed. It really was Tyson Croft standing there.

"Janelle, you're here," he said happily. "You…you look—"

"Tyson," she said quietly, releasing a breath she hadn't even realized she'd been holding.

"Yes, it's me," he said softly. "God, it's so good to see you. Your father and I were so worried about you." He paused. "Is everything okay? Are you okay?"

Speechless, she nodded her head slowly.

"Good. Well, welcome home. You look exhausted."

Fate has a wicked sense of humor, Janelle thought to herself. It had taken her two years to get over the anger and pain of not having him in her life. Now here he was all over again. "What are you doing in my father's office?" she asked, looking around the room. "Where is my father?"

"Ben stepped out. He'll be back in a few minutes." He smiled, concern still shadowing his face. "Janelle, you have no idea how relieved I am to see you. When you called earlier, we were…" He paused. "I'm just glad you're home safe," he said, staring at her. "Are you going to scowl at me all night?"

"Probably. Answer my question, Tyson. What are you doing here?"

He looked down. "I'm working."

She scoffed. "What do you mean? My father would never agree to have you working here."

"I am. I'm working with your father."

She shook her head. "No, that's impossible." She boldly moved to the center of the room.

"Nonetheless, here I am," he said, gesturing around the office. "Your father said you were still in Africa. When did you get back?" Tyson talked as though nothing had ever happened between them, as if he had never walked out on her and their life together. He came from behind the desk toward her, talking, but she didn't hear what he said.

She looked at him, astonished. The audacity of his presumption was mind-boggling. But that was typical Tyson— totally arrogant and completely self-absorbed. The world revolved solely around him. How dare he presume he had the right to comment on her looks, on her life, as though what had happened between them had never happened?

"No. No," she said, seething with anger and holding her hand up to silence him. "You don't get to just come up in here and chat with me like there's nothing between us."

His expression instantly changed. "Janelle, I know you're probably still angry and upset, and you have every right to be."

"I'm not. I got over that a long time ago."

He shook his head. "You're angry, trust me," he said.

"How dare you?" She smiled and chuckled.

"Janelle…" Tyson began.

"Don't 'Janelle' me!"

"I understand your feelings. I just need you to know that I…" He paused.

"That you what?" she said slowly. "Tell me—what could you possibly say to me that would change what happened between us? You see, silly me, I believed you back then. I believed in you, and you turned your back on me. So, no, sorry, I'm not that naive person anymore. You tore my life apart once before, but never again. You walked out on me. You don't get to just walk back into my life now like it was no big deal. Like I said, I got over you a long time ago."

He nodded slowly and lowered his head. "Why don't you just ask me what you really want to?" he said softly. When he looked back up at her, his eyes were piercing. "How could I leave you?"

She looked at him, hurt. All of a sudden the old pain became fresh again. With one question, it had all come back. Yes, she'd wondered about the answer to that one question, but she refused to give him the satisfaction of asking what it was. She had vowed a long time ago that he would never affect her again. But right now, just seeing him standing there, brought up feelings she had thought long buried.

"Janelle…"

"Where is my father?" she asked. Her eyes narrowed in mistrust as she planted her balled fists on her hips.

"He's unavailable."

"You're starting to sound like a broken record. Where is he?" she repeated.

"He's getting coffee in the break room."

She looked around her father's office. It was usually neat, but now there were half-open boxes, files and paper everywhere. It was a cluttered mess. "What's going on with my father's company? Is this your next acquisition?"

He looked hurt. "Do you seriously think that little of me?"

"You're kidding me, right?"

He smiled and nodded. "Yeah, I guess I deserved that." The raw, intense hunger she saw in his eyes made her take a step back. Her stomach shuddered. She swallowed hard, needing to regroup quickly. "Janelle…"

"You need to leave."

"I can't. I promised your father I'd do what I could to help him, and I will."

"He doesn't need your help anymore. He has me now."

"Yes, he does. But you can't help him with this."

"Tyson, leave now or I'll call security and have you physically thrown out of here—your choice."

"Janelle, this isn't about you and me. This is about your father, his company and his freedom."

"What do you mean?"

"You'll have to ask him."

"I'm asking you. Tell me."

"He needs my help and I promised him I'd do whatever I can. Your father is a brilliant businessman, but sometimes solely focusing on winning at all costs causes you to lose everything in the end."

"What do you mean?" she asked. He didn't reply. "You're not going to tell me? Fine." She marched over to the desk, reached around him and grabbed the office phone from the cradle. Before she could lift it, Tyson quickly covered her hand with his to stop her.

Just inches apart, their eyes locked. Intense emotions slammed into her like an anvil falling at high velocity. Her heart thudded in her chest as she held her breath. This wasn't supposed to be happening. She wasn't supposed to be feeling anything, but yet she was. She was over him and he wasn't going to get to her again. "Save it. I'm immune. Your bad-boy charm doesn't work on me anymore."

"Doesn't it?" he asked quietly.

She glared at him, holding her ground. They both knew he was lethal to any woman. But she wasn't going to back down. "Move your hand now, Tyson," she warned through gritted teeth.

"I left for a reason."

"I don't really care about your reason."

"Yes, you do."

"Understand this, Mr. Croft. You don't know me anymore. You knew that quiet, shy, young woman right out of medical school more than two years ago. She wore rose-colored glasses and thought there'd always be a happy ending in her life, no matter what. Well, she was wrong and she's long gone."

"I hope not. I missed her. I missed you," he whispered gently.

Janelle's heart lurched. His voice was too tender and

his eyes were too sincere. "Why are you doing this?" she asked.

He looked away and gently squeezed her hand. "Because I can't stop thinking about you, because I can't stop wanting you and because I can't stop loving…"

"Stop! Enough! I don't want to hear it." She raised her voice.

"Janelle, is that you?"

Janelle turned around quickly to see her father standing in the doorway, holding two coffee cups. A radiant smile instantly spread across her face. She snatched her hand away from the phone and ran over to him.

Setting down the cups, he met her halfway and they embraced long and hard. Moments later he pulled back and gently held her face in his hands. He stared closely, then nodded. "Yes, you're okay?"

She smiled and nodded as tears rolled down her face. "Yes, I am now."

"God, I missed you," Ben said.

She laughed, half crying for joy. "I missed you, too, Dad."

Janelle and Ben hugged again, and then he held her close as he turned to Tyson, smiling. "My little girl's back."

Tyson grinned. "Yes, she certainly is. I'm gonna fax these letters out. I'll be back in a few minutes."

"Dad, you look so tired."

Ben eyed his daughter happily. "Funny, I was just about to say the same thing about you. When did you get here?"

"Just now," she said.

"No. I mean when did you get back from Africa?"

"About three hours ago. I was stuck in Customs for a while. It feels like I've been on the road forever. I left Dar es Salaam over twenty-five hours ago."

"What? It doesn't take that long to get here from Tanzania."

"I know, but I grabbed the first flight, and unfortunately, the last-minute plans made travel a nightmare."

"Well, you're here now and that's all that matters."

"Dad, tell me what's going on. Why, of all people, is Tyson Croft here in your office? He said he was working with you."

"It's nothing for you to be concerned about, sweetheart. He's working a few things out for me.... Just some minor business matters."

"Dad, you know Tyson can't be trusted. You know what he does for a living. The man gobbles up businesses and breaks them apart and sells them to the highest bidder. There's no way he's here to help you."

"I am," Tyson said, standing in the office doorway.

Janelle turned and glared at him.

"Janelle, you're going to have to trust me on this. He is here to help. I know you and Tyson have a strained past and, from the sound of it when I walked into the office earlier, a questionable present, but I'm going to need for you to put all that aside, at least for the time being. I need Tyson, I need you and I need a truce," Ben said.

She looked away, refusing to answer.

"So—" he began, smiling again "—not that I'm not delighted to see you, but what are you doing here? You weren't supposed to come back until next year. What happened?"

"I'm fine. My relief arrived early, so I decided to surprise you and come home for the Christmas holidays. I guess the surprise was on me since I went to my house and found my neighbor Mrs. Ivers there with a little girl. She told me it was your idea for the child's family to move in."

"Yes, it was my idea. I needed them here quickly and they needed a place to stay. Your house was empty and it was perfect."

"I don't understand. Admittedly, the little girl is absolutely adorable, but why was it so important for her family to live in my house? Who's her family?"

"I'm her family. Aneka is my daughter," Tyson said.

His pronouncement stunned her. Tyson had a daughter? She had had no idea. Her heart tumbled. The math wasn't that difficult to figure out. The girl had to be at least four years old. That meant that Tyson had been a father the whole time they were together and he'd never said a word.

Suddenly it all made sense. The months of romantic bliss they had spent together had just been a momentary interlude for him. The reason he'd left her was to go back to his real family. "Your daughter? You have a *child*," she said incredulously.

"Ben," he said, "I'm almost done here. We just have a few more things to tie up. I can move us to a hotel for a few days and..."

"It's the holidays," Ben protested. "I'm sure Janelle wouldn't want you and your daughter out in the street this time of year. Janelle, what do you think about coming home and staying at the big house with your dear old dad for a few days? It'll be good to have my daughter back under the roof again, at least for a little while. And I could certainly use the company. The house gets awfully quiet sometimes. What do you think?"

Both Tyson and Ben looked at Janelle. But she couldn't focus on her dad. She was still stuck on the fact that Tyson had been a father the whole time they'd been together. It took her a moment to catch up with what was going on around her. "Um, yeah, sure, that's fine. Stay at the house with your daughter...your family," she said awkwardly.

"Thank you," Tyson said.

"Good. That's all settled," Ben declared. "Tyson, why don't we call it a night and pick this up tomorrow evening?" Tyson nodded his agreement and walked over to

Ben's desk. "Janelle, give me a few minutes to get some things put away and then we'll head out."

"I just have to go by my house and pick up my suitcases. I left them in the foyer. Also, I borrowed Mrs. Ivers's car, so I'm going to need a ride to the big house."

"I'll take you." Tyson spoke up quickly.

"No," Janelle said just as fast. "No, that's okay."

"She's right, Tyson. It's late. I'm sure Mrs. Ivers needs to get home and your daughter needs you there now." He turned to Janelle. "I'll meet you at your house when I finish up here. It shouldn't be too long." He kissed Janelle's forehead.

Janelle nodded and walked out. Tyson grabbed his briefcase and followed. They shared the elevator down to the first floor and exited the building together. Each got into their respective cars and drove away in the same direction without a single word.

So much for a holiday at home, she thought to herself as she drove off.

Chapter 4

Twenty minutes later they arrived at her town house. In silence side by side, Janelle and Tyson walked up the short path to the front door. As soon as they got to the top step they stopped. Standing beneath the security lights over the door, each had a front-door key in hand. "You go ahead," she said, motioning for him to step up and open the front door.

"No," he said, stepping back. "Please, it's your home. After you." She put her key in the lock and turned the latch. "Are we just going to ignore this and pretend?" he asked.

"I'm tired, Tyson. I don't feel like playing games tonight."

"This isn't a game, Janelle," he assured her.

"Fine, let's pretend. How about we play a game called 'truth or truth'?"

He sighed. "I'll tell you whatever you want to know." His eyes sparkled beneath the lights.

"I can't believe you. One day you were there, we were talking about getting married and starting a life together, and all of a sudden the next day you were gone."

He was stunned by her comment. "Janelle, my leaving

had nothing to do with what I feel for you. It was about me. I needed time. I needed to go. But when I came back you were gone."

She scoffed. "What a surprise, and so convenient. At least be original. Isn't that always the go-to excuse? 'Oh, no, baby,'" she mocked, "'it's not you. It's me. It's not that I'm through with you now, or that I was just using you to kill time. I'm just leaving you to go back to my real family now.'"

"Is that what you think? That I had another family someplace else? That I left you because I was through with you?"

"Are you going to seriously stand there and tell me I'm wrong with your daughter and probably your wife waiting inside?" She stopped suddenly. The thought of coming face-to-face with Tyson's wife sent a stunned shock wave through her system.

An instant later the door opened. Janelle held her breath. Mrs. Ivers stood there, smiling at them. "I thought I heard voices. Why are you two standing out here in the cold? Come on inside."

"Good evening, Mrs. Ivers," Tyson said.

"Hi, Mrs. Ivers. Thank you so much for loaning me your car."

"Hello, Tyson. Janelle, is everything straightened out?"

"Yes, I'm going to stay at my dad's house for a while. I just came back to drop off your keys and pick up my luggage." Janelle handed her the car keys.

"Oh, dear, I already put your bags upstairs in the master bedroom. I can go get them."

"No, no, that's okay. I'll get them," Janelle said, walking toward the stairs quickly. Then she stopped and turned. "Mrs. Ivers, is there someone upstairs?"

"Someone, yes. Aneka is upstairs, asleep in her room," Mrs. Ivers said, looking at Tyson curiously.

As she climbed, Janelle glanced behind her and saw Tyson watching her. She quickened her pace. She wanted to get her things and get out—and away from Tyson—as soon as possible.

She continued down the hall, opened the already-slightly-open door wider, stepped inside and looked around. A dim light shone from a lamp on a night table beside the large king-size bed; the drapes were open, allowing moonlight to beam in, giving the room a warm, cozy glow. Just as the living room downstairs, it was fully furnished and beautifully decorated with stunning furniture that wasn't hers.

She spotted her bags on a cozy love seat in the alcove beneath the bay window. Grabbing one of the handles, she pulled it to the floor. As soon as she did, it tumbled open and a mass of clothing fell to her feet. She knelt and began stuffing things back inside.

"Here, let me help you."

She stiffened, hearing Tyson's voice as he knelt beside her. He picked up her hair dryer, curling iron and several pieces of intimate apparel.

"I have it," she said, quickly taking everything from him and zipping the suitcase up again.

He stood and reached down his open hand to her. She stared at his hand without responding. "I won't bite you, Janelle. I promise." She took a deep breath and took his hand and stood.

A few seconds passed, her hand still in his. They stood toe to toe, staring at each other in the muted darkness. Neither spoke; Janelle didn't even dare to breathe. For the first time that evening there was a silent moment of peace between them.

"You're wrong," he said softly, answering her earlier question. "I'll take these downstairs." She nodded and followed, and then she stopped when movement in the bed caught her eye. He set the bags down, then walked over to

lean down at the side of the bed. Janelle watched his move-
ments. That was when she saw the tiny figure snuggled beneath the covers, holding tight to the bride doll Janelle had
brought back from Africa. She walked over and stood near.

"Daddy…" The little girl moaned softly and reached
out to him.

"Shh, I'm here. Go back to sleep," he whispered, giving her a hug and a kiss on her forehead.

After tucking the covers over the child, Tyson straightened and smiled. Janelle instantly saw the unconditional
love he had for his daughter in his eyes. It was heartwarming to see.

"That's not her doll," Tyson said, turning to Janelle.

"No, it's not. It's mine."

"It's beautiful."

"It's a handcrafted Ndebele bride doll. A friend of mine
gave it to me before I left. It represents a bride on her wedding day. It's supposed to be a blessing for a happy, healthy
family and future."

"It looks expensive."

"I don't know about that, but it's sentimental. It was in
the side pocket of my luggage. I guess Aneka found it. That
would explain why the suitcases were open."

He sighed heavily while shaking his head. "I'm sorry.
She's in a curious stage right now—she's into everything."
He reached down to retrieve the doll, but Aneka's little fin-
gers gripped it tightly as she rolled to the side.

Janelle touched his arm. "No, don't take it away from
her," she whispered. "I'll get it another time."

"Are you sure?"

"Yes, of course."

"Thank you. I'll get it back to you. I promise."

"No problem," she said softly, then paused. "She is beautiful."

He smiled proudly. "Yes, she is, and she's a handful."

"I bet. How old is she? Four?" Janelle ventured.

"Almost. She'll be four years old next month. But, to tell you the truth, she's more like fourteen."

"Let me guess. Nonstop energy and fiercely independent."

He nodded continuously. "Oh, yes, and then some. Running, jumping, skipping, dancing… You name it, she does it. Her favorite storybook character right now is Tigger, the tiger from *Winnie-the-Pooh*. She hops and jumps everywhere. And of course she wears her princess dress and her crown when she does."

"Of course," Janelle said, smiling.

"But she's also kind, generous, creative and wonderfully imaginative. She loves to draw and play make-believe. She insists on choosing her own clothes, even if nothing matches, and she's a sponge for learning new things. And, admittedly, she has me wrapped around her little finger."

Janelle smiled. "Daddy's little girl."

"Yes, she certainly is," Tyson said as Aneka stirred.

"She has your heart. That's how it should be." Janelle looked closer at the little sleeping angel. Her features were soft and innocent and her skin was honey-toned, far lighter than Tyson's deep, rich cinnamon complexion. Her hair, a light brown hue, was lightly tinted with reddish-blond highlights. All at once it occurred to her that Aneka bore very little resemblance to Tyson. "She must look like her mother," she said without thinking.

"Yes, she does," Tyson replied.

Suddenly, Janelle realized where the conversation might lead. She wasn't ready to talk about Tyson having another woman in his life. She took a step back. "I'd better go. My dad is probably waiting outside for me."

"Janelle…" Tyson began, turning to her.

"Daddy," the little girl muttered again.

Tyson turned back to his daughter.

"Don't worry about the bags. I'll pick them up tomorrow. Take care of your daughter." She turned and walked out.

Seconds later she was opening the front door and stepping outside.

She took a deep breath. A sudden rush of crisp cold December air chilled her lungs. It was a welcome sensation; she needed the intense shock to her senses. Exhaustion and jet lag had apparently gotten the best of her. She'd actually had a civil conversation with Tyson Croft.

She looked up at the full moon and wrapped her hands around her arms and shivered. It seemed a lot colder than it used to be around Christmastime, or maybe she just needed to get used to the seasonal weather again.

The door opened behind her. She didn't have to look to know it was Tyson.

"Janelle, can we talk?" he asked.

"There's nothing left for either of us to say," she said.

"Yes, actually there is. I'm sorry."

She turned to him. "Is this your attempt at closure?"

"No, it's a sincere apology for walking away like I did. I know it's long overdue, but I still need you to know that I'm sorry for what happened between us."

Janelle looked away without responding. Car lights turned the corner a block away. A few seconds later she recognized her father's car approaching. "Here comes my dad," she said, stepping down to the walkway.

"Aneka's mother—"

"Look, it's your life. It's none of my business. I really don't need to know this," she quickly interrupted.

"Yes, you do. Aneka's mother died two and a half years ago in a car accident."

Janelle paused and took a deep breath. "I'm sorry for your loss and I'm sorry for Aneka. It's difficult growing up without a mother," she said, knowing from her own past experience.

"Her father is— Her father was my cousin, Girard. He survived the accident, but died a few months later from his injuries. Aneka is my goddaughter and as of two and a half years ago, I'm her legal guardian."

Janelle looked at him, speechless. This wasn't what she'd expected to hear. "I'm sorry. I know you and he were very close."

"We were, and now his daughter is my daughter."

Neither spoke for a few minutes.

Janelle sighed heavily. "I was surprised to see you here. You're the last person I ever expected to see again."

"Yeah, I'm full of surprises these days."

She looked at him sternly. "Nothing's changed. Just because my father seems to need you doesn't mean I do or ever will again."

He nodded. "I deserve that."

"Yes, you do. And stop being so damn understanding. You were never that way before."

"Really? What was I like?"

"Ruthless," she said.

"Yeah." He nodded slowly. "I guess I was."

She grimaced at him. "Wow. Enlightenment. So, what did you do, climb a mountain or chat with a shaman or something?"

He smiled. "Or something."

"What do you want from me, Tyson? A reprieve? Absolution? My blessing to move on with your life? What?"

"Right now I'll settle for a cease-fire." He extended his hand.

She looked at him and then nodded slowly. She was too tired to object. They shook hands and a small smile pulled at her lips. "Cease-fire it is."

"Perfect timing, I'd say," Ben said as he got out of his

car and waved. "Glad to see you two have settled your issues."

Tyson picked up her luggage, which he'd brought down with him, and walked over to the car. Janelle followed, but headed to the passenger-side door as Ben opened the trunk and Tyson put her luggage inside. She waited, listening as the two men stood and talked a moment.

She shook her head. She had no idea what was really going on with her father's business and Tyson, but she was definitely going to find out. The trunk closed and her father walked to the front of the car. She looked into the passenger-side mirror and saw Tyson standing there, waiting.

His apology had been sincere, but there was no way she was going to let him into her life again. He'd hurt her before and she was not going to allow that to happen again.

Ben got into the car and looked over at his daughter. "Well, sweets, are you ready to go home?" he asked.

"Yes, I'm ready," Janelle said.

As the car pulled away from the curb and drove down the street, she glanced in the side-view mirror again. Tyson was still standing at the curb. She watched him watch her until the car turned the next corner.

Closing her eyes, she relaxed for the first time in days. She was on her way home once more.

Minutes later she climbed the stairs to her childhood room and lay on the bed. Within a matter of seconds she was fast asleep.

After standing at the curb and watching Ben's car drive away, Tyson went back inside and climbed the stairs. As he headed for the master bedroom, he glanced in on Aneka to see that she was still asleep, holding Janelle's doll.

He walked over and sat on the love seat beneath the alcove. He laid his head back, thinking about the evening. Hearing Janelle's voice when she had called earlier had been a shock, but seeing her walk into the office had left him speechless.

Granted, she was stunned and furious to see him. Even so, she was even more beautiful than he remembered. Her soft brown eyes still sparkled when she was emotional and her flawless skin still singed red when she was angry. Her full lips were still as luscious and tempting as ever and her body was just as perfect as always.

Her reappearance in his life was far sooner than he'd expected, yet it had allowed him to take the first step back into her life. Granted, it had been awkward and far more difficult than he'd expected, but nonetheless it was a move toward a new beginning.

He had loved her the moment he'd first seen her walk into the hospital cafeteria years ago. He'd known right then she was the only woman for him. It had taken her a bit longer to see that he was the man for her. But together they had worked it out and their union had ended up strong…before he'd left. Tyson needed to remind her of that. It would take time. She may not be ready to accept him right now, but there was one thing he knew for sure—tomorrow was another day.

Chapter 5

Hours later Janelle rolled over and opened her eyes. It took her a few seconds to realize where she was—at her father's home in her old bedroom. Smiling to herself, she stretched leisurely and then slowly leaned up on her elbows and looked around the room. Sunlight streamed in and everything seemed brand-new. She chuckled to herself. Her father hadn't changed a thing since she'd been gone.

Music posters still hung on the walls, trophies and dolls remained on the shelves beneath the crown molding, and CDs, books and DVDs were neatly stacked in her bookcases. It was like stepping into a time warp. Janelle realized the last time she'd actually slept in this room was at the end of her sophomore year in college. After that she'd lived in year-round campus apartments and later on in her own town house.

Her own town house. The instant she thought about her house, she recalled Tyson being there. Of course, now that the home was completely furnished with his things, it seemed more like his than hers. To his credit, the place was stunning. It fit him perfectly—it was stylish, contemporary and tastefully elegant. But she would have expected no less from Tyson Croft. He was the man she thought she'd be with the rest of her life. He was her soul mate, her friend, her confidant and her lover. He was the man of her dreams from the very beginning.

They'd met in the Johns Hopkins cafeteria the start of the second week of her third year in residency. She'd just completed a double shift—all night, all day and well into the following evening. She had been exhausted, too tired to drive home, but also distraught. Her patient, a five-year-old little boy, had been critical.

There'd been about thirty other people in the cafeteria the night they'd met, but she remembered seeing only him. She had grabbed a cup of tea to wind down and take a much-needed break. When she'd walked into the cafeteria, he'd been there, sitting right at the entrance. As she'd entered, he'd looked up at her and she'd stopped. He'd smiled and nodded once. "Good evening," he'd said.

Her heart had jumped. He had unnerved her the instant he'd spoken. She'd taken a deep breath and managed to return his nod. "Good evening," she'd replied and then continued walking until he'd stopped her again.

"Excuse me," he began. She turned around slowly. "Are you okay?"

She grimaced at his question. "Yes, I'm okay. Why, do I not look okay?"

"Actually, you look distressed, like you're carrying the world on your shoulders."

He was more right than he knew, which she admitted to herself. "Thank you for your diagnosis, but I'm fine." She turned and just before she walked away again he spoke once more.

"In that case, are you a doctor here at this hospital?"

She looked down at her blue medical scrubs, white

jacket and badge that clearly stated her name and title. She nodded.

"Good, because seeing you just stopped my heart."

She smiled and half chuckled at the corny remark. "That's the worst pickup line I've ever heard."

"True, but it was effective," he said.

She looked at him, slightly confused.

"It got you to smile. I'm feeling better already."

She grinned again, then turned to walk away.

"Wait! What about my heart?"

"Sorry, you're out of luck. I'm a third-year pediatric resident. The best I can do is to tell you to take two aspirin and call me in the morning." He laughed as she walked away.

When Janelle took a seat on the far side of the room, she turned to see him still watching her. A few seconds later, though, a woman walked up beside him; it was obvious he had been waiting for her.

That was apparently the beginning and end of their first flirtation. She drank her tea while mulling over a troubling case she'd been working. Minutes later, her cell phone rang: her young patient had taken a turn for the worse. Jumping up, she dumped the cup of tea in the trash and ran out, only to discover her five-year-old patient hadn't survived.

An hour later Janelle walked, zombielike, back into the cafeteria. It was empty this time…except for *him*.

He stood as soon as she walked in. Seeing her face, he opened his arms to her without a word. She went to him. He was a stranger, yet all she could think about was being in his arms. Janelle never cried at work because doctors weren't supposed to. They had to be unaffected by human emotion to do their jobs. But the instant he folded his arms around her, she relinquished her detached emotions and sobbed.

He consoled her without a single word.

She didn't see him again until the following week, when he was waiting at her table, their table, in the cafeteria. Janelle asked him about his heart problems, and she knew right then that her heart was lost to him. For the next eleven months, they were inseparable.

"Damn," Janelle said as she snapped back to the present. She closed her eyes and sighed heavily. Her memory was too good. Why did he still have to be so—amazing? She sat all the way up in bed and wrapped her arms around her legs, resting her chin on her knees. Her stomach tumbled the way it used to do long ago when she'd dreamed about Tyson. She tensed and stopped right there. Thinking too much about Tyson had a way of clouding her judgment. He had always affected her that way.

The moment she'd seen him for the first time, he'd taken her breath away. With one smile, he'd taken over her world. Years ago, when they were together, all she'd thought about was being with him. Nothing else mattered—not school, not family, not even being a doctor, something she'd always wanted to be. She'd actually considered dropping out of med school for him. It was a mistake she'd never made. All her life, she had only ever wanted to be a doctor.... She sighed and shook her head.

"This is crazy," she muttered, then glanced over at the small clock on the bedside table. She grimaced. The time seemed wrong. It was much earlier than she'd thought. Still, she felt rested and not as tired as she'd expected. She grabbed her cell phone and checked her messages. There were welcome-home messages from Mia and Stephen, Tatiana and Natalia. She texted them all back and sent a message to her friend and mentor at Johns Hopkins Hospital, Dr. Meg Richardson.

She got up and took a quick shower and then put on a T-shirt and pair of jeans from her suitcase. Then she grabbed an old heavy college sweatshirt she'd found in the back of her closet.

Her cell phone beeped. It was Meg. "Janelle, I just got your message. Are you back in town?"

"Yes, I got in yesterday. I'm gonna hang around for a while. I was hoping we could grab a quick meal and catch up."

"That sounds great. We definitely need to talk. Do you think you can stop by the hospital for a quick coffee later on this afternoon, say about three o'clock?"

"Sure, sounds perfect. What's up?"

"There's a pediatrics position that opened up here at the hospital a few days ago. I haven't had time to put out feelers yet. And now I'm thinking with your talent, background and medical experience with Medics International, you're perfect for the position. That's if you're interested."

Janelle was stunned. She knew she'd have to look for a new job sooner or later, but to have one just fall into her lap was incredible. "Yes, yes. I'm definitely interested."

"Good. I have to go now. Meet me in my office at three."

"Sure, okay, see you then. And, Meg, thank you so much."

"I should be thanking *you*. See you soon."

Janelle ended the call with a grin on her face. Practicing medicine at Johns Hopkins was something she'd always dreamed of doing. She stood and opened her bedroom door to the mouthwatering aromas of bacon and rich, roasted coffee brewing. As soon as she came to the second floor's open foyer, she saw the stunning holiday decorations. She peered over the banister. Christmas had exploded everywhere. A thick strand of evergreen garland, accented with small holiday balls and holly berries, coiled down the railing. A huge wreath, wrapped with red ribbon and red holiday balls, hung in the large window above the front door, and she could see the image of a second matching wreath positioned outside.

The entire first floor had been transformed into a vibrant holiday display. There were colorful garlands, perfect poinsettias, vibrant evergreens, candles, bells, stars and miniature Christmas trees. In the living room, a fifteen-foot Christmas tree stood elegantly poised between one of the front windows and the fireplace. There was another strand of lights twinkling on the mantel, while two giant, red poinsettia topiaries stood on either side. There were ribbons and bows, massive Christmas balls and beautifully wrapped boxes beneath the tree. It was easy to see that her father still loved this season.

On the mantel hung four holiday stockings. She read the names: Ben, Janelle, Aneka and Tyson. She shook her head in wonder. How and when had Tyson become such a big part of her family? She wondered exactly how much had changed while she was away. She continued on to the kitchen, where she saw her father pulling a mug down from the cabinet above the sink.

She smiled to see him wearing the World's Greatest Dad apron she had bought for him when she was twelve years old. He wore it whenever he cooked breakfast, his favorite meal of the day. She remembered that every morning, her father would be in the kitchen cooking her breakfast before she went off to school. "Good morning. I smell bacon and coffee," she said.

As Ben turned around, it was obvious that the joy of having his daughter back safely filled his heart.

"Good morning. Oh, yes. That's still the best way to start the day," he said as Janelle walked over and gave him a big hug. "I didn't expect to see you up for another few hours. Any residual fatigue left over from the jet lag?" he asked, pouring coffee into two mugs.

"No, not at all. I feel fine—better than fine actually," she said, looking at the perfectly crisped bacon on the counter in front of her. "It's good to be home again."

Ben smiled proudly. "It's good to have you home again."

Janelle sat at the counter and grabbed a slice of bacon and took a bite. "Turkey bacon? It's pretty good. Not that I'm not happy to see you this morning, but what are you still doing here so late? It's after nine o'clock. You're usually at the office by six."

"Things have changed. I've changed," Ben said as he placed two plates of food on the island counter and sat across from Janelle. "No more smoking cigars, no drinks at lunch meetings and no more fatty meals. Now I get at least seven hours of sleep every night, I hit the home gym for an hour every morning and I eat right—turkey bacon, only one cup of decaffeinated coffee and one egg-white omelet with scallions. I've also lost a little bit of extra weight."

Janelle smiled. "Yes, I noticed. That's great, Dad," she said. "I'm proud of you. And this looks delicious."

"I guess everything you told me for years finally sank in. I'm feeling better than ever. I'm taking care of myself, and I have Tyson to thank, as well."

"Tyson?" she questioned after sipping her coffee.

Ben nodded. "Seeing him with his daughter got me thinking. I need to take care of myself for my grandchildren. I'd like to be around and be able to play with them in a few years. That is, *if* my daughter ever decides to settle down."

"Thanks for the pressure, Dad," she joked, eating a forkful of omelet.

He chuckled. "No pressure, I promise," he said, smiling. "I'm just very hopeful."

"Speaking of Tyson…tell me what's going on with the business. How is he really involved?"

"Janelle, I'm handling this," he assured her.

"With Tyson."

Ben sighed heavily. "When the economy tanked a few years back, we got hit hard, very hard. Real estate and new development projects just weren't moving. A lot of other companies were going bankrupt or imploding. I was determined to hold on, and I did for a while. I was neck-deep in three major housing development projects. One went belly-up almost immediately. I sank everything into the last two projects, but by then the business was hemorrhaging money. I tried everything to save the projects. Nothing was working. Money just wasn't there.

"I initially borrowed against a balloon payment I anticipated making, but when the time came, the cash wasn't there. I borrowed again. The interest rate was astronomical. I put the house and the company up as collateral. I eventually filed Chapter 13 for protection. There was nothing more I could do. The business is circling the drain." He shook his head in despair.

"Dad, why didn't you tell me? You know I have my trust fund. I've never touched it. I could have helped," Janelle said softly.

"No, absolutely not," he said firmly, standing to take his empty plate over to the dishwasher. "That money is from your mother and her family. It's for you and your children."

"Dad…"

"Absolutely not," he insisted. "End of discussion."

She nodded her agreement, but knew this wasn't the end. She was going to find a way to help her father's business. "So what about Tyson living at the town house? How does he fit into all of this?" she asked, following him to the dishwasher.

"I called him for help and he came immediately. He brought his daughter…. They needed a place to live."

"Dad, you know what he does for a living. He buys troubled businesses and then sells them off on a chopping block. He'll do the same thing to your business. Why would you call him, of all people?"

"No, he won't. His business had changed. *He's* changed."

"How could he change? That's what he does for a living. He's a shark and he's very good at it. When we were together, he was here in town to buy and take over two different companies. He's merciless."

"Yes, I agree. I despised his tactics. But that's not who he is—not anymore. He's a troubleshooter now. Croft Enterprises is a consulting firm that handles businesses in financial and management crisis. He fixes businesses. He used to tear companies apart. Now he knows how to save them."

"No, that doesn't sound right."

Ben nodded. "It's true. For the past two and a half years, he's been consulting with failing businesses and helping them turn things around. His services are well-known and very much in demand. I was lucky that he put me at the top of the list and came here so quickly. His success rate is excellent. His client list is a who's who among the top Fortune 500 companies. And believe me when I say this— his waiting list is endless."

"I find this hard to believe."

"Believe it," Ben said seriously. "I think his change had a lot to do with you."

Janelle considered his words for a moment. She didn't know what to think or to believe anymore. But right now Tyson wasn't her main concern. "Okay, fine, so he's turned from Sheriff of Nottingham to Robin Hood. What's happening with your business now? What exactly is he doing to help you?"

"I had creditors and banks breathing down my neck. The IRS was ready to file charges. Tyson stepped in and, to tell you the truth, I don't know what I would have done if he hadn't. I think we're close to finding the light at the end of the tunnel. There are no easy solutions. He's given me some viable options, including taking on a business partner."

"A business partner," she repeated distastefully.

Ben nodded. "Yes, Tyson and I have narrowed down a few interesting prospects. One in particular is very impressive."

"What about me? I could be your business partner."

"No, this isn't your life now, Janelle. You're a doctor."

"Dad, be careful. You always said business partners were trouble. You never wanted someone to take what you built."

"Don't worry. For the first time in a long time things are looking up. And speaking of time," he said, looking at his watch, "I need to get to the office. I have meetings all day, starting in about thirty minutes." He hung up his apron and left the kitchen, heading down the hall to his home office.

"With Tyson?" Janelle surmised, following him.

"No, it's with a bank. Tyson set it up. So, tell me, what are your plans?" he asked.

"I'm having lunch with Nya at twelve and a quick coffee with my friend Meg at the hospital at three."

"Meg Richardson?" he asked. She nodded and he smiled. "I always liked her. She was good for you. So, you're really gonna stay?"

Janelle nodded again. "Yep, so far that's the plan. I still have to look for a job and officially give my notice to Medics International, but looks like you're stuck with me for a while."

Ben reached over and squeezed her hand lovingly. "It's my pleasure. It's good to have you home again. When I returned your call last night and you didn't answer, I was worried sick."

"I didn't get a call from you last night," she said.

"I used Tyson's cell phone."

"I did get a phone call, but I didn't recognize the number, so I didn't answer." She paused, watching her father gather his things to leave. "Dad, how did you know where to find Tyson after all this time?"

"We've kept in touch over the years," Ben said, putting a few files into his briefcase.

"You kept in touch how? Why?" Janelle asked, surprised.

"I know, I know," he began, nodding his head as he closed and locked his case. "Tyson and I weren't exactly the best of buddies when the two of you were together, but I guess things changed."

"That's too much change. Talk about a Christmas miracle. If I remember correctly, you despised him when we were together."

"*Despised* is a strong word," Ben corrected as he slipped his suit jacket on and turned to her. "I felt Tyson was distracting you from your goal. I didn't want that to happen. You always wanted to be a doctor. It was your dream. I didn't want you to one day look back and have regrets. When you told me you were considering quitting your residency, I knew you were confused."

"Dad, I don't have any regrets and, for the record, back then I considered quitting my residency every other day. Medical school was hard."

"I'm glad you didn't. You know your mother quit her dreams for me. She wanted to be a doctor, too. This was way before you were born."

Janelle frowned. "I never knew that. Why didn't you tell me?"

Ben nodded. "I guess maybe I always felt guilty for standing in the way of her dream. She never said it, but I always felt she regretted giving it up to be my wife."

"Dad, no. Mom would never even think something like that. She loved us fiercely. I'm sure she never regretted her life."

Ben nodded solemnly. "No, you're right. She didn't. But when she died I promised myself I'd never stand in the way of your dreams. I'm very proud of you, Dr. Truman." He hugged her, then grabbed his keys and started toward the front door. She followed. As he walked, he unfastened one key from the loop. "Here's the key to the other car. It's got a full tank. Go out. Enjoy your day."

"Thanks, Dad," she said, taking the key and kissing his cheek.

"Hey, how about I take my favorite girl out to dinner tonight?" Ben said as he opened the front door.

She nodded. "Yeah, that sounds perfect." He turned to walk away. She called out to him. "Dad, wait. What aren't you telling me? You're hiding something. I can tell."

He sighed, turned back to her and leaned down to kiss her cheek. "There's nothing. I've told you absolutely everything about the business. Now, give my best to Nya and Meg. I have to go."

She nodded slowly, knowing in her heart there was more to his story and his hasty retreat. She was to meet Nya at twelve, which gave her just enough time to catch up with Tyson to find out what was really going on.

She went back inside and quickly grabbed her phone and dialed Tyson's number from her call log. He answered on the second ring, and his deep voice instantly sent a warm tremor through her body. "Tyson."

"Good morning, Janelle. How are you feeling today?"

"I'm not sure yet."

"Jet lag?" he asked.

"No."

"What's wrong?"

"Can we talk?"

"Of course. Where are you now?" he asked.

"I'm at my dad's. I know you must have a busy work schedule, but do you think we can meet sometime today? This morning if possible?" she asked.

"How about right now?" he offered.

"Yes, perfect. I'm on my way out the door this minute. I can meet you wherever you'd like."

She opened the front door and stopped and gasped.

Chapter 6

Tyson stood in the doorway with a smile that instantly sent her senses into emotional overdrive. As usual, *gorgeous* didn't do him justice. He wore a charcoal-colored business suit with a white shirt and a dark tie. "Tyson," she muttered breathlessly.

"Good morning again, Janelle," he said, ending the call and smiling warmly. "I'm guessing this is soon enough."

She stared at him with her cell phone still up to her ear. It was as if thinking about him all morning had, by magic, conjured him up. She didn't know how, but ever since the very beginning of their relationship, he always had a way of knowing exactly when she needed him. "How did you...? What are you doing here?" she asked.

"You called me. I came. I thought that was obvious."

"I'm sorry. You just took me by surprise again. I didn't expect to see you immediately."

"Actually, I wanted to catch up with Ben before he left for work this morning."

"You just missed him, but I'm glad you're here."

"May I come in?" he asked, still standing on the top step.

"Yes, please, come in." He stepped inside, paused and

then turned to her. They stood there a moment until she spoke again. "Um, can I get you something to eat or drink?"

"No, thank you. I'm fine. Are you okay? You seem uneasy."

"How is it you always know when I'm troubled?"

He smiled. "I don't know. I guess I just do. What can I do to help?"

"It's about my father. He's…"

Tyson's expression instantly changed. "What happened? Is he okay?" he interrupted, obviously concerned.

"Yes, he's fine," she said, noting his abrupt reaction and seeing his strained expression. "Apparently he's better than fine. All of a sudden he's eating right, exercising and taking care of himself. I couldn't be happier."

Tyson nodded with relief. "Good. I'm glad to hear it."

"Come, we can talk in the living room," she said, walking past him. He followed, looking around at all the decorations.

"Wow. I see you're all ready for Christmas. This is incredible. I forgot how much your father loves the holiday season."

"Yeah, he does," she said. "He always tried to make it extra special for me because of my mother's death. He never wanted me to feel sad." She watched as he walked over to the Christmas tree and then to the fireplace mantel, where he fingered the stocking for his daughter. "He put up Christmas stockings for you and your daughter."

"Yes, I know," Tyson said, then turned to her. "He told me. He also invited us over for Christmas dinner, but that was before you came home. I'm sure he'll want to spend the holiday with you."

"There's no reason for plans to change on my account. There's always room for one or two more."

"Thank you. So, tell me, what's troubling you?"

"I need you to tell me the whole truth about what's going on with my father. Is his business in real danger?"

"Yes, it is. Ben has made some questionable business decisions, and unfortunately, it's put his company in serious jeopardy."

"If it's about money, I have a trust fund from my mother and her family. It's worth quite a bit of money. I want to use that to help him."

Tyson shook his head. "Ben has taken that off the table."

"I'm putting it back on. I have a stake in the company, too."

"We've talked about opening the company to public shares or taking on an investment partner."

She shook her head. "I can't see him doing that. He's a very private man. I don't think he'd be happy to have others involved in running it. But isn't the real-estate climate improving?"

"Yes, it is, but at this point he's in too deep and time has already run out on him. Maybe you can talk to him. He's stubborn. And unfortunately, he may have no choice. Whether or not he is reluctant, private investors may be his only alternative."

She nodded. "I'll try."

"Good. Thank you. I guess I'd better go." He walked away.

"Earlier, when I asked about my father, you seemed worried." Tyson stopped and turned to her. "You know something else about him, don't you?" she prompted. "What aren't you telling me?"

"What do you mean?" he asked innocently.

She shook her head, knowing his expressions too well. Just like her father, he was hiding something. "Please don't play games with me, Tyson. This is too serious. I know you just as well as you think you know me. You're hiding something, just like Dad. What is it? What's going on?"

"You need to talk to your father about this."

"He'll give me the same double-talk I get from you. Tyson, please, if you know something about my father, tell me. I have to know."

Tyson took a deep breath. "Why don't we sit down?" he offered.

Her insides tensed. This didn't sound good already. She quickly assumed that there was more bad news about her father's business, which might be in worse shape than she'd originally thought.

He took her hand and led her to the sofa. They sat side by side. "Janelle, I came back about eight weeks ago to help your father."

"Yes, I know that already."

"What you don't know is this isn't the first time I've been back to Baltimore to help him. I was here shortly after you left for Tanzania six months ago. I stayed in your home for about two months."

"I don't understand," she said. "Why?"

"Ben had a problem and he asked me to come."

She shook her head. "Another business issue?" she asked.

"No, he had some medical trouble."

Her heart jumped instantly. "What? Wait, I don't understand. He had medical problems and he called you and not me? Why?"

"He didn't tell you because he didn't want to worry you. He knew that if he told you, you'd come back to the States and stay here for him, and he didn't want that."

Her mind was a-jumble with a million questions. "No, this makes no sense. What kind of medical problems?" she asked, trying to think rationally. But all her years of self-composed medical training had gone out the window.

"Ben suffered a minor heart attack and a TAI."

"You mean a TIA? A transient ischemic attack—a mini-stroke?"

He nodded.

Janelle gasped. Suddenly she couldn't breathe. The air in the room seemed to evaporate. She jumped up and ran to the front door. In an instant Tyson was right behind her. He stopped her before she could get to it.

"Janelle, stop," he said, standing between her and the door.

"Get out of my way, Tyson. I need to go see my father." She stepped to the side, but he blocked her way again.

"Janelle, stop and listen to me."

"Move," she demanded angrily, then pushed past him.

"Janelle," he said, grabbing her arms and turning her around to face him. Tears began streaming down her face. "Listen to me."

"No, I don't want to listen." She didn't need a medical degree to know that her heartbeat was elevated, her breathing erratic and her pulse out of control. She tried to push away from him, but he held tight to her arms. "Tyson, you need to let go of me now."

"Calm down," he said.

She glared at him. "Are you kidding me? You want me to calm down after hearing that my father almost died and I didn't know anything about it?"

"Yes, that's exactly what I want. You can't just run off to him like this. Please, let me finish. Ben is fine. With medical treatment and preventive care, his cardiologist is very encouraged by his progress. He had a procedure and he's changed his lifestyle. He's doing fine. You wanted the truth? This is it. He's fine. I would never lie to you. You know that."

She did know it. She swallowed hard and looked at her hands on his chest. His heartbeat was just as elevated as hers. She tried to push by him again, but this time he quickly wrapped his arms around her and held her tight.

At first she struggled. Then knowing it was futile, she held her breath and tensed. Everything inside her wanted to explode as the memory of her mother dying on Christmas Day and the image of her father collided in her mind.

Then she exhaled and crumpled against him, giving way to the feelings long buried in her heart. As always, he was here for her. She closed her eyes and breathed in the sweet, spicy scent of his cologne. Yes, this was what she remembered so well. Tyson—strong, commanding, powerful, yet tender, gentle and forever loving.

Being here in his arms, hearing his soothing voice, feeling him this close… The memories washed through and flooded her heart, bringing back feelings she had tried for so long to deny. This was where they had started and she knew in her heart that she had never stopped loving him. "I can't…I can't lose him."

"I know," he whispered softly in her ear as he stroked the length of her back. "You won't lose him. I promise."

He kissed her forehead, tenderly soothing the tears and sobs away.

She reveled in the strong protection he offered. Here, in his arms, nothing bad could ever happen. He had a way of always making everything all right.

She didn't know how long they stood there, but after a while she took a deep breath and stepped back. He released her and gently tipped her chin up with his finger. She looked up into his dark, loving eyes. They were safe and assuring. Right then she knew she was lost once more. Falling in love with Tyson had been easy the first time. Loving him now was as natural as breathing.

"He's all I have left, Tyson…" she began.

"Trust me. You have more than you can imagine. I'm here. I will always be here for you."

His words washed through her like a warm wave of calm. Trusting him had never been an issue. He had never lied to her. Years ago, when he'd told her that he was here for a job and would be leaving as soon as it was over, it had been the truth. But she'd thought she could persuade him to stay. He hadn't and she'd been crushed. That was when she'd left.

"I'm okay. I'm sorry. I shouldn't have…"

"No, please don't apologize," he said, smiling. He cradled her face in his hands as his thumbs wiped away the last of her tears. "Are you okay?"

She nodded. *Why does he have to be so wonderful?* "I'm fine."

He released her and she stepped back and looked away. "My heart breaks every time I see you cry. Did you know that?" She turned back to him and shook her head. He smiled. "Remember the first night we met?"

She nodded. "I'm surprised you remember that night," she said.

"Of course I remember. How could I forget? That was the night my life changed, the night I fell in love with you."

The lump in her throat instantly dissolved and her nerves stilled. It felt as if, all of a sudden, the world had slowed, just for that moment. Without thought or hesitation, she wrapped her arms around his neck and kissed him. It was completely impulsive, but it felt so right. He kissed her back and then everything she had been feeling exploded. All she could think about was being with him just one more time. The kiss deepened and the passion escalated. Then, suddenly, everything stopped. He pulled back.

"Janelle. Janelle, wait," Tyson said, breathing hard and holding her from him. "We can't. Not like this. You're upset and vulnerable. I can't take advantage of you and I don't want you to have any regrets when we make love."

"Tyson, I'm fine," she assured him, moving closer.

"I know, but I'm not."

"You're turning me down."

He leaned in and kissed the sweet underside just behind her ear. "You have no idea how much I want you right now. Believe me, when I walk out of here in the next few minutes I'm gonna hate myself, but this isn't enough for us, not anymore."

She licked her lips, took a deep breath and nodded slowly. He was right. She was upset and vulnerable, but she also wanted to be with him. Still she nodded. "Yes, you're right. This is too fast."

"I think I'd better go," he said, turning to the door.

"Wait…" she said. He turned around. "Thank you."

"For what?" he asked.

"For telling me the truth, for being here for me," she said, half smiling. "For always being here for me."

"Janelle, I will always tell you the truth, and there's no other place I want to be except here with you." He leaned down and kissed her lips tenderly. "I'll see you later."

"Later," she said softly. She watched as he got into his car and drove off, then closed the door, walked over to the stairs and sat.

This was information overload. Her father seemed fine medically, but she still intended to talk to both him and his doctor. She grabbed her cell phone and called her father's office. His voice mail answered, but she decided not to leave a message: she didn't want to upset him. She went back into the living room and walked over to the mantel. Four Christmas stockings—it looked as though they were one big happy family.

She still couldn't believe her father had called Tyson and not her. But if her reaction to hearing the news was any indication, then maybe he had been right not to do so. She was out of control and completely irrational. Going to her father at that moment would have gotten him upset and that was the last thing she wanted to do. Tyson was right. She needed to calm down before talking to her father.

She walked over to the sofa and sat, taking a deep breath before dialing her father's office phone number again. He answered. "Hi, Dad. Got a few minutes?" she began.

"Hey, sweetheart. Sure—just a few, though. Everything okay?"

"Yes…well, not really. I spoke with Tyson a few minutes ago. He told me about your heart attack and stroke." She heard her father sigh. "Dad, why didn't you tell me? I could have come home. I could have been with you."

"And that's exactly why I didn't tell you. I didn't want you rushing home upset, and had I told you, that's exactly what you would have done. I had the best doctors and the best medical care available. Believe me, if any further problems arose, I would have called you, but they didn't. And now I feel better than ever."

She couldn't deny that. Her father looked better than he had in years. He'd lost weight, he was eating right and he was taking care of himself.

"That's not the point. You should have called me."

"To do what?" he asked. "There was nothing you could have done at the time except sit and worry, and I didn't want that. Now, I need to get to a meeting and get my business back in just as good shape."

"Okay, but I still want to talk about this."

He chuckled. "Of course you do. Now go enjoy your day and don't worry about me. I'm just fine."

"All right. See you later." She hung up, feeling a little better. Tyson was right. She thought about their conversation in the foyer and her reaction. He had always been the calm in the middle of her emotional storms. She couldn't believe she'd kissed him! It was totally out of character for her, surprising both of them, even as he kissed her back.

Janelle reached up and touched her lips. She could still feel the pull of his mouth on hers.

He seemed different, that much was without doubt—certainly not the arrogant and aggressive man he had been before. There was a gentle calmness about him now. Maybe it was his young daughter's influence. Children had a way of changing a person's world for the better—what was important one minute suddenly wasn't anymore. But was he really different?

She didn't know what to think. Her father obviously trusted him.

Her cell phone beeped with a text message from Nya, who was on her way to the restaurant. Janelle grabbed her purse and hurried out. Time enough later to worry about Tyson, her father and her future.

Chapter 7

Janelle parked her car a block away and hurried to the restaurant. When she tried to open the door handle, it was locked, and the dark, smoky glass obscured her view. She looked at the decorative sign in the window. The Chesterfield was one of the most prestigious restaurants in the Baltimore area. Its chef was world renowned and reservations were almost impossible to get... So where was Nya?

She looked around and then started to leave. A few steps away, she heard the restaurant door being unlocked and opened. She turned, seeing a gorgeous man dressed in jeans and a T-shirt standing in the open doorway. With blond hair and sea-blue eyes, he looked as if he'd come right off a movie set.

"Excuse me. Are you Janelle?" he asked.

She nodded. "Yes."

He smiled and deep dimples cut through his handsome face. "Hi, I'm Brad. Come on in. We've been waiting for you." He held the door for her to enter. Once inside she looked around, amazed by the sheer splendor and ambience of the entranceway.

"Follow me. We're in the kitchen, and lunch is almost

ready," he said, heading around the bar to the main dining area. "Nya's already sipping champagne."

"Of course she is," Janelle confirmed. She knew her sister too well. Even in muted light and empty, the place sparkled and shone with stunning radiance.

"So, you're Nya's sister."

"Yep, one of them."

"I've known Nya for a while. I didn't know she had sisters," he said.

"She has two. We're all stepsisters. Different mothers and different fathers," she said. Brad turned and looked at her, confused. She smiled. "It's complicated. Trust me, explaining it will probably give you a headache."

They snaked through the spotless stainless-steel counters and wait stations to a small room beside the main kitchen, where Nya was sitting at a small round table, talking on her cell phone. When she saw Janelle she smiled, waved and quickly ended her conversation. "Thanks, Brad."

He blew her an air-kiss and went back to the kitchen.

"Hey, girl," she exclaimed with her arms open wide.

Janelle smiled and walked over to her. They hugged and laughed. "It's so good to see you. Oh, my God, you look sensational."

"You, too," Janelle said.

"Well, yeah, of course I do, but I wasn't exactly working in the middle of the desert. You're practically glowing. Come on. Let's sit down. Brad made us something amazing for lunch."

"Brad, huh? Nice. He's gorgeous."

She smiled and winked. "We're just friends. Long story, great ending," she said just as her cell phone rang again. Nya looked at the number and smiled. "I need to get this." She pressed the FaceTime accept button and smiled. "We're here," she said, turning the phone around so Janelle could speak.

"Hello, ladies," Mia said, sing-songing a greeting to her two sisters.

Janelle beamed with delight at seeing her other sister on the video app on Nya's cell phone. "Oh, my God, Mia, look at you. You look fantastic. How are you and how's everybody?"

"I'm fine. We're all fine. Everything's great. I'm so sorry to miss our pre-Christmas lunch and shopping this year. But how are you?"

"I'm wonderful. It's so good to see you. How's my godson?"

"*Our* godson," Nya joked.

"He's amazing. Hold on a second. I'll let you see him. He just went down for his nap." Mia held her phone down to her sleeping baby in the crib. Both Janelle and Nya squealed with joy at seeing him and then silenced quickly. But it was too late. He began to stir and his lower lip pouted.

A second later his eyes opened. He whimpered and then started crying. "Aw-ww," Janelle and Nya said in unison.

"Oh, well, ladies, looks like I'm back on mommy duty. I'll call you guys later tonight. Have a great lunch. Welcome home, Janelle. I love you both," Mia said, waving.

Janelle smiled as Nya ended the call. "It feels so good to be home. You have no idea."

"It's good to have you back. So, tell me, how's my stepdad?" Janelle's expression instantly changed. "What's wrong? Is Ben okay?"

Janelle sighed heavily, shaking her head. "He's fine, but to tell you the truth, I don't know what to think."

"What do you mean?"

"My dad had a heart attack and a mild stroke."

"What? When?" Nya asked quickly.

"About six months ago. I didn't even know about it. He didn't tell me. Apparently, I had just left for Tanzania when it happened."

"Oh, my God. And he's just telling you this now?"

"No, that's just it. He didn't tell me. Tyson told me. Dad called him instead of me after it happened."

"Whoa, wait a minute. Tyson, as in Tyson Croft—*your* Tyson Croft?" Nya asked. Janelle nodded. "Okay, wait, I don't get it. Why did Ben call him and not you—or me, for that matter?"

"He told me that he hadn't wanted to worry me and have me rush home to be with him. If Tyson hadn't told me, I never would have known what happened."

"Okay, start from the beginning. What does Tyson have to do with this and when did he come back into the picture?"

Brad brought their lunch. After a brief conversation, the two began eating as Janelle told Nya about her homecoming and seeing Tyson again and meeting his daughter.

"A four-year-old daughter," Nya exclaimed.

"Wait, there's more." Janelle continued the story.

By the time the meal was done Janelle had told Nya everything about her father's business problem and Tyson living in her home with his daughter.

Nya shook her head. "This is too unreal. I can't believe it. I had no idea. I spoke with Ben a couple of weeks ago and he never mentioned anything to me."

"I know the feeling," Janelle said sarcastically.

"Okay, so Tyson is working with Ben now. You talked to him. He told you about what's been going on, but what about the two of you?" she asked.

"What do you mean?" Janelle asked.

"You know exactly what I mean. Two and a half years ago you and Tyson were headed down the aisle. Then all of a sudden he's gone and you leave for Africa. Now you're back and he's back. What happens now?"

"I don't know," Janelle said, taking a deep breath and shaking her head. She looked at her sister and sighed. "I kissed him." Nya smiled without responding. "Nya, you don't understand. I mean I *really* kissed him," Janelle reiterated.

"Yes, I do understand. You're my sister. Yeah, maybe not by blood, but with us, that doesn't really matter. I know you, and deep down in your heart you still have feelings for Tyson, and I know that he has some pretty strong feelings for you, too." Janelle shook her head as Nya nodded. "You're gonna have to relent, Janelle. You two had the romance of the century, and fine, things fell apart at the end, but you and I both know that wasn't the end—not really. My advice—grab all the love and happiness you can and, in this case, it's with Tyson."

"Since when did you become a romance guru?"

"Apparently since now," Nya said, smiling.

"It's not that easy, Nya. I wish it was. He's leaving again."

Nya reached across the table to hold her sister's hand. She squeezed gently. "Actually, sis, it *is* that easy. Love is the easiest thing in the world. Just follow your heart."

"Okay, now you're starting to scare me."

"If I learned nothing else from watching Mia and Stephen come together, it's that love will always find a way. So, tell me, how did he look?" Nya asked.

"He was still as handsome as ever. The instant he looked up at me, I swear my heart skipped a beat. It was as if time had stood still and the past two and a half years of my life had evaporated. I told myself that I was over him. I was wrong."

Nya giggled and smiled. "I love the sound of romance in the afternoon."

The two went on talking about men, jobs, family, vacations, the holidays and then back to men. Two hours later they were still laughing and talking.

"Come on. Let's get out of here. I can't stand looking

at that old college sweatshirt any longer. You and I have some serious shopping to do."

Janelle stood, following her sister. They thanked Brad and his kitchen crew, left a very generous tip and then continued outside. Nya put on her dark sunglasses. "I think we need Bergdorf."

"Newsflash—there's no Bergdorf Goodman near here," she said.

"Sure there is. There's one on Fifth Avenue."

Janelle chuckled. "Fifth Avenue, as in New York City? No way. We're not going all the way to New York to shop for clothes," she insisted as her cell phone rang.

"Sure we are. I have my dad's private plane sitting on the runway right now. We can fly there, shop and get you back here by midnight, one at the latest. Come on. It'll be fun."

"Can't, sorry. I'm meeting with a friend at Johns Hopkins in a few minutes. Hold on," Janelle said, answering her cell. "Hello?"

"Hello, Janelle, this is Mrs. Ivers. I need your help."

"Sure, Mrs. Ivers. What's wrong?"

"My son was in a car accident. I need to go to him. Tyson is in D.C. and I can't take Aneka with me. Would you come by and stay with her for a few hours? You're the only other person she knows and I know Tyson won't mind."

"Um, sure," she said tentatively, "okay. I'll be right there." She ended the call and looked at Nya. "I gotta go."

"What's wrong? Is it Ben?"

"No, that was my neighbor. She stays with Tyson's daughter. She needs someone to stay with Aneka. Looks like a rain check on shopping and my meeting," Janelle said, holding her arms out to her sister. They hugged one another tightly. When they finally let go, they smiled at each other. "You take care and have a safe trip back to New York. I'll talk to you soon."

"Okay, but I'm still going shopping for you," Nya said.

Janelle hugged Nya again then waved and headed to her car. She called her friend Meg and postponed their meeting until the next day, then drove off. When she got to her house, Mrs. Ivers was standing out front with Aneka. "Hi," Janelle said. "Any word about your son?"

Mrs. Ivers shook her head. "He's still in the emergency room being examined."

"Is there anything I can do? Anyone I can call?"

"No, but thank you. I'm going to get over there and see what's going on. Aneka, you remember Ms. Truman from last night?" The little girl nodded and looked at Janelle suspiciously. "Good. Now, I have to leave, but Ms. Truman is going to stay here with you until your father gets home, all right?" Aneka stared at Janelle then nodded slowly. "Ms. Truman is going to give you your snack and then you can take your nap and be a very good little girl the rest of the day, okay."

Janelle smiled. "Go. Take care of your son. Don't worry about us. We'll be just fine. Any food allergies?"

"No allergies, but she is asthmatic. Her inhaler's in the kitchen, but she hasn't had an attack in some time. Thank you so much for coming. I knew you were the perfect person to call," Mrs. Ivers said, then hurried to her car.

Janelle and Aneka waved and watched as she drove off. When the car turned the corner, Janelle looked down at the little girl, who was still looking up at her, frowning. "Well, I guess it's just the two of us for the rest of the afternoon. What would you like to do?"

Aneka shrugged her shoulders and looked down at her shoes without answering.

"Okay, well, I guess we can color or paint or maybe

I can read you a story or we can watch one of your animated movies."

Aneka shrugged again, still avoiding Janelle's gaze.

"Why don't we get inside out of the cold first?" Janelle said as she held her hand down for Aneka to take. The girl did so, reluctantly. They went back into the house. Janelle looked around. The place was as neat as a pin. She headed to the kitchen and found a cut-up apple on the counter. Aneka followed silently and stopped in the doorway. "Okay, I guess this is your snack." Aneka nodded, then turned away.

Janelle smiled. "Okay, I have an idea. While you eat your snack, I'll look around to see if I can find the ingredients to make my special Christmas cookies."

Aneka's eyes instantly brightened. "Cookies?"

Janelle nodded. "Yes, a special Christmas cookie. One I learned to make from a friend of mine who lives very far away in a place called Africa. But you'll have to eat your snack first and hopefully I can find the ingredients."

Aneka quickly sat at the kitchen table, grabbed the sliced apple and began eating. Janelle started looking in the cabinets. "What is ingredients?" Aneka asked, repeating the word slowly.

"What *are* ingredients," Janelle corrected. "Ingredients are different things that all go together to make up a finished product," Janelle said, continuing her search. "And ingredients—" she paused and sighed heavily "—are what we don't have." She turned around to Aneka sitting quietly eating her apple. She hated to disappoint Aneka after promising her special cookies, but she didn't have a choice—or maybe she did. She turned to Aneka and smiled. "How about we go on a field trip first?"

Chapter 8

Having received Mrs. Ivers's message, Tyson immediately cut his workday short and headed home. He wasn't getting much done anyway. Ever since his conversation with Janelle earlier that morning, all he could think about was her and the kiss they'd shared. He wanted to be with her, but he knew it wasn't the right time for them to be together. He also knew that it had been the right thing to do to tell her about her father, but seeing her so upset had nearly broken his heart.

He had tried to call her a few times to make sure she was okay. But then getting the message that she was with Aneka was the best news all day.

He wanted Janelle and Aneka to get to know each other. Aneka, having lost her parents so young, barely remembered them. She called Tyson "Dad," but knew about her father and mother. She was a wonderful little girl, but often closed herself off with those she didn't know. He hoped one day she and Janelle would grow to love each other like mother and daughter.

As soon as he walked into the house, he heard music

playing, joyous laughter and loud singing coming from the kitchen. "Hello," he called out. There was no answer.

An instant later Aneka came running around the corner and right at him, her hands and face powdered with flour. "Daddy!" she squealed with joy.

Tyson leaned down and picked her up as she wrapped her arms around his neck, talking excitedly about her day.

"Hey, hey, look at you," Tyson said. His suit jacket was instantly covered with flour and frosting, but he didn't mind at all. Still holding his daughter, he continued to the kitchen, seeing Janelle place a decorated cookie on a plate with several others. "Hello," he said as Aneka continued talking. "What in the world do we have here?" Tyson chuckled, seeing the kitchen in a complete mess.

"Hey, you're early. We didn't expect you for another few hours," she said.

"We're making cookies, see?" Aneka said happily.

"Yes, I can certainly see that," he said, chuckling at the mess in the kitchen and at her face sprinkled with flour. "It looks like you've been having fun," he added as he set Aneka down. She hurried back to the kitchen table and continued icing a cookie with a plastic spoon. "What kind of cookies are you making?"

"Christmas-ball cookies," Aneka said proudly, holding her half-frosted cookie up to show her father.

"Yes, I see. They look delicious. May I have one?"

Aneka shook her head. "No, no, we can't eat cookies until after dinner. We promised." She turned and looked at Janelle, smiling. Janelle nodded her agreement.

Tyson nodded and smiled. "That's a very good idea," he said, looking at Janelle as she began to clean up some of the bowls and cookie pans on the countertop.

"I hope you don't mind," she said. "I usually make cookies at Christmas. This seemed like a good time to get a little help."

"Yes, I know," he said. "I remember we made Christmas cookies together once." She turned to him and nodded as they shared a glance. "And, no, I don't mind at all. I'm delighted you're doing this with Aneka. She needs this. Thank you." He took his jacket off and rolled his sleeves up to help. He washed his hands, picked up a cookie and a spoon and began frosting it.

Aneka smiled happily as she added an abundance of sprinkles on her frosted cookie. "See, Daddy? Janelle showed me how to color in my cookies like my coloring books. Then we put on red and green and yellow and blue sprinkles. They are pretty."

"Yes indeed, they look beautiful," he said, still looking at Janelle. He finished his cookie then walked over to Janelle, who was standing at the sink. "I got Mrs. Ivers's message about her son. Any word on how he's doing?"

"No, I haven't heard anything yet," Janelle said as Aneka began singing along with the Christmas carols again.

"Daddy, can Janelle stay for pizza night?"

"That's a great idea, sweetheart," Tyson said, then turned to Janelle and smiled. "Yes, please stay."

"Actually, I already have dinner plans."

"Oh," he said, disappointed.

"Dad and I are having dinner out tonight," she added.

"Perfect. We can all do dinner out. I'll call Ben and invite him, too," Tyson said, grabbing his cell from his jacket pocket. He dialed quickly and spoke to Ben. A few minutes later he ended the call, smiling. "Ben was just about to call you about dinner. His meeting is going to run late and he's going to grab a quick bite at the office. So, it looks like you're joining us for pizza night."

Janelle smiled and then looked at Aneka, whose bright, excited eyes shone happily, waiting for an answer. "Yes, I'd love to join you and Aneka for pizza night."

Aneka began cheering and then stopped suddenly. "And cookies after, right?" she asked.

"Definitely," both Janelle and Tyson responded.

Three hours later, after pizza and cookies, after cleaning up the kitchen and during the second animated holiday movie, Aneka crawled into Janelle's lap. By the time the movie ended they were both sound asleep. Tyson looked over and smiled. This was his dream come true—to have this family.

He picked up the remote and turned the television off. As soon as he did, Janelle woke up.

"Hey," she said sleepily, then yawned.

"Hey, sleepyhead," Tyson responded.

She smiled. "I guess I'm still on Tanzania time." She looked at Aneka cuddled on her lap. "Looks like we both fell asleep."

Tyson walked over to her. "It's the perfect picture. Here, I'll take her up to bed." Janelle shifted Aneka as Tyson wrapped his arms around his daughter and lifted her up. Aneka immediately twined her arms around his neck. "I'll be right back."

"I'd better get going. Thank you for this evening. I had fun," Janelle said.

"Please don't leave yet. Please," he said.

She nodded and watched as Tyson took Aneka upstairs. After a few minutes Tyson came to the upstairs rail. "Janelle."

She looked up at him. "Aneka wants to say good-night to you."

She nodded and went upstairs. What was once a nice-size guest room was now a perfect little girl's princess bedroom. Aneka was sitting up in her canopy bed, holding Janelle's African doll. Janelle walked over to the bed. "Hey there," she said.

Aneka rubbed her eyes. "Good night, Janelle. Thank

you for helping me make Christmas cookies." She looked at her father and continued. "And here's your doll back. I'm sorry I took it."

Janelle smiled. "You're very welcome, and I'll tell you what—you hold on to her for me, okay?" Aneka smiled happily and then lay back with the doll in her arms. "Good night, sweetheart. Pleasant dreams." Aneka sat up and opened her arms for a hug. Janelle embraced her, then stepped back as Tyson gave her a kiss and a big hug. He tucked her beneath the covers and moved a curly tendril from her forehead.

"Good night, Daddy."

Janelle turned to leave and Tyson followed her. They stopped when Aneka sat up and called out, "Janelle, can you come see Santa Claus with me tomorrow?"

"I'm sorry, sweetheart. I don't think I can," Janelle said.

Aneka frowned and nodded sadly.

Tyson and Janelle went downstairs. She gathered her coat and purse and then yawned again as she turned to the front door. "Good night."

"Janelle, you're exhausted. Why don't you stay here? Please. I promise to be on my best behavior."

She smiled. "No need. I'm fine," she promised.

"No, you're not. You're exhausted."

"Tyson, I'm a doctor. Of course I'm exhausted. I've been exhausted for the past eight years of my life. Trust me. I'm used to existing on fumes. I'm fine."

"At least have a cup of tea with me. Please."

It was obvious that he wanted her to stay awhile longer. And not surprisingly, she wanted to stay as much as he wanted her to. "Tea sounds like a great idea."

He smiled. "Good. Sit, relax. I'll be right back."

Janelle reclined on the sofa. She closed her eyes and began thinking about the last time she and Tyson were together. The kiss they'd shared was soul-moving, heart-stopping, toe-curling incredible. The man had a way of turning her world upside down with just one glance. Everything about him made her heart beat faster. There was no denying her attraction to him. She sighed, wondering if she would ever get enough of Tyson Croft.

She opened her eyes, smiling, just as Tyson came around the sofa and handed her a cup of hot tea as he sat. "Music or television?" he asked.

"Music," she replied quickly.

He picked up the remote control and pressed a button. Smooth jazz music began to play. She smiled at the familiar selection. He remembered. It was her favorite CD. Janelle took a sip of her hot tea, then placed the mug on the coaster in front of her. "You remembered. Earl Grey with a twist of lemon. Thank you."

He nodded. "Yes, of course I remembered, and thank you again." She turned to him, puzzled. "For staying with Aneka," he added. "She told me that she really had a great time. She likes you. And trust me, she doesn't warm up to a lot of people instantly, but she did with you."

"She's an adorable little girl. I like her, too."

"I'm glad. I have to admit, I hoped you two would hit it off. Making cookies was a brilliant idea and they were amazing."

She smiled. "I haven't made Christmas cookies in years. The last time was with…" She stopped and looked at him. He smiled, knowing it had been with him—and they had done much more than just bake that night. "I remember making cookies with my mother. It was our annual tradition. Every year we'd choose a dozen different recipes and spend the weekend in the kitchen singing Christmas carols, laughing, baking and decorating. I forgot how much fun it was."

"Well, they were definitely a big hit with Aneka."

"Aneka—that's a beautiful name. Does it have a meaning?"

"It's Hawaiian for Annette. It means 'full of grace.'"

"It's very pretty for a very pretty little girl."

Tyson smiled. "It amazes me every time I look at her. She looks just like my cousin." He paused. "I think about him not being here to see Aneka grow up and—" he paused again "—everything he's gonna miss…"

Janelle reached over and held his hand. He looked up at her. "I know it's hard missing a loved one, especially around the holidays. But remembering them keeps them alive in our hearts. And keeping traditions alive keeps their joy close to us. Baking cookies with Aneka this afternoon did that for me. It felt wonderful being with her today. And one day I hope I'll be baking cookies with my daughter and then eventually my granddaughter."

"You will," he said assuredly. "So, tell me about working with Medics International. Is it as challenging as it sounds?"

She nodded. "It's extremely challenging. The intensity was unreal. It was scary and exhilarating. Nothing I had ever imagined prepared me to do the job. There's no adjustment period and no time to test the waters to see if you'll fit in. You just have to do the job and save a life. And there are so many lives to save. Just the basic essentials that we all take for granted are terribly needed in some places. It's desperate and it's real."

"And that was good?" he questioned. "It sounds overwhelming."

"It was. In the past two and a half years, I gained a lifetime of medical knowledge. I loved it. Being there took me away from myself and allowed me to focus on others. I needed that."

"But now you're home," he said.

She nodded and took another sip of tea. This time she held on to the mug for courage. She cleared her throat and asked the question that had been on her mind since she'd first seen him. "So, when are you leaving?"

He chuckled. "Are you trying to get rid of me already?"

"I know you'll have to leave. I was just wondering when."

"There's a big job in New York. If I decide to take it, we'll have to leave Christmas Day."

"Are you going to take it?" she asked cautiously.

"I don't know yet. There's also a very special project I've been working on here. It's complicated and I'm not sure if I'm making any progress. I hope so."

"I'm sure it will work out. I hear you're very good at what you do."

He smiled and nodded. "I hope so," he said, then paused. "You were right. Years ago, you told me that fixing things and making them better was a lot more rewarding than tearing them apart. Before, when I just bought and sold businesses, it was automatic, no feeling. I'd go in and start cutting it up. Now what I do is challenging and I enjoy it."

"Good. But you're still moving around the country a lot. What about Aneka? When school begins for her it's going to be very difficult—even with homeschooling and with private tutors."

"I know. It's time to stop and plant roots, settle down."

"Wow. That's a big step for you," she joked.

He chuckled. "No, not really. I've been thinking about this for a long time. I'm ready for a home and a real family. I just need to do this one last project."

"It'll work in the end."

"I hope so. How about you? When are you headed back?"

"I'm not."

"You're not?" he said. Happy surprise was clear on his face.

She shook her head. "No. I didn't actually resign from

Medics International, but I've decided that I'm staying here, at least for a while."

He smiled. "I'm glad to hear that. So, Africa…are you going to miss it?"

"Yes, I will, very much. Some places are stunningly beautiful and then there are places that aren't so nice. Those I won't miss so much. But overall, I will definitely miss it."

"And the people…?" he questioned.

"Yes, I'll miss the people, too."

"Any one person in particular?" he asked clumsily.

She laughed. "Tyson Croft, are you asking me if I'm seeing someone?"

"Too obvious?" he asked, not at all embarrassed.

"Yeah, just a little," she said. "And to answer your question, yes, I will miss several people in particular." She watched as he nodded and looked away. "They're all under twelve years old, of course."

He grinned back at her. "Good."

"What about you? Seeing anyone lately?" she asked.

"Lately, no, but actually, there was this one woman I was seeing a while back. She was amazing—funny, smart, talented, beautiful. I fell in love with her as soon as I saw her. But I kind of messed it up."

"Really? How'd you do that?" she asked.

"By thinking my career was more important than my heart."

"And it's not now?"

"No, it never was," he said, setting his mug on the table. "I missed you. I missed us."

"Tyson…"

He eased her mug from her hands and placed it beside his on the table. "Come, dance with me," he said as he stood and reached his hand out to her. She took his hand

and he gently pulled her up into his arms. He moved her close and wrapped his arm around her waist.

They began to move slowly, falling into a comfortable silence as the music played and they danced. Their bodies moved in perfect rhythmic sync. She closed her eyes and completely relaxed as time passed—how much, she had no idea. He held her a little closer as the song ended and another began.

She eased in closer as their bodies melded into one. He rubbed his hand along the length of her back, then cuddled against her shoulder and neck. She inhaled the sweet, spicy scent of his cologne as she rested her head on his shoulder. With slow, deliberate ease, he released her hand. She wrapped her arms around him as he encircled her waist, dipping his face to her neck. He kissed her tenderly. The moment was pure romance.

Janelle vowed to hold on tight to this image for the rest of her life. No matter what the future brought, she would always have Tyson and this moment. She sighed. This day was perfect—making cookies with Aneka, having dinner together with Tyson and now this. It was the perfect family evening and she wished it could be like this forever. But they weren't a family and she had to remember that. There was no way she was going to be hurt again. Instinctively she stopped dancing.

He slowly released her and they gazed into each other's eyes. Neither said a word. The silence between them spoke louder than either of them could ever do. With their mouths just inches apart, she knew the inevitable was going to happen. But she also knew once she started, she'd never want to stop. She took a small step back.

"Tyson, this is wonderful," she began, then smiled. "Actually, it's amazingly wonderful, but probably not a good idea. I'd better go." She turned to leave, but stopped when he held on to her hand. "I guess we just weren't meant to be."

He released her.

Sadness pulled at her heart as she walked out.

As she drove away, tears fell and her thoughts flowed in complete chaos. She had always known the direction of her life and never afforded herself the opportunity to question her choices. She always knew what she wanted, set goals and achieved them. Tyson was the only person to ever make her question her direction. Now here she was again asking, "What if?"

She shifted the gear into Park and realized she had driven all the way to her father's home without knowing it. She got out and went inside. As soon as she entered, she saw that the Christmas decorations were lit up and heard humming coming from the living room. She peeked in. Her father was wrapping a Christmas present. He looked up, smiling. "Well, hello. Welcome home. How was your day?"

"Hi, Dad," she said, kissing his cheek. "It was good. I had lunch with Nya and then hung out with Tyson's daughter and made cookies. Afterward we had pizza."

"Sounds like a delightful evening."

"It was," she said happily, remembering the kitchen mess.

He stood and then placed the wrapped present beneath the Christmas tree. "You look happy."

"I am. I'm glad to be home."

"So how did it go with Meg—a job offer, perhaps?" he said, hopeful.

"I had to cancel Meg when Mrs. Ivers called about staying with Aneka. We're going to meet tomorrow morning."

Ben nodded. "Good. Oh, before I forget—you got a delivery this afternoon."

"A delivery for me? From who?" she questioned.

"I don't know. I put them upstairs in your bedroom."

"'Them'?" she repeated curiously. "Okay, thanks. So, how did your meetings go today? Any progress?"

"It was long and arduous and a complete waste of time."
Ben shook his head slowly and sighed. "It wasn't what I
expected. Giving up full control of a business it took an
entire lifetime to build out of nothing is tough. I guess
I'm going to have to think about this next move." He half
smiled. "But right now, I'm going to bed."

"Yeah, me, too," she said, yawning. "Good night, Dad."

"Good night. Pleasant dreams."

Janelle went upstairs and opened her bedroom door, where
she saw three large boxes sitting on her bed. She read the la-
bels. They were from a local boutique. She knew instantly
that Nya had gone shopping for her.

Chapter 9

"Thanks again for everything, Meg," Janelle said, leaving her friend's office the next morning. "The hospital's offer is very exciting. Working here has always been a dream of mine."

"Trust me. We'd be lucky to get you. With your past two years working with Medics International in Africa, you could get a position on staff just about anywhere in the country. So, please, please, consider this position. We'd love to have you here. You were a brilliant young doctor when you left. Now the sky's the limit."

Janelle looked around, smiling. The pediatric ward was fully decked out with decorations representing every end-of-year seasonal holiday. There was even a posting saying when Santa was coming to visit later that afternoon. This was, at times, one of the busiest places in the hospital. Today was no exception. There were medical staff and visitors everywhere. It was just days to Christmas and to every hospital across the country there was an unwritten strategy to get every capable child home with their family. "I'd love to be a part of the Johns Hopkins family."

"Fantastic. Let's make this happen. We just need to

take care of the usual Human Resources formalities and then we'll be all set. I'd say you can sign on just after the first of the year."

Janelle nodded. "Sounds good. That will give me time to take care of the formal notification to Medics International and maybe take a few days off for the holidays."

Meg smiled. "Perfect. So, any plans for the rest of the day?"

"Yeah, I have some last-minute Christmas shopping to do."

Meg shook her head sadly. "I do not envy you that challenge. Two days before Christmas, last-minute shopping…the stores will be loaded and crazy with the shoppers about the same."

"I know." Janelle chuckled. "Plus, I'm headed to a toy store."

"Oh, you are really pushing it. Well, good luck with that," Meg said, chuckling just as her cell phone rang. She grabbed it and glanced at the number. "I gotta go. I'll get everything started on this end. Human Resources will be in touch." They hugged quickly as Meg started walking away backward and waving. "Have a great holiday. I'll call you next week."

"Thanks again, Meg. Happy holidays, and my best to the family," Janelle said. She smiled joyfully. Getting an offer to work at Johns Hopkins pediatric ward was a dream come true.

She turned and headed to the bank of elevators near the main pediatric nurses' station. As soon as she pressed the elevator button, she heard her name called. She turned to find Tyson and Aneka walking toward her. Her heart skipped a beat at seeing him. Dressed in blue jeans, a black shirt and black leather jacket, he looked exactly as he had the first time they'd met—bad-boy dark and dangerous.

Several nurses walked by and openly stared admiringly.

Aneka ran and grabbed her. "Hey, what are you two doing here?" Janelle asked, kneeling to hug Aneka. Then she stood and kissed Tyson's cheek.

"Good morning. Wow. You look beautiful."

"Thank you. I didn't expect to see you here."

"Actually, we're on our way out," Tyson said.

"I was in the hospital all night," Aneka announced.

Janelle frowned and looked at Tyson. "You were in the hospital all night. Are you okay? What happened?" Janelle asked, taking Aneka's hand and moving to the side. Tyson followed.

"A few hours after you left last night, I heard her coughing. She was having difficulty breathing. We used the inhaler, but it didn't seem to help much. I brought her into the E.R. They took good care of her."

"Who's your pediatrician?" Janelle asked.

"Dr. Andrea Jenkins, but she's away for the holidays," Tyson said, then explained the rest of their visit there.

"I'm all better now. The doctor said so."

"Princess Aneka, you are a very brave little girl," Janelle said to Aneka, then stood and turned to Tyson. Aneka nodded and smiled proudly. "May I?" Janelle asked, seeing the discharge paperwork in his hands. He handed it to her. She quickly read the medical report, nodding. "This looks good. She should be just fine."

"Thank you. I feel much better knowing that," Tyson said, rubbing his chin stubble. "Thankfully, she slept most of the time."

"And we're gonna see Santa Claus and get a Christmas tree and decorate it with lights and see fireworks and everything right now," Aneka said excitedly.

"Wow. That sounds like a whole lot of fun," Janelle said as Aneka smiled and nodded happily.

"Actually, we're going to change clothes and grab something to eat first," Tyson clarified.

"Did you see Santa Claus?" Aneka asked.

"No, actually I haven't seen Santa in quite a while."

"Can you come see Santa Claus with us?" Aneka asked, grabbing and holding on to Janelle's hand.

"If you don't have any plans, you're very welcome to join us."

Janelle hesitated.

"Please, please, please," Aneka said hopefully.

Tyson and Janelle traded soulful looks as Aneka continued to tug on her hand. How could she possibly resist?

"You know what—I think I'd like that," Janelle said. "But I need to make a few stops first. I can meet you."

"I'll pick you up at Ben's in two hours."

Janelle glanced at her watch and nodded. "Perfect."

Tyson nodded his thanks and the three of them walked over to the elevators to leave. As soon as they stepped outside, they saw the flurries. Aneka, holding both Janelle's and Tyson's hands, was overjoyed to see snow. She let go and started grabbing at the flakes. "Looks like we're going to have a white Christmas," Tyson said. "We'll see you in a couple of hours."

"Try to get some rest," Janelle said before saying goodbye and heading to her car. Fifteen minutes later, she was walking through the biggest toy store in the Baltimore area. She picked out a number of toys she thought Aneka would enjoy, and then she went to another store and purchased something for her father and Tyson.

Afterward, she hurried home, grabbed a quick shower and dressed. She chose one of the outfits Nya had bought for her—gray slacks and a burgundy cashmere sweater. It fit perfectly. She pulled her hair back into a bun just as the doorbell rang. As soon as she opened the door, Aneka, dressed in a little red coat and matching hat, came rushing inside excitedly. "We got a Christmas tree. We got a Christmas tree!"

"You did? That's wonderful," Janelle said as Tyson followed Aneka inside. He had changed into a charcoal cashmere sweater, black slacks and black overcoat, looking just as handsome as before.

He looked her up and down. "You look gorgeous."

"Thank you. You look pretty handsome yourself," she said, closing the front door.

"I look pretty, too," Aneka said, twirling around and clicking her black patent-leather shoes on the marble floor.

"Yes, you look very, very pretty," Janelle told her.

Aneka looked up at the beautiful Christmas decorations in the foyer and in the rest of the house. Her eyes shone brightly as she gasped in delight, then started cheering. Janelle took her hand and walked her into the living room, where the enormous Christmas tree stood. Aneka's face lit up and she ran over to look more closely at it. Janelle turned on the tree lights and the train beneath began circling as the locomotive's whistle played "Jingle Bells." Aneka applauded and knelt to watch the train.

"Thank you for coming out with us today," Tyson said, standing very close behind Janelle.

She turned and smiled. "Thanks for inviting me. I'm looking forward to it. Can I get you anything?"

"No, but we'd better get going. We have a lot of ground to cover."

"What do you mean? I thought we were just going to see Santa."

"I promised Aneka that I'd take her to the aquarium today, and I have tickets to a Christmas puppet show in D.C."

"She's going to love that."

Tyson nodded. "Yes, I think so, too. Come on. Let's get started."

After Tyson pulled Aneka away from the tree lights and train, the three of them headed to the foyer. Tyson helped

Janelle put on her coat then opened the front door. They stepped outside and Aneka skipped to the car. Tyson stopped and turned to Janelle as she closed the door. "I'm glad you're back."

She nodded and smiled. "I'm glad you are, too."

Chapter 10

The first stop was a trip to Santa's House in Inner Harbor. When it was Aneka's turn, she whispered to Santa, telling him all the toys she wanted for Christmas. Then they, including Tyson and Janelle, took pictures with Santa. Aneka was thrilled.

Afterward they ate lunch and then strolled along the Harbor walkway, entertained by jugglers, magicians and carolers. Janelle took Aneka on the merry-go-round followed by a playful walk through a children's gingerbread house and a life-size dollhouse, while Tyson disappeared into a nearby toy store to pick up items he had previously ordered online.

They continued their outing with a trip to the National Aquarium, Aneka's favorite place to go. As soon as they walked in, Aneka led the way to her favorite exhibits.

They drove to Washington, D.C., for an early dinner and a special holiday puppet show at Union Station. By the time they headed back to Baltimore, everyone was happily exhausted and Aneka had fallen asleep in her car seat.

In Tyson's car, Janelle relaxed back into the blissful comfort of toasty warmth and soft holiday music. She closed her eyes and exhaled, feeling absolutely perfect. She turned around to see Aneka fast asleep.

"She is so adorable. How do you like being a single father?"

"It's more difficult than ever I imagined. But I love it and I got great tips from your father."

"My dad? Really?" she said, stifling a yawn.

"Yeah, really." He turned to her. "Tired?"

"No, not really—more happy and contented."

"I like the sound of that."

"Yeah, me, too. I think I could get used to this."

"I hope so." He reached over and grasped her hand, squeezing gently. "Thank you. You made our day very special. I couldn't have imagined it without you."

Janelle smiled to herself. "It's funny. I'm usually working through the holidays. It gives the doctors with young children a chance to spend the day with them. So, I've missed out on most Christmassy things."

"Like baking cookies, riding on merry-go-rounds and taking pictures with Santa," Tyson suggested.

She chuckled. "Yes. Exactly. I forgot how much fun it can be just to let go and enjoy life. I don't get a chance to do that."

"With the right person," Tyson added.

Janelle nodded in agreement and looked at him. "Yes, with the right person."

"So, right person, what happens next?" he asked.

Janelle took a deep breath and sighed. "Well, Dad has the neighbors over tomorrow night for the annual Christmas Eve party and neighborhood luminaries."

"What are those?" he questioned.

"The neighborhood does it every year. My mom and dad started it years ago. We place white bags with candles and sand throughout the area. At sunset the candles are lit and the whole area looks like Santa's runway. Afterward Dad has everyone over for cookies, hot chocolate and champagne."

"Sounds nice," he said.

"It is. The kids in the neighborhood love it and Dad looks forward to doing it every year no matter what. He invites his staff and their kids. It's a huge thing for him.

"Aneka will love it," she added, then continued in a whisper. "Later on in the evening, Santa will drive his sleigh through the neighborhood."

He smiled, nodding. "You're right. She will love it."

They fell into a comfortable silence for the next few minutes. Tyson said, "Janelle, when I asked you before about what's next, I mean with us—you and me. Where do we go from here?"

"Yeah, I know," she said.

"I never lied to you, Janelle. You always knew I had to leave eventually. It was my job."

"Yes, and I also knew that we talked about having a life together. You know I would have followed you anywhere."

"That's just it. I couldn't let you do that."

"It wasn't your choice, Tyson. It was mine."

"And I couldn't let you make it," he said as Janelle shook her head. "Your father was right. You were destined to be a doctor, to save lives. You wanted to help children. How could I let you give up on your future?" he asked as he turned into her father's neighborhood. The area glowed brilliantly, but they barely noticed.

"How can you say that? You were my future, Tyson. Yes, I wanted to be a doctor and help children, but I also wanted to have you, to love you."

He smiled and gently touched her face. "Janelle, don't you know? You have me. You will always have me," he added softly.

"You didn't call. You didn't write or text or anything. You just left me, like I didn't even matter."

"That was just it. You mattered too much."

"But you still left me," she said sadly.

He nodded. "I had to leave."

"'Had to'? Why?"

He shook his head without responding.

She could see he was keeping something from her. "Tyson, this conversation isn't getting us anywhere. We had our chance. It's over. That time has passed."

"No, I don't accept that. I love you, Janelle, and I know there's some part of you that still loves me. We can be together. We will be together. We just need to—"

"Ohh-hh…pretty lights."

Tyson instantly stopped talking and glanced up in the rearview mirror at Aneka. Janelle turned to look back. Aneka was half-awake and looking out the window at the homes in the neighborhood. Most of them were elaborately decorated and brilliantly lit for the holidays.

"We need to finish this conversation," Tyson said quietly.

"Not now. Not tonight," she said.

Tyson drove up into Ben's driveway and parked. He got out, opened Janelle's door, then extended his hand to help her out of the car.

"Can I see? Can I see?" Aneka exclaimed excitedly, wanting to get out to see the lights and animated reindeer up close.

"No, sweetheart, we'll come back tomorrow," he said. "You can see the reindeer then. I promise."

Disappointed, she slumped down in her car seat, frowning. Tyson closed the front passenger door to keep her warm inside and turned to Janelle. He didn't speak. He just smiled.

"Thank you again for today. I had a wonderful time," Janelle said. She started to walk away, but Tyson still held her hand. She stopped and looked up at him. She knew what he was asking without him saying a single word, but she wasn't ready to answer.

"Tyson, today was perfect. I don't want to ruin it by talking about the past and what-if." She sighed heavily. "I don't want to look back. This is my life now and I'm happy."

He nodded, reached up and stroked her face. "I want you to be happy. I always did and always will."

"Yes, I know," she said softly. "Now, you'd better get your little princess home. She needs her rest and so do you."

"Forever the doctor," Tyson said as he stroked her cheek and the soft underside of her chin.

Janelle nodded. "Yep, that's right. So do as the doctor says."

He moved close and kissed her. Everything she thought she knew about love and life and forever disappeared. All she knew was Tyson. It was undeniable. She still loved him. She would always love him. The kiss was passion, desire and need all rolled in one. When it ended she stepped away, smiling. "Hmm, that was nice."

"There's a lot more," he whispered.

Her smile brightened as she slipped her hand from his. "Good night, sir." She backed away, turned and headed to the front door. When she opened it, she looked back to see Tyson still standing there watching her.

She nodded, went inside and closed the door. But that was as far as she got. She leaned back against the door and closed her eyes, feeling incredible. She felt like a kid on Christmas morning, seeing everything she ever wanted right in front of her. Right now, this moment, her life was absolutely perfect.

Chapter 11

Smiling to herself, Janelle headed to her father's office. He wasn't there, so she grabbed a cup of hot tea from the kitchen then went upstairs. Noticing her father's bedroom light still on, she knocked. There was no answer. Peeking inside, she saw that he was asleep in the bed, surrounded by papers. She went in, moved his laptop and gathered the papers, putting them on his nightstand along with his reading glasses. Just as she turned to leave, she heard his voice. "Hey, hi, you're home," Ben said huskily.

She turned back to him. "Yeah, I got in a few minutes ago. I knocked, but you were asleep. I just cleared the papers off the bed. I didn't mean to wake you."

"That's okay. I'm glad you did," he said, sitting upright against his pillows. "You look happy. You have a good day?"

"I am happy and it was a good day." Janelle smiled contentedly. "No, actually it was a great day. It started off with a job offer from Meg at Johns Hopkins medical center."

"A job offer from Johns Hopkins? That's fantastic. For years you talked about being a doctor at the hospital. You were so set on it—and look, you did it. I knew you could."

She smiled proudly. "Yep, looks like it's gonna happen."

"Congratulations, sweetheart. I'm so proud of you, baby."

They hugged warmly. "Thanks, Dad. I'm excited about it."

"When do you start?"

"Not until the beginning of the year. I still have to hand in my resignation at Medics International and do the paperwork."

"Well, now...a job offer. You did have a good day."

"Actually it got better. After my meeting with Meg, I ran into Tyson and Aneka. She had an asthmatic episode last night."

"Is she okay?" he asked, concerned.

"Yes, she's fine. They were leaving when I was headed out. They invited me to join them to go see Santa."

He chuckled. "Now, that's something I hadn't heard in a very long time."

She nodded and sat on the side of the bed. "Yeah, it was a lot of fun. You know, I forgot what Christmas is like through the eyes of a child. I guess I get so caught up in helping children and trying to make them feel better that I forgot the simplicity of just being with them. She's a sweetheart."

"Indeed. And there's nothing like seeing the holidays through the eyes of a little one. They bring a certain kind of joy that's unmatched by anything." She nodded.

Ben hesitated. "So...you and Tyson again?" he asked.

"I don't know." She shrugged. "There's so much water under the bridge for us. I wouldn't know where to start."

"It looks like you already have. Do you still love him?"

She paused and thought a moment. "Do we ever really fall out of love with someone?" she said evasively, catching Ben's smile. "You're smiling. I thought you'd be the last person to want me and Tyson to be together again."

He reached over and took her hand. "Sweetheart, I want

you to be happy. Tyson makes you happy. I can see that now. The two of you have something special. You know, your mother told me something very important before she died, but I didn't listen."

"What did she tell you?"

"She told me to relax and that things always work out as they should in the end." He shook his head. "I'm sorry to say that I didn't always listen to that advice."

"Why, what do you mean?"

"I mean with you and Tyson."

"What about me and Tyson?" she questioned.

Ben nodded and took a deep breath as if to release a heavy burden he'd been carrying. "Two and a half years ago I told Tyson to leave."

"You what? Dad…"

He nodded. "I told him to go back to the West Coast and to leave you to your future."

"Dad, no."

"Yes, I'm afraid so. The night he proposed and you accepted, he came to me. We talked. I told him that I wanted you to follow your dream and he was standing in the way of that. I told him that if he loved you he'd leave. I didn't even want him to say goodbye to you. To his credit, he put up a hell of a fight and an indisputable argument, but in the end I persuaded him that you needed to have your life and that meant being a doctor like you always wanted."

"Dad…"

"I didn't have enough faith in his love and your heart. But then…"

"But then…what?" she asked.

"When I had the heart attack I called him to make things right. He came and he stayed. I tore his world apart and he came and stayed with me, like a son."

"I don't know what to say."

"I do. I'm sorry I interfered. I was doing what I thought

best for you, but now I see that your mother was right, as always. Everything works out exactly as it should, especially love. I already asked Tyson to accept my apology, and now I'm asking you. I'm sorry I interfered."

She nodded. "Apology accepted." She kissed his cheek. "So how did the meeting with the bank go today? Good news?"

He shook his head. "I'm afraid not. We did everything we could think of, but it's not going to be enough."

"Even with taking on a business partner?" she asked.

Ben shook his head. "No one wanted to take the risk. I'm afraid it's over."

"Dad, I'm so sorry."

"No worries. We have a big day tomorrow, lots to do and the kids are depending on us."

"'Tomorrow'?" she queried.

"Yes, for the Christmas Eve party. They're still some things to take care of…the caterer, the florist, things like that."

"I'll take care of all that. You relax. I'm here to help, remember. Plus, I have a few ideas I think you're going to like."

"Sounds good. We'll get started in the morning."

She rose from the side of the bed and nodded. "Good night, Dad," she whispered as he turned off the light.

Janelle walked back to her bedroom and closed the door. Her thoughts immediately went to her father's business and the people who worked for him. There was nothing anyone could do. Then she thought about Tyson. All this time she'd thought he had just walked out on her, but she'd been wrong.

She pulled out her laptop and video-called her sisters. When they logged in, she told them about the past few days and what her father had said.

"Wow," Mia said.

"Yeah, wow," Nya added.

"So, am I crazy or what? How can I fall in love with him in one day? I'm right back where I was two and a half years ago and the moral of the story is still the same—don't fall in love."

"Honey, you never stopped loving him," Nya said.

"That's true," Mia agreed.

After a short period of reflection, Janelle conceded with a nod. "I know." She sighed as she cupped her chin in the palm of her hand and stared at her sisters' images on the laptop screen. Then she smiled. Although she would have certainly preferred to be with them right now, the FaceTime program would have to do. "I'm sorry, guys. This isn't exactly what we were supposed to be talking about the day before Christmas Eve."

"Sure it is," Mia said. "We're sisters. It's what we do."

"Okay, the way I see it, you have two choices. Be happy with him or be miserable without him. Now, I may be biased, but I'm rooting for you to be happy with him," Nya told her.

"I second that," Mia said. "Just enjoy being with him now."

"Not thinking about it obviously didn't mean it wasn't going to happen. But it's inevitable. Tyson is leaving as soon as he's finished with Dad. And since nothing can be done about the business, that's going to be soon. He already has something lined up in New York. It's only a matter of time," Janelle conceded.

"So, the question is, do you want to follow him?"

Janelle didn't need to think long about her answer. "I can't live my life on the road. I'm a doctor. I worked too hard and I love what I do. I don't want to give that up."

"Of course not," Nya agreed. "So, talk to him. Tell him how you feel, tell him you love him."

Janelle shook her head. "Thanks, guys, but I don't think

being together is ever going to be an option. I'll be here working at the hospital doing what I love and he'll be traveling all over the world doing what he loves. What kind of life is that? It's not as if I can ask him to stop working and stay here with me."

"Why not?" Mia said.

"Yeah, why not?" Nya added. "David left Hollywood for Natalia, Spencer left Atlanta for Tatiana and Chase left Alaska for Nikita. So, it does happen. And I'm a firm believer that you can never say what a man in love won't do." She smiled coyly.

"You got that right," Mia agreed wholeheartedly.

Janelle smiled, daring for the first time to even consider hoping there might be a happily-ever-after ending with Tyson in her future. "Thanks."

"No problem. You do what you need to do and let us know."

"I will. Merry Christmas," Janelle said to her sisters as she kissed her fingers and touched the screen.

Mia and Nya did the same. "Merry Christmas."

Janelle ended the connection, took a quick shower, sipped her cooled tea and crawled into bed. She grabbed her laptop and checked the movie listings. One of her favorite holiday movies, *A Christmas Carol,* was just coming on. She reached over to turn off the lamp and settle back just as a message notification beeped. Thinking it was one of her sisters on FaceTime again, she logged on.

Tyson's smiling face appeared on the screen. "It's about time you showed up."

She smiled. "Hey."

"Is it too late to call?"

Her smile widened. "No, not at all. I was just getting ready for bed." His brow arched with interest.

"Don't get any ideas," she said.

He laughed. The rich, deep sound made her stomach flutter.

"I am a very patient man when I have to be. I just called to thank you again for everything you did today. We both appreciate it."

"You're very welcome. Is that it?"

"Not quite. I miss you."

She blushed openly. "I miss you, too," she said as she leaned back against the pillows. "Is Aneka asleep?"

"Yeah, she passed out as soon as her head hit the pillow. She told me that she had a fun day and she'd remember it always."

"It was my pleasure." They both paused. Then she saw him frown in frustration. "What are you doing?" she asked.

"Believe it or not, I'm trying to put a dollhouse together."

She chuckled. "How's that going?"

"It's not. I gave up twice already. This is my third attempt. Much to my chagrin, I can completely build and refurbish an actual building, but I can't put together this dollhouse. That amazes me."

"Did you even look at the instructions?"

"I don't read instructions." He snorted boastfully. "I'm a man."

She started laughing. He smiled, then joined in. "So typical," she said, shaking her head. "Okay, grab the instructions. I have a feeling we'd better start from the beginning."

They spent the next hour and a half laughing and talking while Tyson put Aneka's dollhouse together. When it was done, he angled his laptop screen to show her the end result.

Janelle nodded her approval. "She's gonna love it," she said.

"I hope so. I had it specially designed as a miniature model of our new house."

"It's beautiful," she said, feeling her heart tremble when he mentioned their new home. She wanted to know more, but she couldn't bring herself to ask. "It's getting late. I'd better let you go. Will I see you tomorrow?" she asked.

"Yes, of course. I'm looking forward to it."

"Good night," she said softly.

Neither disconnected the signal. They just looked at each other.

Finally, Tyson spoke. "I love you. Good night."

She nodded and hung up. The movie she'd forgotten all about popped back up on her screen showing the ending credits. She closed her laptop just as it ended.

Chapter 12

The dream Janelle had that night felt too real. In it she had lost everything and, like Ebenezer Scrooge in the movie, she had grown old with nothing and no one in her life. She woke Christmas Eve morning in a panic. The realization that her sisters were right was undeniable. She needed to tell Tyson how she felt. She loved him. She got up, got dressed and hurried out early. Soon after, she was ringing the doorbell at the town house.

Mrs. Ivers answered. "Good morning, Janelle. Come on in."

"Good morning, Mrs. Ivers. How are you and how's your son?"

"I'm fine and, thank God, he's just bruised. It could have been a lot worse. Can you believe he had a car accident two weeks before starting college?"

"I'm glad to hear he'll be fine. Is Tyson here?"

"You just missed him. He's in D.C. all day," she said just as the oven alarm rang. "Oh, there's the oven." She headed to the kitchen, Janelle following.

"Janelle!" Aneka ran to her.

Janelle knelt and hugged her before Aneka took her hand

and pulled her into the living room to see the Christmas tree and presents. There was wrapping paper and ribbon all over the coffee table. "This one is for you," Aneka said, grabbing a shirt-size box wrapped in Santa-and-reindeer paper. "Me and Daddy picked it out special. But I can't tell you what it is. I promised."

"I have a very special gift for you, too, but you'll have to wait until Christmas Day to open it."

"Can I have it before me and Daddy go home?"

"You're going back home on Christmas Day?"

Janelle stilled as Aneka nodded and the affirmation hit her—Tyson was leaving again. With nothing left to do for her father's business, it made sense. She looked around, seeing several pieces of luggage sitting by the stairs.

"Sorry about that," Mrs. Ivers said, walking into the living room. "It's going to be a crazy, busy couple of days. I don't know why I waited to start wrapping gifts. Anyway, Tyson's not here, but if it's an emergency I can—"

"No, it's not important. I'll catch up with him later."

Mrs. Ivers nodded. "I'll let him know that you stopped by."

"No need. I'm glad your son's better. I'll see you this evening, Mrs. Ivers." Janelle said her goodbyes and quickly hurried out to the car. She sat a moment, collecting her thoughts. Telling Tyson she loved him was no longer an option. It was too late. He was leaving. She drove back to her father's home just in time to see him rushing out the front door. "Hi, Dad. You're leaving? Everything okay?"

"Yes. I just got a call from the bank. They're reviewing my application again. Looks like there might be a glimmer of hope."

"I hope so. Good luck. Don't worry about the party. I'll take care of everything. Drive safe." She watched him drive off, then went inside.

Thankfully, the rest of the morning was nonstop craziness and the perfect mental distraction. By ten o'clock there was a constant flow of deliveries, as well as caterers, florists and workmen. Janelle took care of the details and finalized the evening's events. Wanting the night to be really special for her father, she went into the attic and pulled out some of her mother's family decorations. They were the perfect finishing touch.

By late afternoon the Truman home was a spectacular holiday display and a magical winter wonderland. Large white lanterns filled with pine branches, glass balls and candles guided guests to the front door as huge white poinsettias brightened the entrance foyer and flowed throughout the house. Gingerbread houses, candy canes, holiday cookies and edible delights topped every table with a spectacular buffet feast centered in the dining room.

Dressed and smiling, Ben watched as Janelle walked down the front staircase to the foyer. He smiled and hugged her. "You look beautiful. I still can't believe how fantastic this place looks. You did an incredible job. I never took the time to really appreciate how truly remarkable you are. Your mother would be very proud of you. I'm very proud of you."

Janelle beamed with delight as she straightened her father's bow tie. "Thanks, Dad. So, how did it go today with the bank?"

"They'll call me this evening with a final decision."

"You'll get the loan." She nodded, assuring him.

"Either way, let's just have a wonderful evening."

The doorbell rang. "Ah, saved by the bell. It looks like we have our first guest of the evening." Janelle stood by the stairs as Ben opened the front door. A tiny red coat rushed in excitedly. Ben knelt and scooped Aneka up, swinging her around. She giggled and laughed happily as she hugged Ben and talked nonstop about Santa coming to town. Janelle walked over, smiling, as Tyson appeared in the doorway a second later.

Ben set Aneka down, shook Tyson's hand and then hugged him. "We tried," Ben said.

"There's always a Christmas miracle," Tyson assured him.

Aneka tugged on Ben's jacket, wanting to see the Christmas tree and train set again. They went into the living room, leaving Tyson and Janelle in the foyer.

The realization that he would be leaving hit her again. She smiled solemnly. "Hi."

He kissed her tenderly. "You look stunning, as always," Tyson said after a rakish smile and a thorough examination.

"Thank you," she said.

"I have something for you." He pulled a mistletoe sprig from his jacket pocket and held it over her head. Just as he leaned down to kiss her, the doorbell rang. She smiled, shrugged and opened the door, welcoming more guests to the party. In no time the house was packed with family, friends and with children everywhere. Guests continued to arrive in a steady flow. They mingled, talked, laughed, ate, drank and enjoyed themselves. Ben was the perfect host and the life of the party. No one would have guessed that his business was hanging by a single thread.

At dusk the neighborhood luminaries had been lit. Everyone stepped outside to see Santa's runway as the illuminated glow curved and coiled along the sidewalks. The children played along the luminaries as the adults stood by, admiring the spectacular sight. Then to everyone's delight Santa came through, waving and wishing all a merry Christmas.

After a while everyone went back inside to hot chocolate and warm beverages and gathered in the conservatory to watch as the fireworks display began. With the children sitting up front, all eyes marveled at the spectacular night sky.

Janelle noticed her father wasn't there. She looked around, finally finding him in his office. He'd just hung up the phone.

"Dad, is everything okay?"

He turned and smiled. "Yes, everything is more than okay. The loan went through. The company's going to be okay."

She hugged him. "Dad, that's great news. Congratulations."

"I have to say, it didn't look good when I left this afternoon, but whatever Tyson did…"

"'Tyson'? What do you mean?"

"He said he'd talk to them. Whatever he said worked. Looks like I have a new business partner. All I have to do is accept the offer. Ah, there's the man of the hour."

Janelle turned to see Tyson standing in the office doorway. Ben walked over and they shook hands. "Thank you."

Tyson nodded his agreement. "It was my pleasure."

Ben nodded and turned to Janelle. "You two talk. There's a lot to say. I'm gonna celebrate a new beginning by watching the fireworks." He walked out as Tyson entered.

"You've been avoiding me all night," Tyson said.

"Is it that obvious?"

"Yes, it is." He walked over to her. "Why?"

"To make it easier," she said, feeling her heart breaking.

"I don't understand. Your dad's company is fine."

She turned. The desperation of lost love, hurt and pain filled her eyes. "Yes, I know. You did another amazing job. So, I guess this is it. Thank you for helping my father and for staying around to say goodbye this time."

"What?"

"Your work here is done. You're leaving," she said. "I saw the luggage at the house this morning."

"No, Janelle. The luggage is a gift for Mrs. Ivers's son. He's leaving for college."

"But what about the job in New York? And your project?"

"New York was never an option. And you are my special project," he said tenderly. "Janelle, I'm not leaving. There's no way I could walk away from you again. I love you. I've always loved you, now and forever. From the first moment I saw you. I can't picture the rest of my life without you."

She looked into his eyes. The adoration in them reflected her love for him.

"Sweetheart, I can't do this without you. I can't exist without you. You're every breath I take. I need you in my life and I don't mean just as friends. You are my heart and I am yours. We are meant to be together. Say you love me. That's all I need. That's all I'll ever need."

"I love you, Tyson," she said. "I love you."

An endless swell of love washed over them as they kissed. Then he pulled back. "Don't move. Wait here." He ran out then a minute later returned with the box she had seen under his tree earlier. "This is for you."

She opened it, seeing a different African wedding doll inside. She picked it up, smiling. "She's beautiful." Then she looked closely and saw a ribbon around the doll's neck. On the ribbon was a ring. He untied the ring and took her hand. "Marry me, Janelle. Be my life."

Janelle's heart filled with joy beyond belief. "Yes. Yes."

He instantly took her in his arms and kissed her.

Ben, with Aneka by his side, peeked into the office. Janelle smiled happily. "Dad, we're getting married," she said excitedly.

"Well, it's about time," Ben said, walking over to shake Tyson's hand. "Welcome to the family. Looks like I have a new business partner and a son all in one."

"Your business partner?" Janelle repeated, turning to Tyson.

Tyson nodded as he picked up Aneka. "Merry Christmas, little one," he said.

"Merry Christmas," she said, then reached out to Janelle and hugged her, too.

"Merry Christmas, sweetheart," Janelle said.

They all went back to the conservatory to join their guests and watch the Christmas fireworks.

Tyson wrapped his arm around Janelle.

She was surrounded with love. It was the perfect Christmas…with many more to come.

* * * * *

MINE BY CHRISTMAS
Janice Sims

DEDICATION

Mine by Christmas is dedicated to my husband, Curtis, who is my very own tech nerd, like Adam Benson in this story. And to you, the readers, who have loyally followed me since *Affair of the Heart* (1996) to the present. Thank you!

ACKNOWLEDGMENTS

A story is written by an author in isolation, but it comes together with the efforts of many people. Thanks to my editor, Rachel Burkot, for her valuable advice on how to make *Mine by Christmas* a more pleasurable reading experience for you. Thanks also to editorial assistant Caroline Acebo, who keeps us writers on the right track at Harlequin.

Chapter 1

Adam Benson awoke with a start. He reached over, switched on the lamp and groaned as he sat up and swung his long muscular legs over the side of the bed. What was wrong with him? Why was he dreaming about Sage so frequently? What was even more disturbing was the fact that they weren't erotic dreams. No, these dreams left a lasting impression of real emotions. His heart was still beating wildly in his chest and he vividly remembered the taste of her sweet lips. As he sat there in the bedroom of his Seattle mansion, his entire body was infused with the unmistakable feeling of being in love. He should recognize that feeling because Sage Andrews was the only woman he'd ever loved. Sure, he still thought of her fondly, but it had been years since he'd been face-to-face with her. Did she ever dream about him?

Coming to a decision, he picked up his cell phone from the nightstand and ran his finger across the touch screen, selecting the messages option. He listened to his mother's voice asking him to come home for Christmas. He had not planned to go home to New Haven, Connecticut, this year, but now he reconsidered. There was a certain neighborhood Christmas Eve party he had to attend.

Sage Andrews loved Christmas in New Haven. She never missed going to see the Fantasy Lights at Lighthouse Point Park. Every year she and her father, Earl, went to a local Christmas-tree farm to cut down their own tree. She even liked the quirkier aspects of Christmas in New Haven, including some guy named Noel climbing the Christmas tree on New Haven Green and getting tangled in the branches, which were laden with thirty thousand LED lights. Firemen had to rescue him.

She smiled at the thought as she drove to her parents' house for their annual Christmas Eve party in her old neighborhood. Her cell phone kept buzzing, but she ignored it. She'd had a long day in court substituting for her partner, Jim Douglas, a divorce attorney, who had been called away to be with his wife, Sha-Shana, in the delivery room. They were now the proud parents of a little girl. Sage usually dealt with custody issues, and listening to a couple tear each other apart in court today had been depressing. She just wanted to relax. Whoever was phoning her could leave a message.

Driving down these streets flanked by houses lavishly decorated for Christmas reminded her of her childhood. She'd been a happy kid with parents who loved her and who loved each other. Back then, the Andrews were struggling financially, but so were other families in the neighborhood. It was a close-knit community, though, and everyone helped each other. As times grew more prosperous, the houses improved. Today the neighborhood was one of the most prominent in the city.

She looked sadly at the Cape Cod across the street from her parents' Tudor-style home. The Bensons lived there. Seeing their home always made her think of their son,

Adam, her first love and the only man to ever break her heart.

She sighed deeply and then perked up. Tonight was not for reminiscing about the past but for having fun!

She managed to find a parking space among the other guests' cars on the street and got out to walk to the front door. Just as she started up the solar-powered, lamp-lined walk, wrapped in a hooded woolen coat, it began to snow. She paused to look up at the flurries and held out her gloved hand to catch some flakes in her palm. *We're going to have a white Christmas after all,* she thought with a pleased grin.

She barely had time to pull her hand back after ringing the bell before her mother was pulling her inside.

"Sage!" Patricia Andrews cried, a panicked expression on her attractive chestnut-brown face. "Why didn't you answer your phone?"

Sage had a momentary glimpse of the tasteful holiday decorations such as poinsettias and red-velvet bows on the banisters of the stairs directly in front of her before her mother grabbed her arm in a viselike grip and pulled her through the foyer directly to the kitchen, bypassing the great room, where the party's guests were mingling.

"What's wrong, Mom?" Sage asked. "Can I take my coat off?"

"In a minute," Patricia, a petite, attractive woman in her mid-fifties, said as she yanked her daughter into the chef's kitchen. "You can hang it in the pantry."

The kitchen was bustling with catering staff. Sage, who hadn't eaten since lunchtime, went to grab a canapé from a tray on the counter and her mother slapped her hand.

"Mom, what's gotten into you?" Sage asked as she snapped back her hand and began pulling off her coat.

"I tried to warn you," her mother said cryptically. She took Sage's coat, walked over to the pantry and hung it on a hook in there. The two of them stood in the large space, whispering so as not to be heard by the catering staff.

"Warn me about what?" Sage was getting worried now. "Has something happened to Dad?"

Exasperated, Patricia looked up at her daughter. "Adam's here."

With those two words Sage felt as if her stomach had just taken a nosedive into her Louboutins. For a moment she couldn't think, let alone form coherent words. Then she took a deep breath and exhaled. "You never said he would be here." She sounded more accusatory than she'd intended.

"I didn't know," her mother said in defense of herself. "Millie and Adam Senior showed up with him in tow. What was I supposed to do, tell him he couldn't stay? I'm his godmother, for heaven's sake!"

"Of course not," said Sage, removing her gloves and shoving them into the coat's pockets. She narrowed her eyes at her mother. "Wait a minute. How did you know seeing Adam would upset me? I never said I was avoiding him."

"I'm your mother. You don't have to tell me," Patricia said, rolling her eyes. "It's been nine years since you two broke up, and whenever he's home and Millie and Adam Senior invite us over for dinner, you make up an excuse as to why you can't come. I don't have to be a genius to figure that out!"

Sage willed herself to calm down. She laughed nervously. "He's a family friend visiting his folks for the holidays. No big deal."

"Well, if my instincts are on the money, you're the only reason he's here," Patricia said.

"What makes you say that?" Sage asked, feeling the panic rising again.

"Every time the doorbell rings, and I walk back into the great room with new guests, he cranes his neck to see who the new arrivals are. He's definitely waiting to see you. Who else is he eager to see again? Certainly not any of my other guests whose average age is fifty. That's why I pulled you in here for this little chat."

Sage breathed in deeply and let it out slowly. She was not going to let Adam Benson's presence at this party unnerve her. So what if he'd thrown her over and gone on to become an electronics billionaire who hobnobbed with the likes of the president and Bill Gates?

She was no loser herself. At twenty-eight, she had the reputation of being one of the best family-law attorneys in the state. She looked her mother in the eyes. "Well, let's get out there."

Patricia let out a relieved sigh and beamed. "That's my girl!"

They turned and walked out of the pantry. "And thanks for not letting me eat anything," Sage told her mom. "I'd hate to meet Adam for the first time in nine years with food in my teeth."

Adam was surrounded by people vying for his attention. He'd thought that at an intimate party for twelve couples, as his mother Millicent had described it to him, he would be left alone. But he had people in his face telling him how proud they were of him, a hometown boy who'd succeeded beyond everyone's expectations. He smiled and thanked them while surreptitiously keeping an eye on the entrance.

His patience was finally rewarded when his godmother walked in grasping Sage's hand. His breath caught and he heard himself sigh softly. At five foot nine, she was a statuesque beauty in a killer emerald-green dress. The same shade of green as his tuxedo vest. He smiled, thinking that he and Sage looked like a couple who'd chosen to dress similarly tonight.

He was nervous. How would she react to his being here?

He didn't have to worry, though, because as their eyes met across the room, she gave him a welcoming smile that made her warm brown eyes sparkle.

Then she and his godmother were standing directly in front of him. "Adam," Patricia Andrews said, "you and Sage are the odd ones out since neither of you arrived with a date. I hope you don't mind sitting together tonight."

Adam grinned. "Are you kidding? It would be my pleasure."

Patricia smiled in parting and went to attend to her other guests.

Adam and Sage stood awkwardly for a moment and then he impulsively pulled Sage into his arms for a hug. He expected her to stiffen, but instead she returned his hug. When they parted she looked up at him and said, "This is a surprise. If I'd known you were coming, I'd…"

"You would've made an excuse not to be here," he said, eyes twinkling with good humor.

Sage laughed. "You're probably right," she said softly.

He took her hand in his and they began walking toward the dining room. "It's wonderful to see you again, Sage. It's been way too long."

Sage looked up at him, a smile tugging at the corners of her mouth. "You're as charming as ever."

Adam laughed abruptly. "That's not how you described me the last time we spoke."

"That day I broke the record for the number of cusswords spoken by me in one day. I haven't matched that record since then."

Still smiling, Adam gazed down into her upturned face. "I deserved every word."

"Yes, you did," Sage said. "Are you back for more?"

In the formal dining room, Adam pulled Sage's chair out for her. After she was seated, he sat next to her and turned to face her. The room was abuzz with the soft voices of the other guests, and a John Legend song was playing on the sound system.

The waitstaff was currently serving the wine. The tinkling of crystal wineglasses and the hollow sound of the wine being poured added to the background noise.

Adam's focus was on Sage. He took in the golden-brown smoothness of her skin. How her heavy fall of curly black hair framed her heart-shaped face so beautifully. His gaze drifted downward to her mouth, which was full and sensual. They used to spend hours kissing, so he knew how utterly kissable her lips were.

"Do you remember the promise we made to each other—that we'd always be honest with one another, no matter what?" he said after a minute of simply enjoying looking at her.

"I do," Sage said at once. "And you weren't."

Adam winced. He couldn't have guessed how she would react to him after all these years. But he'd hoped that most of the animosity she'd felt toward him would have dissipated by now. He saw that she was still hurt by his behavior.

"No, I wasn't honest with you," he said. "I told you we should stop seeing one another because our long-distance relationship couldn't last. The fact is I broke up with you because I was ready for intimacy and you weren't. And since you weren't ready, I wasn't going to be that guy who manipulates his girl into something she's not ready for."

"I knew that was the reason," Sage muttered.

"You were only nineteen."

"And you were twenty-one and unwilling to wait," she whispered. Her eyes were momentarily fierce and then her gaze softened.

She briefly looked around, wondering if anyone had noticed them arguing, but the other couples were engrossed in each other. "Adam, that's water under the bridge." She looked at him expectantly. "Mom thinks you came here tonight specifically to see me. Is that true?" She smiled as she waited for his reply.

Adam couldn't hide his astonishment at hearing this. "What is your mother, a psychic?"

Sage laughed shortly. "I've often thought so. Was she right?"

Adam reached for her hand and she placed it in his. "I'm going to assume our truth-only agreement still stands."

Sage nodded. He thought he read genuine affection mirrored in her eyes as she watched him.

"For some reason I've been dreaming about you, Sage."

Her brows arched in curiosity. "What kind of dreams?" she cautiously inquired.

Adam felt his face flush with embarrassment. "Innocent dreams, I assure you. But they're persistent, several nights per week, every week for about three months now."

"I wonder why?" Sage said. "I was sure, until you showed up tonight, that I never crossed your mind."

"Why would you think that? You were my first love."

Sage sighed softly. "You're Adam Benson, electronics wunderkind. You rub elbows with the president. You could have any woman on earth. Why waste your brain cells on me?"

"Because you're special, Sage," Adam answered immediately. "You're the only woman I've ever loved. And I'm here because I think there may be a reason I'm dreaming about you. Maybe we should give us another try."

He could tell Sage was truly shocked by his words. Her big brown eyes were startled. Her hand went to her chest as though doing so would quiet a rapidly beating heart.

"Well, you wanted honesty," Adam quipped.

They were presently being served by the waitstaff. After the waiter moved away, Sage met Adam's eyes. "You're the only man I've ever loved. But, unfortunately, I don't believe in fairy tales anymore." She gestured to the snow falling outside the big picture window in front of them. "During the years we've been apart, my heart feels as though it has frozen over. That's why I haven't fallen in love with anyone else. I never *let* myself fall. I feel like a snow queen whose heart can't be pierced by love. So don't come here talking about trying again, Adam."

Adam felt as though his heart had been run through by a sharp knife. Seeing Sage again confirmed for him that he had indeed been dreaming of her because he still had feelings for her. But if she didn't feel the same way about him, what good would it do for him to try?

Then he remembered something; a gift he'd picked up for Sage at the last minute. He reached into his pocket and brought out a small package of peanut M&M's. He handed it to Sage.

"Merry Christmas, darling Sage," he murmured.

Sage took one look at the M&M's and tears immediately appeared in her eyes. Adam knew she was remembering that when they were poor, he would give her peanut M&M's in lieu of a more expensive box of candy. If she remembered that, Adam hoped, maybe she would recall other things about him that endeared him to her.

Seeing her reaction gave Adam hope. He was determined to make her believe in fairy tales again. He wondered what it would take to melt a snow queen's heart.

Chapter 2

A year later...

Sage stood at her office window on a Friday morning in the first week of December, looking down on the street below. There he was, like clockwork. Adam on his daily run. She couldn't resist a sigh filled with longing at the sight of his tall, well-built form. She turned away, a frown marring her pretty face. Did he jog past her office building every day just to vex her? If so, it was working.

Logically she knew that New Haven, Connecticut, was equally as much Adam's hometown as it was hers. He had a right to move back here after years of living in Seattle. But did he have to buy property in her neighborhood, build a huge house with a security gate *and* join her church?

Benson Electronics provided much-needed jobs for several thousand grateful citizens, which made Adam Benson a local hero. That didn't mean *she* had to jump on the bandwagon, too.

She'd been two grades behind Adam in school, and they had been sweethearts, dating throughout high school and into college. Their friends and family had all thought

Adam would eventually propose. But shortly after she began her second year of college, he told her he'd been offered a full scholarship to study applied mathematics at the Massachusetts Institute of Technology, and that he didn't believe it would be fair to her for them to continue their relationship. He'd broken up with her. She'd been nineteen and thought she'd never recover from the heartbreak, but she had.

Adam went on to make groundbreaking advances in electronics, and in the past few years he'd made strides that put him on par with giants such as Bill Gates and Steve Jobs. Today, at thirty-one, his inventions were earning him billions.

Sage, now twenty-nine, had become an attorney and settled in New Haven, where she'd opened her own firm specializing in family law. Her family was here, as well as most of her friends. She dated fascinating men who treated her well, but whom she never found fascinating enough to marry, although she'd had a couple of offers.

When Sage had heard Adam was moving back home to be near his elderly parents, she had felt warmth suffuse her heart because of the gesture. She tried not to think of the possibility that he'd moved back home to be close to her, as well. She believed she'd been firm enough with him last year at her parents' annual Christmas Eve party when he'd hinted that he wanted another chance with her, and she hoped that he didn't harbor any hopes of their getting back together.

He'd been back in New Haven about a year and so far she had been able to avoid him. When she saw him in church, she made sure to put several pews between them, and after services she found an excuse to beat a hasty retreat. He'd even phoned and left messages, which she'd never returned. Was she being foolish?

Their parents had been friends for decades. She would

not be able to avoid him forever. She knew from experience that the emotional impact of seeing Adam jog by from a distance would be nothing compared to standing close to him, breathing in his essence, hearing his voice with its rich, warm timbre and possibly feeling the heat coming off his body. She needed more time to prepare herself for the full assault of having Adam within touching distance.

She sat at her desk and opened the calendar on her computer. "Oh, no, is that today?" she said out loud when she saw she was supposed to have lunch with her mother at noon.

She adored her mother, but lately all Patricia Andrews wanted to talk about was Adam and how lucky the city of New Haven was to have him back home.

Adam had glanced up and seen Sage looking down at him as he'd jogged past her office building. He'd smiled to himself and kept running. She'd always been stubborn. All his overtures at being friendly had met with failure. She wouldn't return his phone calls. She hadn't bothered acknowledging the flowers he'd sent on her birthday. Any other woman would have been happy that he'd remembered, but not Sage. She was going to make him work for it. What she didn't know was that everything he'd ever gotten in life had been won by patience and hard work. He was undaunted by the impossible. The impossible just took longer. It didn't matter to him how long it would take to win Sage over. He'd known upon seeing her again last year that he'd never stopped loving her. Breaking up with her was the biggest regret of his life.

He'd confided in his mother how he felt about Sage. Millicent Benson had smiled knowingly and said, "It was only a matter of time before you came to your senses. That girl was *made* for you."

Adam couldn't have agreed more. Now his goal was to

get himself and Sage in the same room together. She was clever. Somehow she had managed to slip out of church every Sunday before he could corner her. It didn't help that it seemed as though every unattached woman in New Haven had joined that particular church since he'd become a member and made it their business to get his attention before he could escape the walls of the sanctuary.

He gave a huge sigh as he punched in the code at the gate leading to his house. Solving problems happened to be his forte. Getting Sage to fall in love with him again might seem like an insurmountable task, but he would make it happen either by using his intelligence or perhaps he'd be lucky and fate would step in and decide the matter. Either way, he would remain positive.

The gate opened and closed behind him, and he walked up the drive. His surroundings were immaculate: the three-story redbrick house was trimmed in white, its columns stately and charming. The grounds were expertly mani-cured. In the driveway was a luxury car and in the garage, a couple more. Yes, he was living the American Dream. By all outward appearances, his life was perfect. He had more money than he would be able to spend in a lifetime. The only thing missing was true love. And even though some people believed he had a hard drive for a heart, he still thought true love was the most important thing in the world.

"Christmas is coming, and you know what that means," Patricia Andrews crowed, smiling at her only child. They were sitting at a table in Pat's favorite restaurant, a bistro downtown called Peaches' Place, which served soul food with a healthy twist.

Sage smiled back and braced herself. Every year her mother hit her up for a huge donation to the scholarship fund sponsored by her mother's women's club, the Silver

Foxes. Last year the Silver Foxes had been able to award two deserving students ten-thousand-dollar college scholarships. Each year the ladies tried to up the ante, so Sage waited anxiously for her mother's next words.

Patricia Andrews, looking stylish and smart in her black Donna Karan slack suit and gold blouse, continued smiling. Her eyes were almost the same color as her blouse, a nice contrast to her rich, dark-chocolate skin. Sage had opted for a skirt suit in winter-white today with brown leather pumps. She shared her mother's eye color, but her skin tone was a combination of Pat's dark chocolate and her father Earl's golden-brown skin.

And while Pat wore her black hair relaxed and cut chin-length, Sage preferred to wear her long black hair natural. It fell in curls down her back.

Sage took the opportunity to eat a mouthful of collard greens as her mother gathered her thoughts. She was feeling kind of relaxed today because her mother hadn't brought up Adam once during their lunch date.

Pat spoke at last. "Sweetie, fund-raising hasn't gone well this year. The economy appears to be recovering, but not fast enough. Some businesses that donated to the fund last year are not donating this year. Or if they are, they're not giving as generously."

"How much are you short?" Sage asked.

Pat frowned. "We've raised a little over ten thousand."

"Then you need ten thousand more?" Sage said, looking into her mother's eyes, which had taken on a pained expression. "You need more than ten thousand?" Sage was confused now.

Pat started talking rapidly and excitedly. "Baby, we'd like to give five scholarships this year, so we actually need forty thousand more. Now, I know you usually make up the slack, what with your firm doing so well. But we thought it would be too much of a burden to ask you to do that—"

Sage stopped her. "I don't have forty thousand to give, Mom. I could handle ten, but forty's out of the question."

"I'm not asking you to donate forty thousand, darling," Pat said sweetly. "What we'd like you to do is go to *Adam* and ask *him* to contribute forty thousand."

Pat sat back expectantly in her chair, her eyes excited, her gaze riveted on her daughter's face.

Sage couldn't believe her mother had asked her to do something like that. For a moment all she could do was stare at her mother. When she spoke, it was in measured tones. "I haven't even said a word to Adam since he's been back, and you expect my first meeting with him to be about a donation to a charity?" Not wanting to call attention to themselves, she purposefully kept her voice down and her gestures to a minimum.

"We all agreed that you would be the perfect person to ask him," Pat went on, as if nothing was out of the ordinary. She paused to take a sip of iced tea. Looking Sage in the eyes, she said after a soft sigh, "I know how this looks to you. You think I'm trying to get you and Adam together to talk. So what if I am? You've told me how he's been trying to get in touch with you, and that you've ignored him. And maybe you think your nosy mother is trying her hand at matchmaking. But the truth is, Sage Elizabeth Andrews, you're going to have to face him sooner or later, so you'd just as well get it over with. If a few deserving kids benefit from that meeting, then it's all good!"

"Oh, you want to kill two birds with one stone, is that it?" Sage asked her wily mother.

"Yes, darling, something like that," Pat said, smiling warmly. "Come on. I know you don't have the heart to let the kids down, so go ahead and agree to do it so we can enjoy the rest of our lunch. This shouldn't be so hard for you to do. You've told me time and time again that you're over Adam. You hold no grudges against him for breaking your eighteen-year-old heart."

"I was nineteen."

"I stand corrected," Pat said, eyes twinkling mischievously.

Sage eyed her mother suspiciously. "This isn't something cooked up between you and Miss Millie?"

"Millie and I were disappointed when things didn't work out between you and Adam," Pat admitted. "We were two peas in a pod, Millie and I. Both of us wanted big families and ended up with only one child each. And when you and Adam started dating in high school and seemed so beautifully matched, we started dreaming of future grandbabies." She laughed. "But life has a way of bringing you back down to earth. We've come to terms with our disappointment, darling. Now we just want you and Adam to be able to be in the same room together without any acrimony. He's reaching out to you. Please, meet him halfway."

Sage picked up her fork and held it poised over her plate. "I'll think about it" was all she'd promise her mother at that point. She smiled to herself. *This has* plot *written all over it,* she thought.

Pat sighed in resignation and continued eating. However, Sage could tell that her enthusiasm hadn't waned in the least. The depths of her golden-brown eyes held just a little too much confidence. That look made Sage think her mother believed her mission had already been accomplished.

"Anyway," Sage added, "it's been over a month since Adam phoned me. Maybe he's given up and won't even take my call. So don't get your hopes up."

"He sent you flowers on your birthday last month," her mother reminded her.

Sage just tore into her salad without comment.

Chapter 3

Adam paced his office a few days later as he waited for Sage to arrive for their appointment. Meeting with heads of state didn't produce this much anxiety in him.

He wore an expensive gray pin-striped suit, gray shirt open at the collar due to his having removed the tie—it seemed to have been strangling him in his nervousness at seeing Sage again up close and personal. He'd ditched the jacket and had rolled up the sleeves of his shirt. He realized that all the effort he'd taken getting dressed this morning had been for nothing. He should have worn jeans.

What had him on pins and needles was the fact that he couldn't figure out why Sage suddenly wanted to see him after nearly a year of trying to get her to communicate with him.

His personal assistant, Jeanne, knocked and then quickly entered. "Mr. Benson, Ms. Andrews is here to see you."

Adam smiled at Jeanne. "Please show her in."

Jeanne disappeared and a moment later returned with Sage. Adam inhaled a sharp breath and let it out slowly upon seeing Sage. He schooled his facial expressions because he didn't want his pleasure at seeing her to show on his face. He could not control the tumult of his heartbeat accelerating, though. Or the general thrum of excitement that coursed through his body.

The coltish teen girl he'd known had turned into a stunner of a woman and was very curvaceous. She'd always been beautiful to him, even though she'd often derided her looks when they were growing up. She'd hated the smattering of freckles across her nose. Her black hair had been so unruly, she'd moaned about the number of combs she'd broken in it, whereas he'd loved her hair. He could see she was still wearing it natural, and it was still gorgeous.

She was wearing a navy blue skirt suit with a white blouse underneath. The suit was hitting on all her curves, the hem of the skirt high enough to display her long, shapely legs to perfection.

Sage smiled uncertainly. From the expression in her eyes, he could tell she wasn't sure she'd get a warm reception.

Adam stepped forward and grasped her hands in his. He smiled, his dark brown eyes inviting her to relax. "Sage, you look wonderful."

She gave him a genuine smile this time and he heard an almost imperceptible sigh of relief. "Hello, Adam. You look wonderful, too."

Indeed, Sage could barely stand upright she was so weak in the knees from just his touch. Here was the answer to her question of how she would react in his physical presence: she was melting. She fought to gain control of her senses. But it was her senses that were turning her to mush right in front of his eyes. They were still holding hands, and the solid strength and warmth of his seemed to transmit a current of electricity to every nerve ending in her body. Adam Benson, the lanky boy with the brilliant mind who had been the object of her first real crush, had, in the intervening years, managed to intensify his sex appeal.

Their eyes met and suddenly they were laughing at the absurdity of the situation.

Jeanne, who was still in the room, cleared her throat. "Would you like anything, sir? Coffee, bottled water?"

"Sage, would you like anything?" Adam asked.

"No, thank you," Sage said to Jeanne, who promptly left, closing the door behind her.

"Have a seat," Adam said, gesturing to the brown leather Queen Anne chair in front of his desk.

Sage sat and crossed her legs. She smoothed her navy skirt before gazing up at him. Adam stood leaning against his desk, his smile inquisitive.

"To what do I owe the pleasure of your visit?" he asked gently.

"Thank you for the flowers," Sage quickly said.

"You're welcome," Adam said with a soft chuckle. "That was over a month ago." His eyes bored into hers, and Sage looked down.

"You were never one to beat around the bush," she said. She looked back up at him. "Okay, I've been avoiding you."

"Tell me something I don't already know," he said with a humorous glint in his eye.

"It isn't funny," Sage cried indignantly.

"It *is* funny, Sage," he disagreed vehemently. "We're adults and have known each other since elementary school. There was no reason for you to hide from me."

"I wasn't hiding from you," Sage denied. "I just wasn't ready for this." She gestured to herself and then to him.

"This?" Adam asked, brows arched in an askance expression.

Sage frowned at him. She was convinced he knew perfectly well what "this" was. It was the magnetic pull that she was feeling right now. Sexual heat, yes, but it was more intense than that. She'd known it would happen if he ever got close enough to her because she'd felt its effects so powerfully last year when they'd finally come back together.

He leaned toward her, his square-jawed, clean-shaven face only inches from hers. "Sage, you don't have to be afraid of me. Deep down, I'm still the nerdy Adam you used to know."

Sage eyed him skeptically. "Really deep down," she murmured. She stood and walked over to the window, which provided a view of the busy street below. Downtown New Haven was bustling with activity this time of morning. Christmas decorations were displayed in every store window.

Adam came to stand beside her. "Did you ever think we'd be living in New Haven at the same time?" he asked.

"Honestly, I didn't spend much time thinking about us, Adam," Sage said truthfully. "I wished you well, but I was too busy living my own life. As I'm sure you were busy living yours."

Adam shook his head solemnly. "I see your point," he said. "Okay, we won't reminisce. Let's take it from here, shall we? No wondering what might have been if I hadn't been foolish and broken up with you when I was too young to know better."

She looked up at him with an astonished expression. "You think you were foolish for breaking up with me?"

"It was the most boneheaded thing I've ever done," Adam said without hesitation.

"When did you come to this conclusion?" Sage asked, curious.

"The moment I saw you last year at your parents' Christmas Eve party," Adam answered easily. "I realized I never stopped caring for you."

"Aren't you afraid you're just being nostalgic?" asked Sage. She was searching his face, looking for doubt or indecision. His statement had started her heart to racing, wondering if it were possible that what they'd had years ago had not been puppy love, as her mother sometimes jokingly described their relationship during that time, but the real thing. "It happens, you know," she continued. "A couple who were childhood sweethearts meets again, familiar feelings start to stir, and before you know it, they're back in a relationship. But a few weeks or months or maybe even years later, they break up again. The high doesn't last."

"I can see why you became an attorney," Adam said as he bent and kissed her gently on the mouth. He broke it off only long enough to murmur, "But you're not going to talk me out of this."

Sage closed her eyes and opened her mind to the sweet sensual assault of his mouth on hers. His lips were soft yet firm, and his breath mingling with hers was fresh and inviting. When his tongue probed between her lips, she let him in and practically swooned as he methodically and with sheer abandon made her so weak in the knees that she literally fell into his arms.

When they came up for air, they looked into each other's eyes for several intense moments. "You never used to kiss me like that," Sage breathed.

"I was a boy then," said Adam. "I'm a man now."

"I don't know what to say," Sage told him, "or what to do." She looked him straight in the eyes. "I guess I should just be honest with you. I came here today to ask you to donate to my mother's women's-club scholarship fund. She wanted me to stop avoiding you and talk to you, and she thought the best way to accomplish that was by making me feel guilty if I didn't come to see you on behalf of the kids. I never thought our meeting would end up like this."

Adam smiled. Sage hoped he knew she was sincere. And that it embarrassed her to have to admit she'd come to see him only for a donation. Her stomach twisted in knots as she stood there looking into his eyes.

"How much do they need?"

She was sure her face registered her surprise. "Forty thousand," she said softly.

"Why not a cool million?" he asked, his gaze resting on her mouth, which made her want to kiss him again. She mentally shook herself and concentrated on the matter at hand: scholarships for needy kids.

"They only asked for forty thousand," Sage said. She sat in the chair because suddenly this encounter was taking on a weird vibe. She'd anticipated Adam being cordial, yes. He'd always had good manners. But that kiss had been unexpected, and she was still weak from its effect. She also sensed that Adam wasn't as warm and welcoming as he had been when she'd first walked in. He seemed more aloof and possibly angry. About what, she couldn't fathom.

He was looking down at her. She sometimes used to be able to tell what he was thinking when they were teens, but now he was inscrutable. He was no longer that sweet boy. She wondered what sort of things the mature Adam could cook up in that superintelligent brain of his.

She didn't have to wait for long.

"I'll give your mother's club a million dollars if you'll agree to do something for me," Adam said, smiling at her.

Sage found the strength to stand now. After that kiss, she was sure that there was only one thing Adam Benson would pay a million dollars to get from her, and he was *not* going to get it!

"What do you think I am?" she exclaimed. "A high-priced call girl?"

He threw his head back and laughed. "Sage, you could always make me laugh. No, I don't want to buy your body. I want to buy your time. I'm attending an international science and technology summit in Vienna next week, and I want you to come as my companion."

"Define *companion*," Sage said, eyes narrowed.

"Being a lawyer again? Okay, if you want the terms laid out for you—you will attend a dinner and a dance with me, plus an awards ceremony. We'll stay in separate hotel suites, of course. Do you have a passport?"

"Yes, of course I do," said Sage a bit testily. "You're not the only world traveler in this room."

"Excellent," said Adam, smiling. "If you agree to those terms, I'll write you a check right now."

"I'll have to speak with my mother's club before deciding," she told him.

"You know they'll jump at the opportunity," Adam said. "And I'd rather you kept the terms of the agreement our secret. I can't have it getting out that I paid for an escort. It might be damaging to both our reputations."

Sage eyed him suspiciously. "Why are you doing this?"

"Because I want you, Sage," Adam said, his tone determined. "And from that kiss, I don't think you're immune to my charms, either. I just think you need time to digest everything. I predict that if you agree to this, you'll be mine by Christmas."

Sage laughed. She'd never been able to resist proving someone wrong when they made outrageous claims as Adam had just done. She would be his by Christmas? Not if she had anything to say about it!

"We'll see about that," she said, offering him her hand.

They shook on it, after which Adam sat behind his desk and withdrew his checkbook from a drawer. "The name of your mother's club?" he asked.

Sage told him, and he wrote her a check and handed it to her.

Sage glanced down at it. She'd never seen so many zeros in her life. "How do you know I'll go through with it?"

"We agreed to be truthful with each other, remember?" he said confidently.

Sage realized that was true. Last year they'd come clean with each other about their past relationship. He'd admitted that he'd broken up with her not because they couldn't carry on a long-distance relationship, but because she was too innocent for him. They'd also admitted they'd never loved anyone else except each other. The ramifications of that revelation still scared Sage.

"I'll hold up my end of the bargain," she assured him. "On behalf of the Silver Foxes, thank you, Adam," she said as she began walking toward the door.

"Oh," said Adam as if it were an afterthought. "You may need some new clothes. And I don't see why you should have to foot the bill for them. I'll have my personal shopper phone you and set up a time to consult with you."

Turning back around to face him, Sage smiled. "You're going to *Cary Grant* me?"

Adam chuckled. Sage guessed he was remembering that Cary Grant and Doris Day romantic comedy she'd made him sit through so many times when they were teens. In it, Cary Grant had purchased a whole wardrobe for Doris Day to wear on their rendezvous in the islands.

"Yes," he said. "I'm going to Cary Grant you, except I don't expect you to sleep with me."

"Good, because it isn't going to happen," said Sage. She gave him a teasing smile and left.

Outside, at the elevator, Sage stood for a moment and just breathed. She was all atremble inside. What had she gotten herself into? It was obvious that she wanted Adam, if her reaction to his kiss was any indication.

What would it be like to spend several days in Vienna with him? As a teen she had been determined to remain a virgin, so she and Adam had not made love. Now adults, they were both no doubt experienced in the art of love.

But it would be a mistake to jump into bed with him. She vowed that not until it was crystal clear that she and Adam were indeed meant to be together would she make love to him.

Chapter 4

After Sage left Adam's office, she went back to work, where she checked her schedule and asked her assistant to move around a few appointments. Luckily, she had no trial dates coming up soon, so that wasn't an issue. She wouldn't have agreed to go with Adam to Vienna if she'd been due in court the following week.

After giving her assistant instructions, she walked down the hall to her partner's office and knocked on his door. Jim Douglas called, "Come in!" in his deep voice.

Sage opened the door, smiling. "Hi, Jim. How's your day going?"

Sitting behind his desk, Jim looked up and grinned at her. He was a good-looking, broad-shouldered brother of average height with mocha-colored skin and dark brown hair, which he wore natural and cut close to his well-shaped head.

"Forget my day," he said dismissively, his dark brown eyes alight with humor. "How did your meeting go with the wunderkind?"

"Well, he's definitely not a kid anymore, so you can stop calling him that."

"But he's still brilliant, I suppose?" asked Jim.

Sage laughed shortly as she sat in the chair across from Jim's desk. Jim was not only her partner, but her best friend. He had gone to school with her and Adam, so he had a unique perspective on their relationship. He'd known them when they were dating in high school and had been a shoulder for Sage to cry on when she and Adam had broken up.

Besides Adam, Jim was the only man who wasn't a relative whom Sage had ever loved. He loved her, too. But his and Sage's relationship was purely platonic—he worshipped the ground his wife, Sha-Shana, walked on.

Sage told him about her meeting with Adam, including Adam's invitation to go to Vienna with him, leaving out the part about how she was earning the million for her mother's club.

Jim laughed. "Whoa, girl. It's obvious the man has had you on his mind for a while now, and he doesn't want to waste any more time." He searched her eyes. "How do you feel about that?"

Sage blew air between full lips and shrugged helplessly. "I'm stunned. I thought I'd get a cool reception after obviously ignoring him. Instead he was frank and open, and he put his heart on the line by telling me how he feels about me. My head's still spinning."

"You could be treading in dangerous territory here," Jim said with a grave expression.

Sage's brows arched in an interested gesture. "Please, share your opinion. I can use all the help I can get."

Jim paused a moment, his handsome face scrunched up in a frown. "I don't know if I should say this. It might sound as if I'm suspicious of Adam, which I'm not. I believe he's a good guy, but the fact is Adam has changed, Sage. He's a mover and a shaker on the world stage. According to *Forbes,* he's worth a couple billion, at least. All that money and power has to change a man. I'm not saying Adam is less human or less loving or less anything. But a man with that much power knows how to get what he wants, and he wants you, Sage. That makes me just a little afraid for you. Be careful—that's all I'm saying."

Jim wasn't telling Sage anything she hadn't already thought about. Of course Adam had changed over the years. So had she.

The difference between them was that her life wasn't under a microscope all the time. When Adam Benson announced a new invention, the whole world wanted to hear about it. The city of New Haven had been beside itself with curiosity about him when he'd first moved back home, but now he could pretty much go anywhere in town and be left alone. Outside of New Haven, he was hounded by the media. Sometimes she felt sorry for him. But then she remembered how competent and even-tempered Adam was. He probably took all of the attention in stride.

Sage smiled at Jim and said, "I know he's changed. At this point we're just trying to see if we still fit or not. You know, they say the easiest way to find out if you can get along with someone is to take a trip with them. We'll see how Vienna goes."

Jim laughed shortly. "I hope you have a ball," he said sincerely. "Every woman deserves to be treated like a princess at least once in her life."

The next few days were a whirlwind of activity. Ruby Gaskins, Adam's personal shopper, came to Sage's office one morning and took her measurements in preparation for outfitting her for the trip. Ruby was a petite African-American woman in her late fifties. She'd been a buyer for Bergdorf Goodman in New York City before she'd retired and moved to New Haven. Being a personal shopper was her second career, and from the enthusiasm she showed for it, Sage could tell she loved it.

Sage stood still and tried not to giggle as Ruby stretched the measuring tape up and down her body, her lips pursed in concentration. A pair of red-framed reading glasses hung from a chain around her neck, and she had a pen stuck behind her right ear. She wore her silver hair in a relaxed pixie cut. The red pantsuit and red strappy sandals she had on suited her vibrant personality to a T.

"You're a size eight," she told Sage after putting her tape measure away. "With very nice curves, I might add, so I'll make sure you have adequate room in the bust and hip area. Mr. Benson tells me you two are going to a dressy dance, and you'll be mingling with people who think nothing of shelling out big bucks for designer clothing. But he also said you'd be embarrassed by too much ostentation." She slid on her glasses and looked Sage in the eyes. "Was he accurate in that assumption?"

Sage nodded. "He was," she confirmed with an apologetic smile. "I don't want to make this harder on you, but if you could keep the cost down I'd really appreciate it."

"You don't want to be too beholden to Mr. Benson, huh?" Ruby correctly deduced.

"It's hard to explain, but no, I don't," Sage answered.

"Oh, honey, I have two daughters around your age," Ruby told her. "Believe me, I understand. Sometimes a man's generosity comes with a price tag. I also know Mr. Benson pretty well, and he's not like that. But I'll adhere to your rules in this matter because as of this moment, I'm *your* personal shopper."

And so they chatted about clothes for a while, after which Ruby left to begin her shopping expedition. Then Sage's cell phone rang. It was Adam.

"Hi," Sage said when she answered, her tone light and welcoming.

"Hi, yourself," said Adam huskily. "I hope I'm not interrupting anything."

"Nah, Ruby just left after a very thorough consultation."

"She's the best. You'll be happy with her results. Listen, you've got to call off your mother and her club. To thank me for my donation, I'm being inundated with cakes and pies and casseroles. Mrs. Harrison, the housekeeper, is starting to give me nasty looks. Especially since I insist that she freezes everything instead of tossing the treats out. I can't toss those ladies' family recipes in the trash. Besides, I love your mother's sweet-potato pie."

Sage laughed delightedly. "I'll make sure they get the message in a tactful way," she promised.

"Thank you," said Adam. He sighed softly. "It's really nice talking with you over the phone. This is the first time I've heard your voice this way in years. Remember the conversations we used to have?"

"Well into the night," Sage said, recalling those days when it was sheer torture to say goodbye to him. The sound of his voice could always curl her toes. It still had that effect on her.

"By the way," said Adam, "our flight leaves very early on Wednesday morning—5:00 a.m.—so I'll be picking you up at four."

"I'd just as well not go to bed at all," Sage said with a smile in her voice.

"You can sleep on the plane," Adam told her. "The company plane's very comfortable, and you and I will be the only passengers, so you can wear pajamas if you want to."

Sage laughed again. "What are you trying to do—spoil me?"

"I'm shameless," he admitted.

"Yes, you are."

"Just making up for lost time," he said in defense.

Thinking their conversation was taking on too intimate a tone, Sage changed the subject. "Tell me something about the summit. Who will be there? Will you have to give a speech?"

"It's a meeting of minds," Adam told her. "The best and the brightest in science and technology get together to discuss how to make the future better for mankind. And, yes, I'll speak at the summit. I hate to call it a speech because it'll really be just a conversation with lots of comments and questions from the audience."

"I'm looking forward to hearing what the great thinkers of our time believe we have to do to make our future brighter," Sage said excitedly.

"And *I* can't wait to see how you look in pajamas these days," Adam joked.

"I'm hanging up now," Sage threatened. Laughter was evident in her tone.

"I'm phoning Ruby and telling her to buy you some silk pajamas," Adam said.

"They would just be a waste of money," Sage told him. "I don't sleep in pajamas anymore."

"What *do* you sleep in?" he inquired.

Sage could tell by the lowness of his voice and the keen interest in his tone that he was waiting with bated breath for her answer.

"Nothing," she said. "Goodbye, Adam." And she hung up, laughing.

When Adam picked her up on Wednesday morning, Sage was packed and ready to go. They both wore casual clothing of jeans and shirts and athletic shoes for comfort on the plane. Adam carried her big suitcase to the car and put it in the trunk while Sage, briefly peering up into the pitch-black sky at that time of morning, followed with a carry-on bag and her shoulder bag.

Adam opened the car door for her and she climbed inside. Once behind the wheel of the SUV, Adam turned to her and said, "We're off to Wonderland."

Buckling her seat belt, Sage smiled at him. "I did some research online, and Vienna does seem to have a lot of fairy-tale palaces."

"It does," he said. "And we'll be staying at one of them."

"What? A real palace?" She tried to keep the excitement out of her voice but failed miserably. She felt like a little girl at Christmastime.

"The Palais Schwarzenberg," Adam told her. "It was built in the eighteenth century by a family descended from royalty. It's in the center of Vienna, and because it's surrounded by eighteen acres of land, it's more like a private home than a hotel. And they boast one of the best restaurants in the city, so I hope you enjoy it."

"I'm sure I will," Sage said breathlessly. "You're really pulling out all the stops, aren't you?"

"I've dreamed of sharing experiences like this with you, Sage," he told her quietly. "Now that I have you all to myself, I'm not holding anything back."

Sage was secretly thrilled at his words, but she was afraid to tell him how good it made her feel that he was eager to share his world with her.

"That's very sweet of you," she said softly.

Adam smiled at her and returned his attention to his driving.

"It's no more than you deserve."

She looked out the window as he maneuvered the car down her street. Except for security lights around their houses, her neighbors' homes were dark.

His last words made her a bit melancholy. He believed she deserved special treatment. Was his opinion based on what he had known of her when they were young? He certainly wasn't basing it on what he knew of her present life because he knew nothing of it, except what he'd heard from secondary sources.

She thought it best to lay her cards on the table. "Adam, I'm not as sweet and innocent as I used to be. In my job I've seen so many marriages dissolve that I've become cynical, and that's probably why I'm not married. I'm beginning to believe the institution of marriage doesn't work anymore."

"What about my parents and your parents?" he asked softly. "They've been together for more than thirty years."

"They come from a different generation."

"That's nonsense," he stated emphatically. "True love still exists."

"Yes, but it's rare. Half of my friends are divorced, and out of those who're still married, their marriages are in trouble. Only one couple I know is still as in love now as they were when they tied the knot, and that's Jim and Sha-Shana Douglas."

"The Jim Douglas we went to school with?" Adam asked incredulously.

"Yes. He's my partner."

"I always thought he had a thing for you," Adam said thoughtfully. "I figured he wouldn't waste time asking you out after we broke up."

"He was there for comfort, but no, Adam, Jim and I never dated. We've never even kissed. He's my best friend."

"Your best friend is a guy," he said.

She couldn't tell how he felt about that from his neutral tone. "Yes. Who's your best friend?"

"Ethan Strauss," Adam answered. "He runs the West Coast office. We've been friends since my first year at MIT. You'll meet him and his wife, Trudi, on this trip. And they're very much in love."

"I'm looking forward to meeting them."

Chapter 5

About half an hour later Sage was stepping onto the plane. Adam had driven them to a private airport on the outskirts of New Haven. The luxuriously appointed plane had seating for twelve. The color scheme was neutral, and the seats were extra large and upholstered in leather as soft as butter, Sage learned when she ran her hand along the back of one of the seats.

"Get comfortable," Adam said, "while I have a word with the pilot."

In his absence Sage strolled down the aisle until she found a seat in the middle that appealed to her. As soon as she seated herself, a tall, good-looking guy in a dark suit, green eyes welcoming, approached her. "You must be Ms. Sage Andrews," he said, smiling down at her. "I'm Georges, and I'll be your flight attendant." He reached for her carry-on bag. "I'll stow that for you if you like."

Sage smiled at him and handed him the bag. "Thank you, Georges."

He took the bag and put it in the overhead compartment. Then he smiled at her again and said, "We'll be taking off soon. Would you like a preflight drink?"

"No, thank you," Sage said, eyes full of humor. She wasn't much of a drinker, and having one at five in the morning seemed excessive.

"Water, coffee, tea?" asked Georges.

"Nothing, thank you," Sage said. "I like to have both hands free at takeoff so I can hold on tight to the arms of my seat."

Georges laughed softly. "You don't like flying, huh?"

"Can't say that I do," Sage told him frankly. "I just see it as a means to an end that unfortunately sometimes can't be avoided."

"I hear you," said Georges.

Adam arrived at that instant and Georges asked him if he could bring him anything.

"No, thanks, Georges," said Adam.

Georges left them alone.

"Is Georges a regular?" Sage asked Adam teasingly. "Or was he hired specifically because you didn't want me to meet the gorgeous female flight attendant who usually works on your company plane?"

"You mean Brigit?" Adam laughed. "I'm afraid she's busy posing for the *Sports Illustrated* swimsuit issue.... No, my dear, Georges has been with the company for years."

Sage looked at Georges at the back of the plane, standing at the flight attendant's workstation that included a small kitchen. "He's a cutie."

"Married," Adam said. "The only unmarried male on this plane is yours truly, so...down, girl."

They were leaning back in their seats, facing one another, smiles on their faces. "Fasten your seat belt, Duck. We're going to take off in a few minutes."

"I was wondering when you'd bring that up," Sage said, enjoying the closeness.

"Don't worry. Your nickname's safe with me," Adam assured her. "No one will ever know that when you started walking as a toddler, you were so cute and chubby that you waddled like a duck, and your mom took one look at you and started calling you Duck."

"I'll never forgive her for that," said Sage.

"You were adorable," Adam said. "I used to love the times your mom would bring out the home movies."

Sage felt her face grow hot with embarrassment even now. "Isn't it peculiar how your most embarrassing moments seem to be adorable to someone else?"

Georges put in another appearance to advise them to buckle their seat belts. "Five minutes," he said as he hurried to the back to buckle up himself.

Adam reached over and buckled Sage's belt. "Only to the people who love you," he said.

Sage didn't say anything. She simply continued to meet his gaze. Some part of her wanted to believe all his sweet talk. She wanted to simply let go and enjoy herself and not worry about being careful. The cynical part of her warned that Adam had broken her heart before and there was a possibility that he would do it again. Either because he was looking for something in her that she didn't possess, or he had truly changed for the worse over the years, and this was all a cruel game to him, a diversion to entertain a jaded playboy.

Adam buckled his own seat belt and smiled at her. Sage yawned. He yawned in response and laughed. "I guess they really are contagious."

Sage's eyes were dreamy. "You really did turn out well," she told him. "I mean, I thought you were cute when you were younger, but you've only gotten better with age. You've got that rough-hewn, masculine thing going for you. Some men look like bums when they miss a day shaving, but you just look hotter for some reason."

"Have you been drinking?" Adam asked. He smiled,

revealing dimples in both cheeks. He simply gazed at her with those beautiful dark brown eyes.

"No," Sage told him with a sigh. "I'm just tired of being Sage Andrews, the lawyer, someone who always does what's expected of her. I'm such a good daughter, a good citizen, the responsible one. Let's make a promise to each other to say exactly what we're thinking on this trip, Adam."

"Okay, there won't be any filters between the two of us," Adam promised.

The sound of the plane's engines got her attention, and Sage braced herself for the liftoff. She closed her eyes and grasped the seat's arms.

Adam put his arm around her shoulders. "Why didn't you tell me you hate to fly?"

"I didn't want to disillusion you," Sage said. "You seem to think I'm perfect."

Adam grinned. "That wouldn't have disillusioned me," he said. "It only makes me want to protect you more." He held her until the plane evened out.

Sage opened her eyes and smiled at him. "I know it's childish. Traveling by plane's supposed to be the safest way to travel."

"Statistically, it is. But try to explain that to your body, which reacts instinctively to the unnaturalness of flying. I don't like it, either. I just have to do it so often that I've gotten used to it. I try not to think about the science behind a metal machine weighing several tons shooting through the air."

"You're not making this better," Sage said with a laugh.

"Oh, hell, I'm sorry," Adam apologized. He bent and kissed her. Sage felt her body relax and leaned into him.

The kiss deepened and she soon forgot everything except the feel of his mouth on hers.

"Better?" Adam asked hopefully when they came up for air.

"Better," Sage said, smiling happily.

Like an apparition, Georges was once more in the aisle. "You can remove your seat belts and relax now." He smiled at Sage. "How about that drink?"

Before she could answer him, Sage stifled a yawn. "No, thank you, Georges, but I will take a pillow and a blanket. I think I'll sleep for a while."

"Make that two, Georges," Adam said. When Georges left, he pulled Sage close. "Finally, we get to sleep together."

Sage laughed softly and snuggled closer.

As she drifted to sleep she heard Adam ask, "Do you still ride horses regularly?"

"Mmm-hmm," she murmured. "Why?"

"Just wondering," he said and left it at that.

It was night when the plane landed in Vienna. En route to the Palais Schwarzenberg, they passed Schloss Belvedere, the Belvedere Palace, and Sage couldn't take her eyes off the magnificent edifice, which was actually two eighteenth-century palaces with painstakingly landscaped gardens between them. The lights inside gave the huge palace a golden glow, and the lights reflecting off the man-made pond out front gave it a surreal quality.

There was one magical building after another, and Sage soaked it all in while Adam watched her with a smile on his lips. He seemed gratified that she was enjoying herself.

"I wanted your first glance of Vienna to be at night," he told her. "It's beautiful, isn't it?"

"Breathtaking," Sage agreed. She couldn't stop smiling.

Adam leaned forward. "Driver, could you drive by one of the squares?"

"I'd be happy to, Mr. Benson," the driver, a native Austrian, said.

"From mid-November to Christmas, Vienna transforms

its squares into Christmas markets. Vendors sell all sorts of Christmas-themed items. People turn out in droves to buy their Christmas gifts and just to eat and socialize."

"There's Christkindlmarkt at city hall," the driver suggested. "We're not far from there."

When they arrived, there was nowhere to park. "Want to get out and stretch your legs?" Adam asked.

Sage agreed, so they got out and Adam asked the driver to come back for them in half an hour.

The square looked like a Christmas wonderland with decorations everywhere, and it was packed. Men, women and children milled around, stopping at several of the more than one hundred stalls where vendors sold everything associated with Christmas, from cookies to Christmas trees.

The smells were so enticing that Sage let her nose lead her. She pulled Adam over to a stall that sold hot chocolate. They purchased two mugs and continued their stroll through the square.

The temperature was in the twenties and they both had donned jackets over their shirts. They were quite comfortable, naturally holding hands as they walked. Sage sipped her hot chocolate and breathed in the crisp, fragrant night air. "Somehow I always pictured Austria with snow."

"It's early yet," Adam said. "It'll probably snow before Christmas."

Suddenly, Adam stopped at a stall that sold ceramic animals dressed in silly Christmas regalia. He picked up a brightly painted ceramic duck wearing a Santa hat. He bought it and handed it to Sage.

Sage laughed as she accepted the six-inch-high ceramic figurine. "I'll call her Duck."

Sage decided Adam had been right about the Palais Schwarzenberg. In spite of its size and obvious ornamentation on the outside and inside, it struck her as a country home. She felt comfortable as soon as they walked into the grand lobby.

They were greeted by a beautifully dressed woman with dark hair with silver streaks who looked to be in her late fifties. "Good evening, Mr. Benson, Ms. Andrews, I'm Greta. I hope you had a lovely trip," she said pleasantly with a German accent.

Adam assured her that they had, and she gestured to a young man in a uniform to get their luggage. Then to Adam and Sage, she said, "Since your assistant arranged everything in advance, there's no need for you to check in. I'll show you to your suites."

As they walked down the long corridor and took the stairs to the upper floor, Sage admired the family portraits on the walls. But that wasn't the only artwork gracing the walls of the palace. There were also paintings by well-known artists such as Renoir. She peered closer. They didn't look like reproductions to her.

"What beautiful paintings," Sage said to Greta.

"The portraits are of the ancestors of the family who owns the *palais*," she said. "As a matter of fact, some of the family still lives in part of the *palais,* so you may run into them during your stay."

"Then you're not part of the family?" asked Sage.

"Oh, no," Greta said modestly. "I am an employee. There is a full staff, of course. And we also have a wonderful restaurant. May I make a reservation for later tonight for you? Or would you like dinner delivered to your rooms on your first night? You must be jet-lagged."

Adam and Sage looked at one another. Adam deferred to Sage. "We'll do whatever you want to do tonight," he told her.

"We'll stay in for tonight," Sage said.

"Very well," said Greta pleasantly.

They arrived at Sage's suite. Greta unlocked the door and handed the key to Sage. It wasn't a card key. It was an actual key, something Sage hadn't seen in a hotel for quite a while.

Highly polished hardwood floors ran throughout the huge suite. Besides a king-size bed and an accompanying ornately carved bedroom suite, there was a sitting area and an en suite bath that was spacious and had both a sunken tub and a shower stall.

"This is gorgeous," gasped Sage.

Both Adam and Greta seemed pleased that she liked it.

"Very good," said Greta, smiling. "This way to your suite, Mr. Benson."

Sage hugged Adam briefly and whispered, "Thank you!" before he left with Greta.

Greta closed the door behind them, and as soon as they were out of earshot, Sage flung herself onto the bed and gave a muffled scream into her hands to avoid being heard. She remembered Jim's words. "Every woman deserves to be treated like a princess at least once in her life." She indeed felt like a princess. A princess who was going to sleep in a palace tonight!

She got up momentarily and explored every nook and cranny in the suite. By the time Adam knocked on her door a few minutes later, she had gone over the entire place from top to bottom.

She stood sheepishly at the door when she stepped aside to let Adam enter.

Adam walked in, smiling at her. "You look like the kid who was caught with his hand in the cookie jar."

"Worse," said Sage, taking her hand from behind her back. In it was a half-eaten chocolate torte. "Austrian pastry," she said, smiling. "This hotel *so* gets a five-star rating from me!"

Adam laughed. Her heart leaped at the sight of his joy at

seeing her so happy. This was the Adam she remembered: a boy without a cruel bone in his body. Someone who would never hurt her and who only wanted the best for her.

Chapter 6

Since the summit didn't begin until their second day in Vienna, they had the next day to go sightseeing. They got up early and had breakfast in the hotel restaurant, after which the driver who'd picked them up at the airport the previous night arrived to take them on a tour of the city.

Sage was wearing one of the outfits chosen for her by Ruby: black fitted slacks with a beige cashmere twin set, black leather riding boots with heels comfortable enough for walking and a shoulder bag to match. She'd combed her thick, black curly hair back, fastened it with a tortoise-shell comb and let the rest fall down her back.

Adam was casually dressed in jeans, a long-sleeved gray shirt and a black leather jacket. He wore black leather Italian loafers. He looked ruggedly handsome.

As they stepped outside, Sage saw the grounds of the *palais* clearly for the first time. The lawn was like a carpet in its perfection. Seasonal flowers abounded as far as the eye could see.

"Good morning, Mr. Benson, Ms. Andrews. I hope you had a restful evening," the driver greeted them.

"Thank you," said Adam. He smiled at the man. "I'm sorry. I didn't get your name last night."

"My mistake, Mr. Benson. Last time I simply told you I was from the agency your assistant booked to drive you. I'm Franz Holtz. I'll be your driver for the duration of your stay."

"It's a pleasure to meet you, Franz."

"And I you, sir," said Franz. "I'm a big fan of your work."

"Well, thank you again," said Adam.

He then turned to Sage. "Shall we go?"

Sage nodded eagerly. Adam helped her into the back-seat of the luxury car. After Adam was also inside, Franz shut the door and then climbed behind the wheel of the car.

"I was told you wanted to sightsee today, sir," Franz said.

"That's true," Adam said. "But first I have a surprise for Ms. Andrews. We have a private viewing of the Lipizzaner."

Sage couldn't believe her ears. Ever since she was six years old, she'd wanted to see the Lipizzaners live. She'd taken horseback-riding lessons from age seven to her senior year in high school. She still went riding whenever time permitted. Her favorite event was dressage. And the Lipizzaner was known for dressage.

All inhibitions gone, she threw her arms around Adam's neck and kissed him repeatedly on the cheek. "Oh, thank you, thank you, you sweet man, you!"

A few minutes later they were pulling onto the property that housed the Spanish riding school—Spanische Hofreitschule. The house and barn were both elegantly appointed. The fence bordering the property seemed to stretch for miles. Horses frolicked in grassy fields.

A man and a woman, both in their mid-thirties, came out of the house upon hearing a car in their drive.

The man introduced himself as Josef Aronsen, and the

pretty blonde was his wife, Hilda. They were both horse trainers.

"It's a pleasure to meet you, Mr. Benson," said Josef, beaming. He was a dark-haired man of average height and weight with powerful thigh muscles. Both he and Hilda wore riding clothes.

"Please, call me Adam," Adam said warmly. "And this is Ms. Sage Andrews. She's the horse lover. She's an experienced rider, and it's always been her dream to ride a Lipizzaner."

"Ride!" exclaimed Sage, unable to contain her excitement. She'd thought she was there only to watch someone else ride the famous horses. She looked to Josef and Hilda for confirmation of Adam's words. They were nodding and smiling.

"Right this way," Josef said.

Josef and Hilda led Adam and Sage to the barn where two more people, a man and a woman, were putting a stallion through its paces in a corral. The woman was riding the handsome Lipizzaner while the man walked alongside, calling out instructions.

Adam, Sage, Josef and Hilda walked over to the corral and Josef called, "Victor, Beatriz, bring Alexi over here, please."

Victor and Beatriz were quick to respond. Victor took Alexi's bridle in hand and led the woman on the horse to the edge of the corral.

Josef made the introductions, and then Sage said, "I don't know about this. I'm nervous. Alexi will sense I'm nervous."

"Alexi is used to people being nervous around him," Hilda assured her. She patted Alexi's head affectionately. "He is such a pretty boy that he's used to people being intimidated by his beauty."

Alexi whinnied and threw his head back, as if he agreed with her assessment of his character.

"Come," said Hilda. "Get to know him before you mount him."

Sage stepped closer to the beautiful white horse, which was a product of Arab, Danish, Spanish and Italian stock.

"What do you know about Lipizzaner?" Hilda asked gently as Sage caressed Alexi's mane and worked her way up to touching his mighty head.

"Just what I've read," Sage told her. "The riding school was founded in the late fifteen hundreds, and the horses have been bred especially for beauty and strength and intelligence. And they can make those wonderful jumps because of their powerful hind muscles."

Hilda smiled warmly. "You've done your homework!"

Sage wasn't listening because Alexi was looking at her and she was looking at him. His huge, beautiful eyes seemed to be assessing her. Then he bent his head as if he wanted her to pat him, and she did.

"He likes you," said Josef, grinning.

Sage was glad. She'd never met a horse that didn't like her and had been hoping that Alexi wouldn't prove to be the exception to the rule. Arabians could be quite unpredictable, and Lipizzaner horses were part Arabian.

"But that doesn't mean he'll let me ride him," Sage said from experience. Horses were like humans. They could have their moods.

"Let's give it a try, shall we?" said Hilda.

Sage was game. She removed her sweater and handed it to Adam.

She glanced down at her slacks and boots and realized that it was almost as if Ruby had chosen them for this moment. She looked up at Adam before she turned and followed Hilda into the corral, silently asking for encouragement. Seemingly reading her mind, Adam gestured toward the corral with a nod. "Go on. You can do it."

Sage took a deep breath and stepped into the corral. Beatriz dismounted and offered Sage the use of her riding helmet. Sage gratefully accepted.

"Thank you, Beatriz," she said softly.

"My pleasure," said Beatriz with a smile. A short brunette with brown eyes, she looked around twenty-five.

Josef held Alexi's bridle while Sage mounted him, and then he and Hilda walked out of the corral along with Beatriz and Victor.

"Is it all right if I record this?" Adam asked Josef.

"Yes, it's perfectly fine," said Josef.

Sage sat atop Alexi, patting his strong neck. "Take it easy on me, boy, all right?"

Remembering her dressage training, she began with the basic passage in which the horse moved forward in a rhythmic manner that resembled skipping. She was astonished when Alexi recognized her signals. She'd been afraid that he wouldn't. She had no way of knowing how his riders had been training him over the years. But either he was exceptionally trained, or she was actually remembering the lessons her riding teacher had taught her over the years.

Alexi trotted around the large corral performing one trick after another, while Sage marveled at the play of his powerful muscles beneath her. After a few minutes she got so bold that she was determined to try a pirouette. She gave the signal with a squeeze of her legs and a gesture with the reins. Alexi pivoted in a circle, his hind legs bearing the weight. He did it in such a smooth motion that Sage felt as if she was dancing with him.

Their audience enthusiastically applauded. Sage signaled for Alexi to stop pirouetting and walk over to the edge of the corral. He followed her instructions without a hitch.

She was beaming as they approached the others. "He's brilliant," she said to Josef and Hilda. "Thank you so much for allowing me to ride him."

"It was our pleasure," Josef said, smiling warmly. "You have a great seat."

Sage thanked him for the compliment, and she and Adam thanked them again for granting Sage's wish to ride a Lipizzaner. Then she and Adam said their goodbyes and were soon in the car again with Franz behind the wheel.

"Where can I take you next?" Franz wanted to know.

"Saint Stephen's Cathedral," Adam told him.

While Franz drove them toward the center of Vienna, Adam and Sage relaxed in the back.

"You really do have a great seat," Adam teased her.

"Oh, stop it," Sage said, blushing. "You know he meant I'm a decent rider." She looked him deeply in the eyes. "That was the sweetest thing anyone has ever done for me. I'll remember it for the rest of my life. Thank you so much!"

"You're welcome," he said simply, but his eyes were full of warmth and kindness. And something else that caused her to melt. It looked like genuine affection.

Sage kissed his cheek. "Now, no more spoiling me, okay? Just let me enjoy your company for the rest of the weekend without your playing fairy godmother—um, god-father, to my Cinderella."

"I'm not making any promises," Adam told her. "You wanted honesty. And, honestly, spoiling you makes me happy."

Sage didn't want to argue the point. Instead she reached into his jacket pocket for the cell phone with which he'd recorded her ride. "Let me see it!"

Adam took the phone out of her hand. His fingers flew over the surface and he handed it back to her. There she was in living color, riding Alexi. The video on the four-inch screen was extremely sharp and the sound was excellent, too.

Sage looked at the screen, then at Adam. "You made this?"

"I didn't actually make it, but I invented it," Adam said modestly.

"I've never seen a cell phone with such a sharp picture. This is high-definition, isn't it?"

"It's due to all the megapixels," Adam told her. "Are you telling me you don't own one yet?"

"No, I'm mortified to say I don't."

"I'm hurt," Adam said. But the laughter in his eyes belied his statement. "Are you one of those people who are wary of new technology?"

"Not wary," Sage said. "I just don't run out and buy every new gadget that comes on the market if my present gadget is still working fine."

"Fair enough," Adam said as he took the phone out of her hand and proceeded to demonstrate all of its features.

"It does everything except bring me breakfast in bed," Sage quipped when he was finished.

"That's my job," Adam said.

Sage laid her head on his shoulder and he put his arm around her. They didn't say anything for a few minutes. Adam gave her the phone again after pulling up her video. She watched it over and over, smiling the whole time.

Adam kissed the top of her head and held her securely in his arms. This felt right to him. He couldn't imagine why he'd foolishly stayed away from her for so long. No, he corrected himself, he knew why he'd stayed away: because he'd felt he had no right to reenter Sage's life after being the one to break off their relationship. She'd demonstrated by her avoidance of him over the years that she didn't want to pursue a friendship with him, and he thought the least he could do was honor her wishes.

But when he'd returned home and learned she was unattached, he'd allowed hope to blossom in his heart. The problem was, even with his supposed intelligence, he couldn't figure out a surefire way of winning Sage's affections again. So that was why he'd started jogging past her office every day. He'd wanted to stay in her mind until he figured out a way to get back in her heart.

Then the opportunity had just fallen into his lap. He saw it as fate intervening on his behalf. He hadn't known at the time that it wasn't fate at all, but Sage's mother who'd intervened. Wherever his good luck had come from, he'd readily accepted it.

Now he simply had to be careful not to mess it up.

He smiled as he watched Sage reliving her ride on Alexi. So far, things were going well.

Chapter 7

"It reminds me of Notre Dame with all the gargoyles," Sage said as she and Adam stood in front of Saint Stephen's Cathedral. "I expect Quasimodo to put in an appearance at any moment."

"Let's see how it looks on the inside," Adam said, taking her hand.

They toured the inside of the Romanesque and Gothic cathedral, along with other tourists. Sage found the dark medieval atmosphere a bit depressing. But the sculptures and paintings with religious themes were interesting. To her they spoke of the glory of heaven and the tortures of hell. When Adam suggested a tour of the cathedral's catacombs, however, Sage declined. "No, thanks. I'm not fond of being underground, and the thought of all those poor plague victims' bones down there makes me uncomfortable."

Adam admitted that he wasn't looking forward to it, either, so they went across the street to a sidewalk café, ordered coffees and watched the crowds in the plaza.

"We haven't talked about what our personal lives have been like since we last saw each other," Sage said. She sipped her coffee. "I want to know what you do when you're not inventing clever cell phones."

Adam's dark eyes were alight with humor as he regarded her.

"You already know I like to run."

"Did you choose that route on purpose?" she asked. "Or is it a coincidence that it takes you past my office?"

"Of course I did it on purpose," Adam said truthfully. "You weren't returning my calls. I wanted to stay on your mind."

"Well, it worked. I could hardly forget you when I saw you practically every day."

"What was going through your mind during my daily appearances?" He wanted to know.

"You irritated me," Sage confessed. "And yet, I couldn't look away."

Adam laughed. "And all those times I'd see you in church and hope that I could have a word with you, only to find that you'd disappeared?"

"I know every escape route in that church," Sage said with a smile. "By the way, was joining my church another way to keep you in my thoughts?"

"You were there," Adam admitted. "So that's where I had to be."

She gave him an askance look. "Religion's interchangeable to you?"

"That's not it," Adam explained. "I simply believe that we can find God in many places, and I could worship Him just as easily at your church. Besides, I like the sense of community your church exhibits."

"I do, too," Sage said. "That's one of the reasons I go to that church. They do a lot of good in the community."

"Then it's all right with you if I continue going there?" Adam asked.

"Of course, and I won't avoid you anymore."

"Maybe we can even share a pew," Adam quipped.

"Now, don't get crazy," Sage joked back. "What else do you like to do besides run?"

"I'm an avid reader. I like watching science-fiction movies and pointing out what's real science in them and what's fiction. I like video games."

"Your company makes games, too, right?"

"We make educational videos so that kids can learn something while sitting in front of the TV."

"But those aren't the kind you like playing?" Sage was guessing.

"No, I'm pretty much addicted to games that deal with outer space."

"Do you want to go into space one day?"

"I haven't ruled it out."

"I heard that for the right amount of money, you can buy a spot on a Russian or Chinese spacecraft."

"I'm waiting until I can book a flight on an American ship," Adam said.

"I have no interest in going into space. I find the world is enough." She picked up her coffee, drank the rest of it and set her cup back down. Then she asked suddenly, "I know you said you haven't been in love with anyone since you and I broke up, but has anyone come close?"

"I thought so at first, but turns out she wasn't the woman for me."

Sage's brows arched with interest. "What happened?"

"I caught her rifling through the dresser drawers in my bedroom."

"Maybe she was looking for a T-shirt to put on," Sage said.

Adam shook his head. "She was looking for valuables." He met her eyes. "It hasn't been easy for me to trust anyone, Sage. These can be desperate times. You have people at the top who're making all the money, and a lot of people at the bottom who're just getting by. The system isn't equitable. That's what my company's foundation is working on, making society more equitable. Until everyone's needs are taken care of, you're going to have desperate people in the world who're willing to do anything to survive."

"What did you do about the woman you caught going through your dresser?"

"We sat and talked, and I learned she'd lost her husband and had a two-year-old son. She apologized for attempting to steal from me, but she was getting ready to be kicked out of her apartment. So I paid her rent and got her in a job-training program with the company, and she's doing well now."

"But you stopped dating."

"Yes, because we were dating for the wrong reasons. I was dating her because I was lonely and she was beautiful. She was dating me because I'm Adam Benson."

"I suppose it *is* hard for you to find a woman who wants to be with you simply for you and not for your money."

"Yeah," Adam said, sounding resigned to the fact. "I've learned to live with it. How about you, Sage? Have you been in love since we last met?"

Sage sighed. "I've dated some very nice men, but none I felt strongly enough about to take the relationship beyond just going out and having a good time. At first I blamed you—you'd broken my heart, and I wasn't about to let another man put me through that again. But then I realized I was being foolish. We were so young when we broke up. I couldn't continue to blame our failed relationship on the fact that I avoided commitment. If I was ever to meet a good man and fall in love and have his babies, I needed to put aside the past."

"What year did you come to this realization?" Adam asked, a smile tugging at the corners of his generous mouth.

"Last year," Sage said, laughing. "I know—I'm pitiful.

My mom reminds me that I'm years behind schedule when it comes to making her a grandmother."

"I get the same from my mother," Adam confided. "When I told her I still had feelings for you, she was deliriously happy."

"You told Miss Millie you still cared for me?" Sage said, shocked.

"I've always been able to talk to my mother about anything," Adam said. "It's my dad I find hard to talk to."

"It's his generation," Sage said. "Give him a break. My dad doesn't handle emotional topics well, either. Back to your sharing how you felt with your mom—don't you think you're getting her hopes up? According to my mom, our breaking up was a tragedy for both of them. You know how they are. They're going to start planning the wedding, and we're just trying to get to know each other again."

Adam nodded in agreement. He looked deep in her eyes. "I know, but what can we do? Mothers want their children to be happy. I've been productive. I've been successful, but I haven't been happy without you, Sage. You haven't been out of my mind since the day we broke up. I always carried you with me in my heart." He grasped her hand in his across the tiny round table.

Sage was looking at him, tears glistening in her eyes. "I, on the other hand, did everything in my power to forget you. I dated men who I thought were direct opposites of you. I went through a 'bad boy' phase, which didn't last long because who can put up with that nonsense when they've had true love? True love," she repeated. "Adam, do you think that's what we had, or are we romanticizing everything?"

"You tell me," Adam said. "When we kiss now, how do you feel?"

"Like I'm high on some very good stimulants," she said,

grinning. "Better than I've ever felt with anyone else… Like I could die happy."

"Like it's the most natural thing in the world," Adam said, affectionately squeezing her hand. "I do get the powerful drug analogy, because I am definitely addicted to you, your smell, your taste, how you feel in my arms. In some ways I'm glad we never made love. I don't know if we would have appreciated it as much back then as we would now. I know we haven't waited for each other, but I believe if we do eventually make love, it'll feel like it's the first time for both of us."

Sage wiped her tears away with a napkin and smiled up at him.

"Even your *rap* has improved over the years," she teased.

Adam laughed. "Did I score points?"

"Lots of points," Sage conceded.

"Am I on the way to making you mine by Christmas?" His dark eyes danced with laughter as he awaited her answer.

Sage laughed. "You're definitely playing to win."

But she wasn't ready to concede yet.

That night she and Adam met his best friends, Ethan and Trudi Strauss, at Steirereck, which Adam said was the birthplace of New Viennese cuisine.

Sage wore a black lace, sleeveless silk dress that showed a bit of cleavage, but not too much, with the hem falling a couple of inches above her knees. Black suede strappy sandals and a matching clutch complemented the dress nicely. A classy, ebony-hued thermal-lined evening wrap kept her warm in the chilly December night air.

Adam helped her out of the car when Franz pulled up to the restaurant. Sage stepped out. She was pleased to see that Adam could not help feasting his eyes on her legs as she exited the car.

Sage smiled up at him. He cut a handsome figure in his black suit and white silk shirt. She saw that he had opted to keep the beard he'd been growing for several days now, although he'd neatened it up a bit. She wondered if he'd done that because she'd told him she liked how he looked with a day's growth.

"Enjoy your evening," Franz said as he closed the car door.

"Thank you," Adam returned. "I'll phone you when we're ready to leave."

"Very good, sir," Franz answered, then got behind the wheel and sped off.

The restaurant's doorman held the door for them and murmured, *"Guten abend."*

"Guten abend," Adam replied.

Sage preceded him into the large restaurant. The decor reminded her of their hotel. There was a lot of ornamentation, from the crown molding to the dining-room chairs with seats upholstered in a brocade fabric of predominantly red and gold colors. The floor was highly polished hardwood, and the ceilings were exceedingly high. The crystal chandelier in the main dining room lent a touch of elegance and illuminated an otherwise dim room full of white-clothed, candlelit tables.

The waiter, a young man in a short white jacket and black slacks, welcomed them and showed them to a table in the restaurant's winter garden, which was a conservatory filled with lush greenery adjacent to an outside wall. There were fewer tables in this area, which afforded them more privacy.

When they walked into the conservatory, a male voice cried, "There you are, at last!"

A powerfully built man in a dark gray suit came forward and hugged Adam. Behind him was a lovely willowy woman in a red dress. She and Sage smiled and shook hands.

"Don't mind them," Trudi Strauss said confidentially to Sage. "They haven't seen each other in months. Their bromance has suffered greatly."

"Hello, Trudi," Sage said, laughing softly at her sense of humor. "It's a pleasure to meet you."

"The pleasure's all mine," said Trudi, who was about Sage's height, but thinner. She wore her auburn hair long and sleek down her back. And her skin was a dark copper tone.

Adam waited for a pause in the women's conversation, then said to Ethan with a note of pride, "Ethan, I want you to meet my dear friend Sage Andrews."

Ethan embraced Sage. She could feel his muscles through his suit as he hugged her tightly. "We finally meet," he said enthusiastically after he released her. "Adam's told me so much about you."

Sage returned his smile and said, "It's good to meet you, Ethan. And please take everything Adam says about me with a grain of salt. He's much too generous with his compliments."

Ethan grinned. He had thick, curly blond hair that he wore a bit too long, and his eyes were dark blue. He wasn't much taller than his wife. But his utter masculinity made up for his lack of height.

"He didn't exaggerate when he said you were lovely," Ethan told her. "And I'm sure he didn't embellish anything else about you, either."

The waiter, who had been standing silently to the side while they greeted one another, now gestured to the table. "Please, have a seat," he said.

The ladies were helped with their chairs and the men seated themselves. The waiter presented them with menus and then said, "I'll give you a few minutes to decide."

After the waiter had gone, Adam looked expectantly at Ethan and Trudi. "How are the kids?"

Sage's ears perked up. She loved children.

"They're all doing well," Ethan said. "They miss their godfather."

"I miss them, too," Adam said.

"We have three kids," Trudi said, turning to smile at Sage. "Ethan Junior, seven. Evan, five. And Tara, four—who, by the way, is aptly named because she's a little terror."

"Don't say that about my precious little girl," Ethan said, smiling. "She's just energetic. She's so brilliant, she gets bored easily."

"She tried to shave Boo Bear," Trudi deadpanned. She regarded Sage. "Boo Bear is the kids' black Lab puppy. I got there just in time. Otherwise he would have been scalped."

Sage couldn't help laughing. "I'm sorry," she said.

The others were laughing, too. "No need to apologize. That was just another day in the Strauss household," said Trudi. "The thing is, Sage, I was under the impression that little girls didn't get into as much mischief as boys. But my boys are saints compared to Tara. I don't know where I went wrong with her."

"I'm sure there's nothing you did that makes Tara act out," Sage said encouragingly. "I was a handful when I was that age, too. In fact, I had so much energy, my mom signed me up for every group she could find to keep me occupied and out of her hair."

"What age were you when you stopped acting out?" Trudi asked. "I'm about ready to have Tara tested for attention deficit disorder or something."

"I was six when I discovered horses and started concentrating on *them,* and everything else kind of fell in line. I became more disciplined. I had something on which to focus my energy."

"That could help," said Trudi. "She likes animals." She turned to Ethan. "You used to ride, didn't you?"

"It's been years," Ethan said. "But I did enjoy it. We'll look into it when we get back home." He regarded Sage. "Do you still ride?"

"Does she still *ride?*" Adam spoke up, and before Sage could prevent him, he whipped out his cell phone and showed Ethan and Trudi the video of Sage astride Alexi.

Sage observed Ethan and Trudi as they watched the video together with smiles on their faces.

"I'm jealous," Ethan said, grinning. "I always dreamed of riding a Lipizzaner." He looked up at Sage. "How was it?"

Sage grinned, too. "It was awesome!"

"How did this happen?" Trudi asked. "I've never heard of anyone riding a Lipizzaner except their trained riders."

She was looking at Sage, but Sage had no idea what Adam had done to make her dream come true.

"I had nothing to do with it," she said honestly, turning her gaze on Adam.

"You must have moved heaven and earth," Trudi said.

"I just asked nicely," Adam said modestly.

To which Ethan and Trudi laughed. Sage laughed, too, but what Trudi had said about his having moved heaven and earth made her think about what Jim had said about Adam being a rich and powerful man.

Was there anything Adam couldn't do? The thought kind of gave her chills.

Chapter 8

The next day was the first day of the summit. Adam had made sure that Sage had full access to any of the seminars she wanted to attend. However, there were exclusive meetings that only Adam and Ethan were invited to. Therefore, Sage and Trudi decided to team up and sample what the summit had to offer to someone who was not a trained scientist or a techie.

They had just sat through a two-hour seminar on the environment and were exiting the conference room, along with two hundred other attendees, when Trudi pulled Sage aside and said, "I don't know about you, but I don't want to sit through another dry lecture. Let's ditch this place until the keynote address at two, okay?"

Sage was in total agreement. She glanced at her watch. It was only 11:00 a.m. "Sounds good to me," she told Trudi. "I've been dying to try a Sacher torte."

"I know just the bakery," Trudi promised with a grin.

So they left the Hofburg Congress Center, formerly the winter palace of Emperor Franz Joseph I, and hailed a cab.

"Demel," Trudi instructed the driver.

A few minutes later they were sitting at an outside table,

eating small spoonfuls of the rich chocolate torte, which was Demel's house specialty. The coffee served with it was black, thick, heady and the perfect complement to the torte.

"You know," said Trudi, smiling at Sage over her coffee cup, "I've never seen Adam look at anyone the way he looks at you."

Sage blushed and Trudi laughed softly. "I take it from the expression on your face that you've noticed."

"Trudi, we've just met, but I'm going to ask you to keep this between you and me."

Sage met Trudi's eyes. After a moment Trudi nodded and said, "All right, this is between the two of us. I won't even say anything to Ethan."

Sage sighed gratefully. "Until a year ago, Adam and I hadn't spoken to each other in about nine years. I hadn't said a word to him since I was nineteen, when he broke up with me. Now...well, we both know we never stopped caring for each other. But where it goes from here, I don't know. I felt like I knew the old Adam, but the new Adam kind of intimidates me."

Trudi was listening closely, her dark brown eyes sympathetic. After Sage finished talking, Trudi laughed softly and said, "Honey, is that all? I thought you were going to say you didn't want him or something else equally absurd. Who isn't intimidated by men like Adam and Ethan? They're uncommon, one in a billion. Something would be wrong with you if you weren't a bit intimidated by them.

"That doesn't mean you can't love them. Take Ethan and myself. We met when he and Adam were at MIT. They were roommates and came to the restaurant where I worked part-time as a waitress. I was working on my bachelor's in business at the time. They came in wearing MIT T-shirts and I instantly knew they were a couple of brains, so I played it cool. Adam started flirting a little with me. I ignored him and flirted with the blond. For the next six months they were regulars, and then something happened—Ethan came in alone and asked me out, and we've been together ever since. Was I intimidated by his intelligence? Yes, but I didn't let that stop me. They may be supersmart, Sage, but remember one thing—they're also living, breathing men who need love like everyone else."

"I know you're right," Sage said. "I just don't know if I'm up to being all Adam wants of me."

"That's probably why he invited you this weekend," Trudi said. "So you'll get the chance to see him in his element. But try to remember, Sage, that all the accolades in the world, all the admirers, all the groupies don't mean a thing to Adam. They're just things imposed on him by society. Next time you're alone with him, ask him what really matters to him and he'll tell you, like Ethan told me eight years ago when we got married, that *you're* what matters to him."

Sage wanted to believe Trudi because it corroborated what Adam had earlier told her, that deep down he was still the Adam she'd always known. Now, she supposed, it was all up to her. Would she be able to let go of the past and embrace the future?

Sage and Trudi got back to the Hofburg Congress Center in time for Adam's speech. Ethan had saved them seats down front, and they flanked him as Adam strode onstage to thunderous applause.

He began by welcoming the five thousand attendees to the summit, greeting them in English, Spanish, German, Italian, Russian and Mandarin. He joked that no matter which language he spoke, he always spoke it with an American accent.

Then he said what he'd come there to say. "When I was a kid, I would race home from school in time to catch reruns of *Star Trek*. I wanted to be Mr. Spock. I wanted to live in

their time, where currency was no longer needed because
society made sure that all its citizens had what they needed
without having to beg, borrow or steal. Everyone had access to a good education and was allowed to develop their
talents. There was no caste system. Everyone was equal.
We're here today to discuss how we can change the world."

He spoke for more than an hour with enthusiastic audience participation. Questions were asked and answered. If
Adam didn't know the answer to an honest query, he referred the audience member to one of his colleagues.

Sage found the whole thing stimulating. She knew that
Adam was a mathematician, but until today she had been
unfamiliar with the practical applications of mathematics
in solving everyday problems.

After the speech Adam joined her, Ethan and Trudi. He
went straight to her and hugged her. They hadn't seen one
another since they'd split up at eight that morning.

Sage smiled up at him. "I'm so proud of you," she said
with admiration. And she meant it. He'd really impressed
her with his depth of feeling for the planet and its problems.

Adam smiled happily at the compliment. "Really?"

"Not only did I understand everything you said, I now
want to go out and do something about it," Sage told him,
her eyes ablaze with excitement.

"Don't lay it on too thick," Ethan laughed. "We don't
want it to go to his head."

Adam playfully shook his fist at his best friend and then
pulled Sage into his arms and kissed her.

Sage kissed him back.

It was only after he'd let her go that she remembered
they were in an auditorium full of summit attendees, to say
nothing of Adam's best friends.

But, shyly looking around them afterward, she noticed
that no one gave any outward indication that their kiss had
been anything out of the ordinary. Ethan and Trudi were

warmly smiling at her. But everything else remained unchanged. There was a buzz of human voices in the air. People were gathering their belongings, preparing to leave the auditorium and move on to some other event on the schedule.

Adam pulled her close. Seeming to read her thoughts, he said, "Don't worry. The media was only invited to the awards ceremony tomorrow night."

Sage was just about to tell Adam that it hadn't even occurred to her that the media was there, but Ethan interrupted them. "Hey, how about a late lunch? I'm starved."

The next thing Sage knew, the four of them were squashed into the back of a cab heading somewhere to grab a bite to eat.

Later that night she and Adam got some alone time when they returned to the Palais Schwarzenberg. Because the day had been hectic, they'd elected to dine in her room and relax in front of the fire afterward.

They were doing just that, cuddled on a love seat, cups of coffee in front of them, when Adam looked her in the eyes and said, "Sage, these past few days with you have been everything I imagined they'd be when I asked you to come with me. I've learned so much about you, and what I've learned I like very much. I challenged you, and you were woman enough to accept my challenge. Now I'm going to ask you to do something that is really going to take you out of your comfort zone."

Sage's eyes had been closed as she enjoyed being in his arms. She'd changed into lounging clothes and taken her shoes off. Dinner had been delicious and she'd had two glasses of wine, which had her in a mellow mood.

Adam's nearness was doing crazy things to her body. She was aroused and very close to suggesting they move this scene to the bedroom, which was what went through her mind when he said he was going to ask her to do something out of her comfort zone.

She gazed up at him, her thick-lashed eyes sultry. "I don't think making love to you would be out of my comfort zone."

Adam smiled. "Nothing would make me happier, darling. But I was going to suggest something more."

Sage sat straighter on the love seat. "Like what?"

Adam laughed. "You should see how big your eyes are now." He turned and took her hands in his, then got down on one knee in front of her. "I'm trying to propose to you, Duck."

"Oh, my God," Sage cried. She didn't know how to react. Adam seemed to like springing surprises on her, but this was a little too much. She had gone along with a trip to Vienna, the ride on a Lipizzaner, but now a *marriage proposal?*

"Adam, you're moving too fast for me. I don't know what to say. I like you. I want to make love to you. But I can't truthfully say a marriage between us is the right thing to do. Give us time to get to know one another again."

"We've already wasted too much time," Adam said vehemently. "I feel like we should have been married years ago and already have a family by now. I may seem overeager to you, Sage, but I never do anything without thinking about it for some time, and you've been on my mind for years. I love you, and I want you to marry me and be the mother of my children. I can't state it any plainer than that."

Looking deep into his eyes, Sage sighed. "Remember the day you told me that it would be best if we stopped seeing each other?"

Adam smiled sadly. "I didn't mean to hurt you, Sage."

"I know you didn't," she said softly. She gently touched his cheek. He grasped her hand and kissed the palm. Desire

shot through Sage, jolting her to the core. He was looking at her with such longing, such utter loneliness that her
heart could not deny him anything at that point.

She kissed him. "Adam, Adam, this is exactly why I
avoided you for a year. I knew that once you touched me,
I'd lose all reason."

"That's a good thing," he said as he leaned forward and
took her mouth once more. This time the kiss was more
insistent and so sensual that Sage lost what little control
she had.

What he could do with his tongue was indescribably
wanton. Her limbs went weak, her nipples hardened, and
she was so aroused she could feel herself moistening and
her feminine center begin to thrum pleasurably.

Breathing hard, she broke off the kiss. "I'll make love to
you, but I'm not going to give you an answer to your proposal tonight, Adam Benson. That's too much pressure."

"Well, I'm not going to make love to you until you marry
me," he countered. "We made a promise, remember?"

He got to his feet, smoothing his pant legs as he did so.

Sage rose, too. "I was a teenager when I made you promise we'd wait until marriage!" she cried, outraged.

"Which was a good thing then," Adam said, "because
I was a horny teenager. And it's still a good idea because
you make me *feel* like a horny teenager. Besides, I want
our kids conceived after the wedding."

"That's sexual blackmail!"

"Call it what you will," Adam said stubbornly. "But you
don't get the goods until you agree to marry me."

"*I'm* supposed to be the one saying that!"

"I guess our roles have reversed," said Adam. He picked
up his suit jacket from a nearby chair, then turned back to
face her, his eyes roaming over her body. "I may regret saying no tonight, but a man has to do what a man has to do."

Sage angrily threw up her hands in defeat and walked

over to the door, opened it and gestured for him to leave. "Go right ahead and see if I care! I'm not marrying you just so I can sleep with you."

"I thought you'd marry me because you love me," Adam said, which took some of the wind out of Sage's sails. Her momentary anger fled.

She appealed to him once more. "Adam, stay."

"No, thank you. I've got a date with a cold shower."

"I'm a lawyer," Sage warned him. "I know how to play hardball. You're not going to win this one, Adam."

"I lost when I broke your heart," Adam said, looking her straight in the eye. "I'll see this battle to the end."

"Good night, then," Sage said.

"Good night," Adam replied softly. He left with his jacket thrown across his shoulder and his head held down.

Sage closed the door and locked it.

In times of stress she invariably turned to tidying up her surroundings, and she began with their coffee cups. She fumed as she worked. Adam Benson was insane. That was the only rational explanation. The billionaire genius was certifiable. He was so used to getting everything he wanted that he thought all he had to do to get her to marry him was dangle a million-dollar wager in front of her eyes, whisk her off to Austria and she'd be his!

After returning the coffee cups to the room-service cart, which someone from the hotel staff would soon come to retrieve, Sage brushed her teeth in preparation for bed. Adam was not going to wear her down.

Tomorrow, she would tell him she was going home, even if she had to take a commercial flight. She wasn't playing his games any longer.

When she came out of the bathroom and sat on her bed, she looked over and saw a small Tiffany bag sitting on the nightstand.

Dread filled her as she reached for it and opened it.

When had Adam come in here and put this beside her bed? She had no idea. She slowly opened it and reached inside. When she pulled her hand out, in it was a ring box. Her heartbeat quickened with excitement. Tears clouded her vision.

Inside was a ten-carat, perfectly cut white-diamond solitaire in a platinum setting. She really started crying then because she could see the care with which Adam had chosen it for her. It wasn't twenty or more carats and gaudy like some of the engagement rings she'd seen on celebrities' fingers. Undoubtedly he'd chosen the purest color and cut. It was a ring he'd known she'd be proud to wear.

Her first inclination was to put it on, but she didn't. Adam should be the one to slip the ring onto her finger. He had obviously anticipated their making love tonight, and that was why he'd slipped in here earlier and put the Tiffany bag on the nightstand.

But what could she do about it now after that argument? If she went next door to his room and threw herself into his arms, wouldn't he think she'd changed her mind only after discovering the ring?

One thing was for sure: she wasn't going home tomorrow. She was going to see this out to the end, whatever that might be.

Why did life have to be so complicated?

Chapter 9

Sage knocked on Adam's room door. There was only one thing to do: tactfully give him the ring back.

Adam opened the door wearing only his slacks. Sage momentarily lost her train of thought, so riveted was she by his naked chest. He was cut. His arms, chest and stomach muscles were clearly defined beneath his brown skin. She smiled. The teen whose chest had been practically hairless now boasted a profusion of hair.

He was smiling at her as he stepped aside for her to enter. "Did you change your mind?" he asked pleasantly. He hadn't seen the ring box in her right hand.

Sage stepped inside, he closed the door and they faced one another. Sage handed him the ring box. "It's a beautiful ring, Adam. Gorgeous, in fact, and I would be proud to wear it someday," she said, smiling and pleading with her eyes for understanding.

He accepted the ring in resignation, but his smile had faded. "Do you know what this does to a man's ego, Sage?"

"The same thing that was done to mine when you broke up with me?" she countered.

"Is that what this is about?" Adam asked. "You want revenge?"

"Nothing so childish." Her eyes flashed in defiance. "It's about wanting to wait until we know we're in love and we aren't caught up in what might have been, Adam."

She breathed deeply and exhaled, shedding the defensiveness. She hadn't come here to argue. She went to him and touched his arm. When he didn't recoil from her touch, she moved closer until he relented and pulled her into his arms. Sage lost herself in his masculine scent and the feel of his body wrapping around hers.

After a couple of minutes, during which both of them relaxed and allowed the acrimony to drift away, he let go of her, and Sage peered up at him. "I still love you in that teenage-girl way I used to. Part lust, part romantic ideal, and now I want to love you like a woman would—completely. That's worth waiting for, isn't it?"

Adam nodded. "Yeah, that's definitely worth waiting for."

He walked her to the door and kissed her on the cheek. They didn't say good-night again; Sage just left.

As Adam turned and walked back into the bedroom, the ring box felt burdensome in his hand. He didn't regret jumping the gun and asking Sage to marry him. He simply regretted she hadn't said yes. But he wasn't going to let that discourage him. He'd give her more time to think about them.

When Sage woke the next morning it was snowing. She noticed it when she went to the curtains and opened them to allow the sunshine to spill in. Her room was on the second floor, and the windows opened outward and didn't have screens. She opened one of them and held her hand out, capturing snowflakes in the palm of her hand as they drifted downward.

She sighed. The grounds, the other buildings nearby and the surrounding woods were covered with a mantle of snow. This was how Christmas was supposed to look.

Momentarily, she brushed the snow off her hand and closed the window. Adam would be knocking on her door in half an hour and she still had to shower.

A few minutes later, as she was coming out of the shower, the room phone rang. She sat on the edge of the bed in her bathrobe and answered it. "Hello?"

"Sage, it's Trudi. Have you been online this morning?"

"I brought my laptop, but I've been so busy I haven't even taken it out of its bag," Sage said.

"Well, I wanted to warn you," Trudi went on, "that when Adam kissed you yesterday, someone recorded it and put it on YouTube. It's gone viral."

"You've got to be kidding me!" Sage said. "Adam told me there weren't any reporters at the summit."

"I don't think it was a reporter. Whoever did it bragged that they captured the moment using the new Benson Electronics phone," Trudi noted.

Remembering the phone's capabilities, Sage wasn't surprised.

"Am I identified?" Sage asked, hoping for a negative reply.

"No," Trudi told her. "The caption reads, 'Is electronics wizard Adam Benson in love?'"

"Has Adam seen it?"

"I have no idea," Trudi said. "I was just looking out for you, girlfriend. Actually, I'm kind of surprised that Adam let his guard down like this. He's never been photographed with anyone he's dated in the past. Did you know that? In fact, he didn't even date anyone who didn't sign a confidentiality agreement. I suppose you've signed one, too?"

"No, he never brought up the subject," Sage said softly, with a note of caution. She wondered why Trudi was asking so many personal questions, but assumed that if she and Ethan were Adam's best friends, it was safe to confide in her.

"Anyway," Trudi continued, "Adam has a thick hide where invasion of his privacy is concerned, but you're a newbie, so I thought I'd give you a heads-up."

"I appreciate your thoughtfulness, Trudi."

"No problem," said Trudi. "See you tonight at the awards ceremony."

"All right. 'Bye, Trudi."

"'Bye, Sage."

After ending the call, Sage went to the closet where she'd stashed her computer and grabbed the black leather case she kept it in. Taking it to the desk in the bedroom, she sat and plugged it into the wall socket, realizing that after all this time without turning it on, the battery probably needed recharging.

While she was sitting at the desk, she looked around for the brochure that explained how to operate the TV and how to get an internet connection. Finding it, she turned to the page with instructions pertaining to the internet. Five minutes later she was online.

Two minutes after that she was looking at the YouTube video Trudi had told her about. She blushed when she saw the passionate manner in which she and Adam were kissing. It was easy to see how a moment like that would be hard for anyone to resist capturing. You couldn't fake those emotions.

The picture was so sharp, she could see the expressions on both their faces. Adam looked…well, he looked as though he adored her. And the tender way she touched his face as he bent to kiss her made her heart skip a beat. They looked like a couple very much in love. She was getting warm just watching the two of them.

As a testament to Adam's popularity, there were already more than a million hits. She calculated the time that had passed since kissing Adam yesterday. It hadn't even been twenty-four hours yet. She moved down the page and read a few of the comments. Most were positive, but some were disrespectful to Adam. She supposed she was saved from their vitriol because no one seemed to recognize her.

And then she had a horrible thought. If AOL had posted the video on their site, her mother had probably already seen it. Patricia Andrews treated AOL like her morning coffee. She didn't come fully awake until she'd logged on.

Sage minimized the YouTube page and opened her email. There were emails from her mother, Jim and several other friends. She opened the one from her mother first.

Sweetie, Millie and I are so happy to see that you and Adam are a couple again. That was some kiss!

The one from Jim she read next.

Wow, Sage. I guess the wunderkind has more going for him than a giant brain. Looks like you two are really into each other. Sha-Shana and I were grinning from ear to ear when we saw you on YouTube. We're happy for you and Adam.

Sage found herself smiling as she read their messages. It was heartwarming to know she had family and friends who wanted to see her happy. Was she being too cautious about letting Adam back into her life? Did she, as he'd accused her last night, subconsciously want revenge for his breaking her heart? She didn't want to believe she could be so petty. She'd gone on with her life. She hadn't been pining away for Adam for nine years. So why couldn't she trust her own emotions and let down her guard?

She didn't have time to dwell on it because someone knocked on her door and she knew it had to be Adam. She hurried over to the door and opened it. Adam took one look at her in her bathrobe and laughed.

"Am I early?"

"No," she said, pulling him inside and closing the door. "I'm late. I got distracted right out of the shower."

They kissed briefly. "It shouldn't take me long to get dressed," she continued as he followed her into the room. She gestured to her laptop on the desk. "Have you seen it?"

Adam frowned when his gaze fell on the laptop. "I was hoping to be the first to break the news to you," he said regretfully. "Who told you?"

"Trudi phoned. But, Adam, I'm not—"

"Listen, Sage," Adam interrupted her, a grim expression on his face. "You don't have to worry about this. I've already taken care of it. They're taking it down as we speak."

Sage looked at him in amazement. "Adam, I wasn't about to complain. I was going to say I don't think whoever uploaded the video did it out of malice. They just couldn't resist their fifteen minutes of fame. You're much more experienced with this sort of thing. So if you think it needs to come down, okay. But I'm not offended by it."

Adam brightened. "You're not?"

She smiled up at him. "Of course not," she said. "My first time on YouTube could have been a lot worse than being caught kissing a hot guy."

Adam laughed as he pulled her into his arms. "You've got a good heart."

Sage peered up at him. Smiling sexily, she said, "You're my hero. You were ready to defend my honor."

"I've already tracked down the culprit," Adam assured

her. "But if you don't want me to take any further action, I won't."

"Let the poor guy off with a warning," Sage said. She *was* curious as to who was behind the video, though. "Who was it?"

Adam grinned. "Trudi."

Sage burst out laughing. "That little sneak!" she cried. "Why would she do that?"

"She said she thought Cupid needed a nudge," Adam said, laughing, too. "To quote her—'Adam, you've never been caught kissing anyone in public. If this isn't proof enough for Sage that you love her, I don't know what is.'"

He gently kissed her mouth and then raised his head to look her in the eyes. "She meant well, darling. Can you forgive her?"

"'Forgive her'?" Sage asked. "She can be my matron of honor."

Adam, for all his intelligence, had to allow her words to sink in a moment. "You mean you'll marry me?" he asked excitedly.

Sage was nodding and smiling. "I love you, Adam. I was a fool not to recognize that I avoided you for more than a year because I didn't want to risk having all those feelings rush back and then find out you didn't feel the same way about me. I was afraid of getting hurt again."

Adam rained kisses on her beloved face. "But I do feel the same way! You don't know how frustrating it's been seeing you every day and not being able to talk to you, hold you and make love to you. I've been in misery!"

"I believe you," Sage told him. "Because I've been going crazy wanting to hold you, too. But I've got to apologize to you first."

"You don't need to apologize…" Adam began.

Sage smiled indulgently and interrupted him with "I

do, Adam. So please be quiet and listen. I let fear of getting hurt again harden my heart to you, instead of going on faith and opening up to you after everything you did to be with me—moving back to New Haven, all the messages, flowers, jogging by my office practically every day. You were right when you said I wanted to exact some kind of revenge for dropping me. It was a childish attitude. And I'm ashamed for behaving that way."

Adam pulled her into his arms and held her tightly, inhaling in her essence and exhaling. He could finally breathe again.

"You're not the only one who was afraid," he said softly in her ear. "After realizing I still loved you, I was so scared that I'd never be able to convince you of that fact. What finally won you over?"

"You never asked me to sign a confidentiality agreement. I gave it some thought after Trudi mentioned you usually ask women you date to sign one. I'm a lawyer, and I know how people in your position have to conduct their personal affairs nowadays, just to protect their privacy. But either you trusted me implicitly, or you simply didn't care if I talked about our relationship."

Adam laughed. "Honestly, it never even occurred to me to ask you to sign an agreement. We've known each other since childhood."

Sage was smiling at him, her love for him reflected in her eyes. "And you can trust me until the day you die."

"Which will hopefully be years from now, after we've been married forever and have many, many children, grandchildren and great-grandchildren," Adam said with a grin.

Sage took a step back, but Adam held on to her hand, reluctant to let go of it. She pried her hand free, though, and smiled seductively, her hands going to the sash of the robe she had on.

Adam's gaze was riveted on her. Sage didn't immediately doff the robe. She untied the sash and exposed one naked shoulder and then provocatively stuck one long leg out.

Adam's heartbeat quickened and a certain part of him started hardening. He removed his jacket and let it fall to the floor. He kicked his shoes off next.

He began walking toward her. Sage smiled saucily as she slowly backed away. Her large brown eyes lowered to the bulge in his pants. "What about the summit?"

"They can manage without me," Adam said huskily. He had removed his tie and was unbuckling his belt.

Sage didn't reply. She simply let the robe fall from her shoulders and pool at her feet. Adam paused in unzipping his pants. He'd been waiting for this his whole life. He was still as a statue as he drank her in, every inch of her. Her tall, fit, golden-brown-skinned body exceeded every fantasy he'd ever had about her, and he'd had many. She had breasts that were full and firm and a tapered waist with a flat stomach. Her butt was high and round, like a juicy peach, and curved into a pair of legs that were long and shapely.

His eyes lingered awhile on the V where her thighs met, and he found that he was salivating in anticipation.

"My God, Sage, you're beautiful," he breathed, his voice awe-filled.

Sage smiled. "I'm glad you think so."

By the time Adam had finished the visual tour of her body, he was harder than he'd ever remembered being.

Sage must have been impatient with how slowly he was undressing because she stepped forward to help him. The moment she was within arm's reach, though, Adam couldn't resist pressing her body against his, and then they were kissing. His hands were everywhere, greedily touching her soft, fragrant skin. His mouth was relentless, demanding pleasure as he gave pleasure.

When they came up for air, he greedily let his eyes rove over her. Her golden-brown eyes had a dreamy aspect to them. He realized he'd never witnessed how her physical being changed while in the throes of passion. She was beautiful. Her skin glowed with vitality. Sensuality pervaded every part of her. He would be happy watching her all day. But she impatiently pushed out of his embrace. "Adam, get undressed now!"

Adam was breathing hard as he broke out of his daydream and did as he was told. His eyes never left her as he quickly removed his pants, hopping on one leg then the other as he took them off. Sage unbuttoned his shirt, pulled it off him and threw it over her shoulder.

Adam pulled his T-shirt off and now he was in only a pair of black boxer briefs and a pair of black socks.

Sage's hands were at the waistband of his boxer briefs. Their eyes met and held. They didn't speak as Adam reached down and rolled the briefs off his hips and past his muscular thighs. He stepped out of them, and Sage got her first glance of him.

He heard her soft gasp of delight. Her nipples hardened further, and he could have sworn she was blushing. She looked back up into Adam's eyes. "My God, you're beautiful, too!"

That was Adam's call to action. He bent and hurriedly took off his socks, and they went the way of the rest of his clothes.

Then he smiled roguishly at her, picked her up and carried her to the bed. After he'd placed her on the mattress, he said, "Condoms?"

"Nightstand," Sage said, her gaze going to the top drawer only a few inches from her head. Adam bent and retrieved a condom from the drawer, hastily closed it and set the one condom atop the nightstand for easy access later. Then he gazed down at her and said, "I've been dreaming about this moment since I was sixteen."

Sage laughed. "Me, too," she assured him.

They kissed between giddy bursts of laughter; they were so happy to finally be naked in bed together.

Laughter aside, though, the lust was in full evidence because their bodies, so long denied this closeness, reacted with fierce sexual desire. After a while the laughter was replaced by moans. Adam kissed, nuzzled and licked Sage's breasts. He was intoxicated by her silken skin and fascinated by the taste of her. He wanted to kiss every inch of her body, and he worked his way from her forehead to her navel. When Sage gave a little start when his tongue flicked out and touched the most tender spot between her legs, he merely smiled and said, "Open up for a starving man, my love."

She relaxed and let him feast. She writhed with pleasure, murmured "I love you" over and over again until she exploded and trembled in release.

Having satisfied Sage, Adam got up and put on the condom and entered her. She wrapped her legs around him as he thrust deeply, exulting in the wonderful warmth and tightness of her welcoming body. Sage held on to the backs of his arms, his muscles playing against her palms, which only turned him on more. Her beautiful face mirrored her pleasure. He could not tear his eyes away. When she wet her lips and started panting, Adam knew he was hitting on just the right spot. Her hips rose off the bed as she met his thrusts.

There it was. She moaned loudly. She'd had her second orgasm. Soon afterward Adam climaxed, and his release was so powerful that he was unable to muffle the sound, even though he shoved his face in her shoulder.

Sage smiled with satisfaction. Adam hoped he hadn't disturbed any of the other guests of the *palais*.

Adam rolled off her and onto his side. Sage turned in bed so that they were facing each other. They smiled. He touched her cheek and softly said, "You're the only woman I've ever loved, and if you'll let me, I'll love you forever."

"Make it so," Sage said, and he knew she was remembering his love for *Star Trek: The Next Generation* and his favorite *Enterprise* commander, Captain Jean-Luc Picard. "Make it so" had been the good captain's favorite choice of words when issuing an order.

Adam grinned. "You know me so well."

Sage kissed his lips and snuggled closer to him with a contented sigh. "I'm finally where I belong, in the arms of my favorite nerd."

Adam laughed softly and murmured in her ear, "At last."

* * * * *

A FAMILY FOR CHRISTMAS

Felicia Mason

For Denise and in memory of Leon

Chapter 1

Trey Calloway wasn't the least bit interested in learning how to do macramé. But Kelly had her heart set on it. And if it made his daughter's six-year-old heart happy, Trey would master the craft and be a better man for having done so. But first he had to untangle the mess of threads he'd created.

"Daddy, your snowflake doesn't look like a snowflake."

"I know, baby," Trey said as he tried to dislodge the knots and tangles that did not at all resemble the ones the instructor at the craft store demonstrated.

Trey was the only testosterone in a veritable sea of pink Hello Kitty hair bows, T-shirts and miniature handbags.

After four years of being a single dad, he was used to it. But he didn't think he was ever going to grasp the fine art of macramé.

"Aunt Henrietta is gonna like my snowflake," Kelly announced, the curls in her high ponytail bobbing as she bounced. "I'm making this one for her for Christmas. Who are you going to give that one to, Daddy?"

"The trash can," Trey wanted to say. Instead he said, "I don't know yet, princess."

"Mine is pretty," she said, holding up her handiwork.

Trey studied it for a moment. "Yes, it is." He then held up his blob.

Kelly wrinkled her nose. "Maybe you should start over, Daddy."

"Yes, Daddy, that sounds like a good idea."

A laughing voice that didn't belong to Kelly. He knew that because it was mature, sexy and belonged to the one woman he wanted to get to know a whole lot better.

Over the past couple of weeks Trey had become adept at noticing his new next-door neighbor's comings and goings. It helped that his home office faced her driveway and backyard.

"Hey there, neighbor lady," he said, standing to greet Renee Armstrong.

"Look what I made!" Kelly said.

"You did a good job," Renee told the girl.

Trey glanced around, looking for Renee's shadow, her daughter a couple of years older than his own. He couldn't remember the girl's name, but it was something with a *K.* He remembered that much because of his own, Kelly.

"Did you and your daughter come for the macramé class?" he asked. "It's almost over."

"No, I didn't know about it. But I came to find something that might interest her. Do you have any suggestions, Kelly?"

The little girl held up her snowflake. "I like macramé."

Trey groaned. "That makes one of us," he muttered under his breath loud enough for only Renee to hear.

She smiled. "Well, I'm going to get going. Keisha is over in the art-supply section. I may have a budding Picasso on my hands."

Keisha. That's her daughter's name.

Trey didn't want Renee to leave. Not yet. He was enjoying her scent of vanilla and—oranges? He'd smelled it before in her house a couple of days after they'd moved in. Whatever kind of perfume it was, it was turning him on as much as the formfitting red sweater with little white snowball puffs that hugged her curves.

"We're going to be baking Christmas cookies tonight," Trey said. "Would you like to join us?"

If she took him up on the invitation, it would give him the opportunity to see her again…and in his house to boot. So far, he'd been in her next-door home along with his toolbox to level and hang pictures for her and to fix a leaky sink.

A moment later, though, Trey remembered.

Renee was a package deal. The irascible Keisha came with her. Renee and her daughter had been living next door to him for only a month, and in that short span of time he'd realized that Renee had little control over the girl who was prone to foot stomping, pouting and back talk. That very thought set his teeth on edge.

Renee gave him an "I'm not so sure that's a good idea" look.

His hopes soared. She would decline and then he wouldn't have to worry about Keisha's bad influence on Kelly. At eight, Keisha was just the right age to impress a six-year-old, and that influence boded ill based on what he'd seen so far.

"You know what?" Renee said. "We'd love to come bake cookies with you. What time?"

Trey could have kicked himself for letting his dormant libido get the best of him. Putting on a smile to hide his dismay at having to host Keisha, he named a time.

With a finger wave, Renee said farewell to both him and Kelly.

Still standing, he watched her head down the aisle of

the craft store. Her perfectly rounded behind and legs encased in tights called to him.

"Mercy," he muttered, still watching the sway of her hips.

"Thank you for volunteering, sir," he heard someone say.

"Daddy?"

Trey glanced down at Kelly. She was busy on her next snowflake.

"What is it, princess?" he said.

"Come on now. Don't be shy, sir. We all want to see your handiwork."

Trey glanced up. Was the macramé instructor talking to him?

"Go ahead, Daddy. Show everybody," Kelly urged, practically bouncing in her seat. "You stood up when she asked if anyone wanted to show off their new skills."

New skills?

What the...?

He glanced at the mangled mess on the table in front of him. Then he looked back down the aisle in the direction that had initially captured his attention. Renee Armstrong had disappeared.

He was left with a tangle of knots on the table and the evidence of arousal in his jeans.

"Mine needs a little work," he told the instructor. "Kelly, why don't you show the class what you made?"

As she jumped up to go show off her craft project, Trey settled back in his chair. *Nice save, Calloway,* he thought.

For the past three and a half weeks since moving into a new house on Stanhope Drive, Renee Armstrong had been telling herself that her next-door neighbor was hot. But was it only because she'd been so long without male companionship? she thought. Her racing heart and suddenly sweaty palms told a different story. Trey Calloway was fine, with a capital *F* and sugar on top.

As she made her way through the craft store to find Keisha, she thought about her neighbor and her reaction to him.

He was the sort of man who carried himself in a way that made you stop to notice when he walked into a room. Not exceptionally tall, he stood about five-eleven, maybe an even six feet. Always impeccably dressed and groomed, whether like today in pressed jeans and a cream-colored ribbed sweater, or in an expensive suit and overcoat for church, as she'd seen Sunday morning from her window. He always seemed ready for a magazine cover shoot.

His little girl, Kelly, was the same way. Partial to pink, Kelly Calloway clearly had her father wrapped around her finger. Why else would a man like him be in a craft store doing macramé, of all things? When she'd spied him at the table with a group of little girls wearing all shades of pink, she'd thought she might be mistaken. But it was him.

As he'd clearly struggled with the craft project, he'd been even sexier than normal. There was just something that warmed her heart—and some other places—about a man who didn't feel or at least didn't look threatened by a bunch of little girls doing craft projects.

She was suddenly glad—very glad—that she'd actually put on a cute outfit for the trip to the craft shop at Commerce Plaza. She'd almost just grabbed a college sweatshirt and a pair of lived-in jeans. After a week in her high-maintenance work clothes, she preferred getting comfortable on the weekends.

She wondered if he'd noticed the outfit. In the event he was watching as she walked away, she put a little extra sway in her hips to give him something to contemplate.

He was kind of hard to read. She knew she'd been sending hot and cold vibes his way. He'd come to the rescue with a tool kit and some male expertise when her kitchen sink had gone crazy. Beyond that, they'd just shared a wave and a hello in the morning or as they crossed paths taking the garbage or recycling to the curb.

He didn't wear a ring and in the three weeks she'd been in the house she hadn't seen a wife. There was just one car in his driveway. Out here in the suburbia of Cedar Springs, North Carolina, wouldn't there be two if he were married?

What if the invite to bake cookies was a family thing—one of those neighborly invitations that folks in the suburbs routinely offered? She didn't want to go waltzing in ready to make a play only to be greeted by a perfect little Mrs. Calloway standing in the kitchen.

Oh, dear.

Her first instinct—hesitation because of Keisha—now had another layer of worry.

She found Keisha exactly where she thought she would—in the fine-arts section of the store, mulling over choices of papers and pencils.

Renee made a mental note to find an art class for her to take. Maybe the Common Ground Recreation Center offered something. This interest in drawing had sprung up out of nowhere. But if Keisha was finally taking an interest in something beyond sulking, Renee was all for it.

"Hey, sweetie. What did you find?"

Keisha sat on the floor, legs crossed with two different colored-pencil sets in her lap.

"I can't decide which one is best."

Renee crouched down so she could see the two options. "That one gives you lots of different colors to work with," she pointed out.

Keisha nodded. "But this one has a book that shows you how to draw cartoons. I want to try that."

Renee smiled and helped her up. "Then it sounds like you've made a decision. Let's get that one."

"Okay," Keisha said. She tucked the chosen pencil set under her arm, but didn't immediately put the other back on the shelf.

When Keisha finally relinquished the second set, putting it back in its place in the display, Renee made another mental note to get that one for a Christmas present for Keisha.

"Guess who I saw in the store?"

Keisha glanced up at her, but didn't ask the obvious question.

"Mr. Calloway from next door and his little girl."

Keisha made a face.

"What?" Renee asked.

The girl poked her lips out. "Nothing."

Renee blew out a sigh. She was going to have to ask Dr. Hendrickson about this new uncommunicative phase Keisha seemed to be in. It had started a few weeks ago and seemed to be getting worse.

"They invited us over to make Christmas cookies tonight. Would you like that? It'll be the five of us."

"Who else is coming?"

Renee blinked. That was more interest than she'd seen from Keisha in anything except the art supplies.

"Mr. Calloway, his wife and his daughter."

"He doesn't have a wife," Keisha announced as they made their way toward the checkout.

"How do you know?"

"Kelly told me."

Kelly told her? Every day after school as they worked through homework, Renee tried to get Keisha to open up about the new school, the new friends she was making—if any—and anything else that might be on the girl's mind. This was the first she had heard of Keisha actually engaging long enough for the briefest of interactions with other kids, let alone in a full-fledged conversation about family.

"Do you and Kelly play together?"

The question seemed ridiculous. Renee knew full well that Keisha hadn't been outside to play with anyone since moving into the new house.

"I see her at school."

"What did she say about her mom?"

"She doesn't have a mom," Keisha said. They reached the checkout and Keisha put her art kit on the counter as Renee opened her purse for her wallet.

She had a hundred questions for Keisha but knew better than to press or rush the girl. Nothing would shut down Keisha faster than undue interest on Renee's part.

With the transaction completed, the clerk handed Keisha the bag. The girl grinned, mumbled a thank-you and then skipped to the door. Renee smiled. Glad to see—at last—a glimpse of the old Keisha.

When they were in the car with the heat's air chasing away the December chill, Renee broached the subject again.

"So did Kelly say what happened to her mom?"

"She died."

Renee gave her a sharp look. "Recently? Oh, that's so sad."

Keisha took the art kit out of the craft-store bag and read the back panel with the explanation of what was in the package out loud before answering. "No. A long time ago when Kelly was a baby."

Renee bit back a smile. A long time ago from a kid's perspective could be anywhere in the past from an hour ago to the time when dinosaurs roamed the Earth. The "baby" part narrowed it down a bit. Kelly looked to be no more than five or six years old, so she hadn't been a baby too long ago.

"She told me we were meant to live beside each other

because she doesn't have a mother and I don't have a father."

When Keisha didn't say anything else, Renee glanced over at her. The eight-year-old was staring at her hands. Renee started formulating one of the open-ended questions that Dr. Hendrickson said would draw Keisha out in times like this. Before she could get the gentle question out, Keisha spoke.

"I didn't tell her you weren't my mom."

Renee's hands tightened on the steering wheel. Her heart felt as if it had been gripped in a vise. Maybe this was what the past few weeks of acting out had been leading to. She so desperately wanted to ask Keisha if that was the case, but she couldn't get past the lump in her throat.

At least she hadn't qualified it by saying Renee wasn't her "real mom."

Renee was starting to feel as if she needed her own fifty minutes in the therapist's chair. Maybe Dr. Hendrickson would make an exception in his practice and take on an adult as a patient.

"Thank you for buying me the art pencils," Keisha said.

You're the grown-up here, Renee, she told herself. *What matters most is what's best for Keisha.*

"You're welcome, sweetie. I'm glad you like them." Then she added, "We don't have to bake cookies with the Calloways tonight if you don't want to."

Keisha tucked her art kit back into the bag and put it right next to her on the seat.

Security, Renee thought. *She's keeping the important things close by.* She'd definitely look into an art class…if Keisha was still—

"I want to," Keisha said, interrupting Renee's thoughts. "It'll be fun. Can we make gingerbread men?"

Renee beamed. "Definitely."

* * *

At exactly six-thirty, the front doorbell chimed.

Great, Trey thought. They *would* be punctual on the one night when he needed more preparation time. Kelly had just dropped a bombshell on him.

"Kelly, our guests have arrived. I want you to be on your absolute best behavior," Trey said. "We'll cut and bake the cookies, put some icing on the tops and make it an early night."

From across the kitchen table, his pint-size princess gave him one of the looks that fathers the world over had fielded on many occasions and hated every time they got one.

"Daddy, I'm not fibbing. It's the truth. Keisha doesn't like me. She doesn't like anybody. She's mean."

But because he had the hots for Renee Armstrong, he was about to put his daughter and therefore himself in miserable company.

Trey sighed.

This "cookie-baking neighbors" thing was going to be a disaster through and through.

In the grocery store where they'd picked up sprinkles, three tubes of Pillsbury cookie dough—one each of chocolate chip, sugar and peanut butter—and something called "edible glitter," Kelly had sulked. Now he knew why.

He couldn't very well open the front door and say, "Go away. My kid doesn't like your kid." So he did the next best thing. He resorted to bribery.

"Can you be a gracious hostess for ninety minutes?"

Kelly eyed him dubiously. "How long is ninety minutes?"

Trey thought about that, trying to compute the time into a six-year-old's frame of reference. An hour and a half would be long enough to bake the cookies and get them cooled, decorate them, eat a few and call it done.

"As long as watching three back-to-back *Dora the Explorer* shows," he told her.

Kelly wrinkled her nose.

The doorbell chimed again.

"That's a looong time, Daddy. And you never let me watch that many *Dora*s."

"If you can be a gracious hostess for Keisha while we bake cookies tonight, we can go pick out a new Dora backpack for you."

"And I can watch three?"

This was his kid, all right.

Trey nodded wearily. He knew when he was beat. "Yes."

Kelly immediately brightened. "Okay."

She scrambled down from the chair and skipped toward the front door with Trey following.

The gracious-hostess concept was from his aunt Henrietta, the Calloway family matriarch, who was apparently running an underground comportment academy for girls from her home.

Kelly had spent a long weekend with Aunt Henrietta and Uncle Carlton a few months back when he'd had to make an out-of-town business trip. Somehow, over the course of three days in that house, Kelly had learned how to host a garden tea party, including the proper way to brew tea and fold linen napkins into intricate shapes.

From then on, tea parties were real, no longer the imaginary kind. At Kelly's insistence along with Aunt Henrietta's coaching, he'd invested in a proper teapot and kettle. All tea bags had been banished from the house and replaced with specially blended concoctions in expensive canisters from Tea Time, a downtown tea shop.

The doorbell chimed again. "We're coming," Trey called out.

A few moments later, he opened the door to find Renee

and Keisha standing there, each holding a full bag of something in her arms.

"Hi there," Renee said. "We were starting to think the cookie party had been canceled."

I wish, Trey thought.

"Not at all," he said. "Come inside out of the cold."

The December evening had a nip in it. The forecast was for a cold front to move into the area over the next few days. But it felt as if the weather prognosticators had gotten it wrong because the cold was arriving earlier than anticipated and their guests were bundled up accordingly.

"Hello," Kelly said as Renee and Keisha entered the foyer. "Welcome to our home."

Trey glanced down at his daughter, who had evidently morphed from a six-year-old into a mini–Stepford wife in the past thirty seconds.

As Keisha passed by him, Trey peeked into the bag she carried.

Then, as if reading his mind or divining his intent, Renee said, "We weren't sure what type of cookies you bake for the holidays, so we brought ingredients to make a couple of different kinds we thought you'd like."

"The orange-marmalade button cookies taste the best," Keisha said.

Orange-marmalade button cookies? That sounds like something that will take longer than ninety minutes.

The four of them stood in the foyer until Renee prompted, "If you'll show us the kitchen, we can get started."

Kelly swept a hand out as if she were Vanna White displaying tonight's big prize on *Wheel of Fortune.* "Right this way," she said.

Trey eyed her suspiciously. Either the whole gracious-hostess bit had been too much or his kid wanted that Dora backpack awfully bad.

A few minutes later, after coats were in the hallway

closet, the kitchen countertop was covered with two kinds of flours, three kinds of sugars, little bottles of flavorings, small containers of spices and assorted canisters with candies.

Troy bit back a groan as he glanced at Kelly.

While the girls were busy pulling mixing bowls from the cabinets under the island, Trey touched Renee's arm. The contact must have surprised her because she looked up with wide eyes.

"What is all this?" Trey asked with a nod toward all of the stuff that had come out of their two bags.

"Ingredients," Renee said, giving him an odd look.

"Ingredients for what? A state dinner?"

Renee put one hand on her hip. "You're the one who invited us over to make cookies. If you'd rather not…"

"Cookies," Trey said. "Not…" He waved a hand at all of the stuff on the island countertop. Then, taking a few steps toward the refrigerator, he pulled out one of the Pillsbury cookie-dough rolls. "Cookies."

Renee gave him the stink eye. "You cannot be serious." She advanced on him and snatched the tube from him. "This is cheater dough."

Trey looked affronted. "Sandra Lee and I beg to disagree."

Renee stared at him openmouthed for a moment. Then a giggle burst through. "*You* watch the Food Network?"

"I have skills," he boasted.

"Oh, really," Renee said, humor still lacing her voice. "Well, we're here to kick it down-home like the Neelys visiting Martha Stewart."

Laughing, Trey placed the ready-to-bake cookies back in the refrigerator. From the pantry, he pulled out three aprons and handed one to each lady.

"None for you?"

Picking up a wooden spoon, he held it forward like a

shield and poked his chest out like a superhero. "Chef Trey doesn't need an apron to whip up gastronomical delights."

Renee laughed. "We'll see about that."

With Kelly standing on a step stool and Keisha perched on one of the counter stools, they began an assembly line of measuring, dumping and stirring as Renee read out the directions for their first cookie recipe.

"Andrea used to love baking," he said. "That's why the kitchen is fully outfitted."

"Who's Andrea?" Keisha asked before Renee could shake her head to stop her.

Trey look embarrassed, but Kelly answered the question with a child's guilelessness.

"She was my mom," the girl said. "But she doesn't live here anymore. She's an angel and looks out for me from Heaven."

Renee and Trey shared a glance that spoke volumes.

"I'm sorry," she mouthed to him.

"It's okay," he said. "We talk openly about it." But he quickly decided to change the subject. "So, are you two all settled in your new place?"

"We're getting there," Renee said as she cracked eggs into a small bowl. "You want to whisk, Keisha?"

"What's 'whisk'?" Kelly asked.

"A whisk is a kitchen tool used to whip eggs or other ingredients," Renee said.

"See?" Keisha held up the metal whisk. "Want to try it?"

Kelly paused for a moment, studying Keisha, and then nodded. Keisha demonstrated. "Just whip your hand around till they're nice and frothy."

Kelly took a turn at the bowl, and eggs sloshed over the side.

"Uh-oh," Kelly said, casting a worried glance first at her eight-year-old teacher and then at him.

"It's okay," Keisha said. "It's your first time. Keep practicing."

Renee lifted a brow as if surprised by Keisha's gentle instruction. Trey noticed that, too, as he watched the girls much like an approving father. He was pleasantly surprised that the foot-stomping pouty-mouthed girl he'd seen from his office window had been transformed into a helpful tutor for his daughter. Maybe Aunt Henrietta was expanding her gracious-hostess seminars to all of the neighborhood kids.

Kelly relaxed and found a rhythm for whisking the eggs. A moment later, Trey's gaze caught Renee's and he winked at her.

A blush rose on her face, a reaction that intrigued him greatly.

While the first batches of cookies baked, the girls disappeared upstairs so Kelly could show Keisha her room.

"This was a great idea," Renee told Trey. "Thank you for inviting us. With my work schedule and Keisha's, *er,* after-school activities, we really haven't met any other neighbors."

"I'm glad you came."

And he was being honest about that.

"I had my doubts," Renee said. "Keisha has been, well… problematic lately. I think the stress of the move and a new school got to her more than I initially thought."

"I've seen a couple of moments in the driveway," Trey admitted.

Renee winced. "Yeah. Then you know what I mean."

"I can't believe how well they hit it off," he said.

Instead of looking pained, Renee looked relieved. "I'm glad she's made a friend. Frankly, I was starting to worry."

Renee looked around at his spacious kitchen with its top-of-the-line appliances, double ovens and granite countertops. "Your kitchen is lovely."

"Thanks," Trey said. "It's actually what sold us on this house. That and the extra bedroom. The kitchen had just been completely remodeled."

"How many bedrooms are here?"

"Five," he said. "Most in the neighborhood have just three or four. When my wife and I bought the place, the plan was to fill every room with a kid or two and then build an addition if we needed more space."

"Wow."

Trey laughed. "Is that horror in your eyes I see? We both came from large families. Of course, we didn't know that she wouldn't be here or that Kelly would have to grow up without her."

"Do you mind if I asked what happened?"

He shook his head in the negative. "A drunk driver slammed into her. He, naturally, walked away with just a couple of scratches. Andrea died at the scene. It was the worst day of my life," Trey said. "Kelly was almost two and cried for her mother constantly. I was thirty-one and had no clue how to raise a child on my own. We both muddled through, though."

"You've done a great job," Renee said. "But I'm curious about something."

He leaned against the dishwasher, his legs stretched out in front of him. "What's that?"

"Her hair. It's always gorgeous, especially on Sundays. You do hair?"

Trey laughed so loud he almost choked.

"Of all the things I imagined you might ask, that's the last thing that would have been on my list."

Renee shook her head in amusement. "What were you thinking?"

His dark eyes took her in, his gaze pausing at her mouth and then traveling slowly down her body before returning again to her face. "Uh, just some other things," he said.

"For hair, I can manage one pulled-back ponytail or one fat French braid with a ribbon or barrette on the bottom to keep it in place. No, I definitely cannot claim any hair skills. I have an aunt who owns a salon. Her name is Patricia, but everybody calls her Tiny. Kelly goes there every week. All I have to do is make sure it's neat for school."

"Hmm," Renee said. "Do you think I can get the number? I'd like to check prices and see what I can manage for myself and for Keisha."

"No problem," he said, giving her a look that seemed to be part of another conversation entirely.

"Is it a little warm in here?" Renee asked.

The oven timer buzzed.

Trey pushed away from the dishwasher. "That's our cue for the first batch."

"I think we permanently lost our sous-chefs."

"Let them play," he said. "We can manage alone."

Chapter 2

Renee was sure that Trey Calloway had more than cookies on his mind. She did, too.

She watched as he pulled out the first and then the second cookie sheet from the oven.

"There are some trivets in there," he said, nodding toward the island.

Renee found them in the drawer and put them on the side counter where he then placed the cookies for cooling.

"The marmalade part is easy," Renee said. "We can leave that for the girls to do."

Trey put the dirty bowls in the dishwasher and pulled out two clean ones for the next batch of cookies. He then produced an elaborate-looking corkscrew. "Can I interest you in a glass of wine?"

She nodded.

He selected a bottle from a built-in wine rack. "Cabernet Sauvignon okay?"

"Sounds good," she said, pulling up one of the high-top stools and settling on it.

"So where did you guys move from?" he asked as he pulled down a couple of glasses, then opened the bottle.

"Durham," she said. "I wanted Keisha in a place that had more stability than a third-floor walk-up in a sketchy neighborhood."

"Well, welcome to Shangri-la, more formally known as the Cedar Grove subdivision. This neighborhood in Cedar Springs is about as sleepy as it gets without actually being Mayberry. Our nearest competition for nothing going on is the Holly Grove neighborhood."

"That's exactly what I wanted. No questionable neighbors like the six registered sex offenders who lived within three blocks of our building. And no TV satellite trucks bearing reporters eager to tell the sad stories of blighted residents."

"Ouch," Trey said.

She looked at him askance. "Oh, dear, please. If you are one of those, please, please, please be the meddlesome TV reporter rather than the sex offender."

He smiled and shook his head. "I'm neither."

"I sense a *but*."

"But I have a cousin who is one of those satellite TV truck 'this just in' types," he said, holding the wine bottle like a microphone before pouring for them both.

He put a glass of the rich Cab in front of her and then picked up his own glass.

"To new beginnings," he said in toast.

Renee smiled. "I like that." They clinked glasses and then sipped the wine. "This is good," she said.

He winked. "At one point I wanted to be a sommelier."

She lifted an eyebrow at that. "Really?"

He grinned and shook his head as he leaned against the island and toward her. "No. I just like that word. *Sommelier*," he said again, giving it the French pronunciation and a waggle of his brow.

"You're a mess."

"How'd you pick Cedar Springs from Durham?" he

asked. "There are some nice places in Durham and the whole Research Triangle area. How did you choose this sleepy little hamlet?"

Before she could answer, the girls bounded into the kitchen.

"The cookies smell good!" Kelly said.

Trey pushed off the island, set his glass down and turned toward the fridge.

"First batch is up," he said. "I thought you two had ditched the operation. We have vanilla and chocolate soy milk and I picked up a quart of whole if you prefer."

"We want chocolate!" Kelly chose for both of them. "And I was showing Keisha my doll collection. I have one of each," she added for Renee's benefit, "but I love Addy the most."

"One of each what? And who is Addy?"

Trey pulled chocolate-flavored soy milk out and reached for two glasses. He poured Kelly's half-full but put barely an inch in Keisha's glass for a small taste.

"See if you like it," he told her.

"I like chocolate milk," she said.

Trey poured more into the girl's glass so each child had an equal amount.

Renee was setting up the ingredients for the next round of cookies.

"Addy would be one of the American Girl dolls," Trey said, answering her unaddressed question. "It's a line of dolls with historical characters. Addy is the black girl from the Civil War. Most of them represent the 1800s, but they also have some from historic decades in the twentieth century. And a new one recently came out."

"Don't forget Kaya," Kelly said. "Her name is a *K* like mine."

"Far be it from me to forget," Trey said. "My credit card takes a hit every time a new one or accessory comes out."

"Who's Kaya?" Renee asked.

"She's the Indian girl," Kelly supplied. "She's from 1764 and is from the Nice Purse tribe."

Trey bit back a grin. "She's Native American and that's Nez Percé, princess."

"Oh, yeah. I keep forgetting. *Nez Percé*," she said, echoing her father's pronunciation.

"The collection is a great way to get girls interested in history. There are American Girl books and…"

"This milk is nasty!"

Three heads turned toward Keisha, who was at the end of the island, holding the glass out from her with her face scrunched up in aversion.

"Keisha," Renee said sharply. "What did we talk about?"

Keisha frowned, but didn't say anything else as she put the glass on the counter and pushed it away from her.

"I'm sorry," Renee told Trey. "I'll finish that."

"No worries," he said as he placed the glass in the sink, reached for a clean one and filled it with white whole milk. "Here you go."

Keisha smacked her lips together as if trying to get the taste of the chocolate milk out of her mouth and then reached for the glass.

"You don't like soy milk?" Kelly said.

Keisha wrinkled her nose.

"It's made from soy beans," Kelly helpfully offered.

"Bean milk! Ewww. Who wants milk made out of beans?"

"Keisha, you're a guest here," Renee scolded.

"Well," Trey said, filling the silence that dropped over the kitchen. "How about you two finish up those button cookies. They should be cool enough now for the marmalade. We'll get started on the chocolate-chip batter."

Neither girl moved.

"I want to pour the chocolate chips in," Kelly said.

"All right," Trey said.

"You and Keisha need to get on marmalade duty while those are still soft," Renee said. "I put the marmalade and two spoons over there for you."

The girls went to the counter, Kelly dragging her step stool with her.

Renee and Trey watched them work for a moment. Keisha showed the younger girl how to make the small dents in the cookies and how much marmalade to add.

"They seem to be getting along well," Trey said.

Renee glanced up at him as she measured out flour. "You sound surprised."

"I mean, well, they're just really getting to know each other."

"I've been worried about Keisha making friends," Renee said, her voice low so it didn't carry to where the girls worked. "Coming into a new school after everyone else has already settled down for the year is hard." She paused. "It can be hard for grown-ups, too," she added, giving him a look that said she might be interested in a grown-up kind of playdate.

"Then that toast to new beginnings was more than appropriate," he said. "How about going out with me? Just the two of us."

She smiled. "I'd like that a lot. What did you have in mind?"

"How about you pick a place? Anywhere you've been wondering about?"

"As a matter of fact, yes," she said. "I hear Trance is a great place."

He nodded but with apparent hesitance. "Give me your number and we can set it up for next week."

"They're rich," Keisha said about an hour later. They had returned to their house, put the cookies and their bags on the kitchen table and shed their coats.

"Who? Help me put these things away," Renee said, handing Keisha bags of both flour and sugar.

"Kelly and her father."

"What would make you think that?" Renee asked.

As they put away the leftover cookie ingredients, Keisha explained. "Kelly showed me the catalog. Those dolls cost like a hundred-fifty each! And you know where she has them all set up?"

Renee had no idea but knew she was about to find out.

"In her playroom. She has *two* rooms—one for sleeping and one for playing, with a big bathroom between them. That's what rich people have. Houses like that," Keisha added in case Renee wasn't following.

"Sweetie, just because Kelly has a room for her toys doesn't mean they're rich. It means that they're organized. Instead of having toys all over the house or using a basement as a playroom, they're just in one of the upstairs rooms. Their house is much bigger than this one," she said.

Keisha nodded. "Exactly. Because they're rich."

Renee put her hand on the girl's head, then tugged at one of the braids. She wasn't going to explain to the child what Trey had said about buying the house with his wife to fill it with children.

Renee didn't know anything about Trey Calloway's finances, but she suspected he was an overindulgent parent rather than an independently wealthy one. She knew the Cedar Grove neighborhood wasn't a wealthy one. It was solidly middle-class, just like its twin, Holly Grove. Residents were working professionals, most in their thirties, forties and fifties; families with kids in school or starting college. The fact that Keisha equated the trappings of middle class with being rich was yet another reason Renee was glad to have made the move out of Durham and to Cedar Springs.

"Your uncle Petey is *rich*," Renee said.

Her best friend had indeed made a bundle as a video-game entrepreneur. If things had worked out between them long ago, maybe she and Keisha would be rich, as well. But Renee knew that if she and Peter had ever hooked up, there would be no Keisha in her life and she would be poorer because of it.

"No, he isn't," Keisha countered. "He lives in an apartment building, just like we used to."

Renee smiled. There were apartment buildings and then there were *apartment* homes. Peter Shepherd *owned* the six-floor building and claimed the penthouse floor as his personal residence. The three bottom floors of the building had two apartments each before hitting the higher-rent whole-floor units. Even if there had been any vacant units on the lower floors, Renee would have needed a salary three times the size of her current income as a manager at a retail store to even be considered for residency in that building.

"Well, the next time we're over there," she said, "I'll have Uncle Pete explain to you the different kinds of rich."

Keisha produced one of her "if you say so" looks that had become all too common in recent weeks.

"Can I have another cookie?"

Renee glanced at the wall clock, then nodded. "You have an hour before it's lights-out."

"Okay," Keisha said, reaching toward the tin with the chocolate-chip cookies. "But, Mom?"

Renee's heart swelled. "Yes, sweetie?"

"That milk over there *was* nasty."

Later that night—long after cleaning up the kitchen and putting Kelly to bed with a story, Trey went to his home office to get a little work done. As his computer powered up, lights from outside threw patterns across the partially closed blinds.

It was nearly eleven, not that late for a Saturday night,

but it was the second time he'd noticed his next-door neighbor getting late-night company.

Even though he knew it was childish, not to mention none of his business, he went to the side of the window to peep outside.

Before the vehicle's headlights winked out, he saw the hood ornament of a late-model Jaguar. A moment later, he saw Renee Armstrong silhouetted in the side door and a man bend low as if to kiss her. No additional lights came on in the house as the man shut the door behind them.

Inexplicably irritated, Trey stomped back to his desk. He had no claim on her. She was a grown woman and could see whom she wanted. Just because *he* would never have female company in the house even if Kelly were sound asleep didn't mean that Renee applied the same moral code to *her* affairs.

It doubly irritated him that he knew he was being unreasonably prudish. But she had been coming on to him just a few hours earlier. Now she was wrapped up in another man's arms.

The next morning he woke up in the same foul mood as the night before due to his neighbor's late-night visitor. The Jaguar, however, was gone, which he noticed when he went outside to pick up the morning newspaper.

He had no claim on Renee Armstrong. She could see whomever she wanted, whenever she wanted.

Still, it grated.

Maybe because it conflicted with the whole fantasy he'd built up about them—neighbors with benefits who could've grown into something even more meaningful. Or maybe it was because Renee didn't jibe with his image of what a mother should be in the same fashion that his wife had been for Kelly. Either way, he knew he was being a sanctimonious fool. Cursing under his breath, he aimed to get on with his day.

It was already shaping up to be a test of his patience.

"Come on, Kelly!" he called toward the kitchen as he tossed the newspaper in a basket for later. "We're going to be late."

Sunday-morning church service started promptly at ten-thirty, and Sunday school, to which Kelly seemed particularly averse, began at nine. If it were just him, he wouldn't go to church at all. But Andrea had wanted Kelly to grow up in the church, the way she had. And taking Kelly to services kept Aunt Henrietta off his back. So every Sunday morning, they went through the motions of being good Christians.

Trey checked his tie in the mirror, then got his overcoat as well as her coat, hat and scarf from the hall closet.

This Sunday morning had been more of a trial than usual. Apparently, too many cookies made his kid cranky the next morning. She didn't want to wear the outfit he'd laid out for her on the daybed in her playroom. Not up for an argument, he'd acquiesced when she'd instead dragged a blue-and-white dress from her closet. The cotton material wasn't for winter, but he'd convinced her that tights and a white turtleneck would go great. He hadn't mentioned the part about them also adding a layer of warmth.

He'd changed the ribbons in her ponytails to match the outfit and then had gone downstairs to prepare the quick breakfast they'd eat before heading to the Chapel of the Groves.

The oatmeal, juice and apple slices should have been a simple affair.

"I spilled juice on my dress," Kelly called.

Probably deliberately, he thought. When he reached the kitchen, he saw Kelly dabbing a napkin on the front of her dress.

"Let me see," he said, stooping to assess the damage. If there was an orange-juice spot on the dress, he couldn't see it. "It's fine," he pronounced. "Put your coat on and get in the car."

"But, Daddy, look," the six-year-old said, pointing to an imaginary spot. She'd apparently wanted to convince him she needed to change, but not so much that she'd actually ruin one of her favorite dresses.

"I don't see anything and neither will anyone else. Stop stalling, Kel. Let's go."

Knowing the jig was up, she accepted her coat and shrugged into it. But she balked at the wool cap.

"It's going to mess up my hair."

Trey sighed. "Fine," he said, weary from their earlier battle.

He stuffed the hat in his pocket and wrapped the scarf around Kelly's neck.

He then shooed his daughter out the mudroom door and to the car that was already heating up and idling in the driveway. Once he got Kelly seat-belted into the backseat of his Lincoln Navigator, he shut the door only to see Renee stepping out of her front door.

She had on superhigh heels, at least six inches, with black fishnet stockings, the kind with the sexy seam up the back of the leg. A short red leather skirt was the next thing he noticed before what looked like a faux fur jacket that barely hit her midriff. When she turned and saw him, she startled.

"Good morning," Trey called.

"Oh. Uh, hi there," she said. "Off to church?"

"Yeah."

She stood there, not moving, and Trey got the hint.

"Well, we're late," he said. "See you later."

She glanced up the street, then back at him before giving a distracted wave.

Trey followed her gaze but didn't see anything. He got

in his truck and pulled out onto the street. Then, with a final glance over his shoulder at Renee, he put his attention on the road even though his thoughts remained on his next-door neighbor.

Now her choice of the nightclub Trance for their date made sense. There was no way the getup she was wearing this morning was for anybody's church. If anything, she looked as if she was headed out to go work a pole somewhere.

That lascivious thought made him squirm in the driver's seat with the image of one of those long limber legs wrapped around...

A noise from the backseat halted that line of thought. He was going to have to double his offering and pay special attention to Chaplain St. Clair's message this morning. Maybe he *and* Kelly needed an extra dose of religion today.

Trey shot a guilty glance in the rearview mirror to check on Kelly.

"What's up, princess?"

"Can we sit with Aunt Henrietta and Uncle Carlton?"

"It'll depend on if there's room on the pew where they're sitting."

"Drive faster."

Trey met his daughter's gaze in the rearview mirror. She was absolutely serious. As if *he* had been the holdup this morning.

Women.

As if she knew exactly what he was thinking, Kelly blew him a kiss. Trey smiled. "Yeah, back at ya, kid."

"Hey there, Renee. Sorry I'm late," Jeremy Knight said, slamming the door of his Mercedes-Benz and tossing her the keys as she came toward him from the walkway. "Keisha up?"

"Not yet," Renee said. "And make something besides

pancakes or waffles for breakfast, will you? We made cookies last night and she had a ton of them. She's had enough sweet stuff to last a week."

Renee made her way to the Mercedes and climbed into the driver's seat.

"Any cookies left?" Jeremy hollered from the front doorway.

"Kitchen table."

She shut the door and drove off. She glanced down at her work clothes and wondered what Trey Calloway had made of her outfit. He'd looked shell-shocked—and not in a good way.

He and his daughter were the spitting image of suburban Sunday-morning propriety and she looked like... Well, Renee knew exactly what she looked like on this particular morning.

Her mobile phone rang then, and as Trey Calloway left her mind, she focused on business.

She touched the Bluetooth control as she headed the sleek luxury car vehicle out of the Cedar Grove subdivision. "Return Engagements, this is Renee. How can I pleasure you?"

Chapter 3

Trance hadn't been open for a full year and already had a reputation for being a place where its patrons could find or pick up *anything* that helped them get their party on, be it a date for the night—or the hour. Trey had never been there, but had gotten an earful about the place from his cousin Sasha, whose idea of relaxing after work differed drastically from Trey's.

After being thoroughly wanded and patted down by security at the door, Trey escorted Renee into the nightclub and immediately realized that Renee was one of the hottest women, if not *the* hottest woman, in the place. If he'd thought Sunday morning's getup of fishnet panty hose and leather made him want to howl, he knew he might have to beat a couple of brothers off of her tonight—literally.

She wore a simple black pencil skirt and a blouse. But the devil, as the saying went, was in the details. Her blouse featured more skin than fabric. A fact that wasn't readily apparent until he helped her out of her heavy wrap at the nightclub's coat check.

When he got the full effect, Trey felt as though he'd been sucker punched.

Renee's top hugged her front in a way that had to be designed to make grown men weep. Trey was absolutely certain that no bra was under it. Two strips of fabric were connected by a large grommet in the back, leaving the rest of the "blouse" falling to the side.

As he watched her walk, Trey remembered how much he'd enjoyed playing peekaboo when he was little. As a grown man who had been without female companionship for way the hell too long, he knew it was a game that still roused his passions.

Trance was hopping. Music pumped from unseen speakers and strobe lights flashed to the beat of the music around the mirrored interior. Wednesday night, billed as Midweek Madness, was packed with people partying as if they didn't have to go to work in the morning. And maybe they didn't, he thought.

Trey couldn't remember the last time he'd been in a nightclub. Being the single parent of a six-year-old had by choice and necessity altered his priorities and perspective, not to mention his social life. Kelly was delighted to spend some time with her great-aunt and uncle, and Renee said she'd gotten a friend to stay with Keisha.

They snaked through the crowd, making their way to an area where counter-high tables were scattered about the perimeter of the room like mushrooms growing wild. Trey claimed a table just as it was being cleared.

"This place is something else!" Renee said, practically yelling to be heard over bass beats of some artist he'd never heard of. When had he turned into a stuffy old man? He was just thirty-five years old, for Pete's sake.

A waitress in black approached, took their drink orders and placed a placard on the table indicating it was now occupied.

"Let's dance!" Renee said, practically dragging him onto the crowded dance floor.

A few moments later, Trey Calloway didn't have a thought in his head except the woman writhing in front of him.

Renee liked the way Trey Calloway moved. Smooth and easy, not enough to break a sweat, but with the grace of a man who knew how to work his body.

She'd been looking forward to tonight's date with Trey. Not only was she out with her sexy neighbor, but this evening was also the first time in almost two years that she'd been able to put on something that made her feel sexy and go out with adult company. Between work, Keisha's evening therapy sessions, work and elementary-school homework, she hadn't been able to do much of anything except keep all the balls in the air as she juggled the demands made of her.

But tonight was for being in the company of a sexy man who found her attractive.

Tonight was for dancing with abandon, for being appreciated for being a woman, not just a mom, an employee or a solution to a problem.

She smiled up at Trey as she raised her arms in the air and partied like she didn't care—because she didn't.

What a liberating feeling.

They danced through two songs, the second one an extended play of something with a driving beat that thrummed through Renee's body in a way that had her wondering if it was the music or Trey making her hot and bothered. She ultimately decided it was a bit of both, combined with the luxury and the freedom of just being all woman tonight.

"We're gonna slow it down now and kick it back a few years. Some of y'all will remember it, and the rest of you are about to get schooled," the DJ said. "This is for all of the lovers in the room. Let your baby hold you tight."

The music shifted to a Luther Vandross song about holding someone tight for just one night.

Renee glanced up at Trey, who'd arched a brow in question.

She shook her head. It was best not to tempt fate. As Luther crooned, Trey led Renee back to the table they had previously claimed. Their server approached with the drinks they'd ordered and placed them on the table.

"Thanks," Trey said, slipping a fifty on the tray as payment and tip.

"I like that they didn't just leave unattended drinks on the table," Renee said, picking up her glass.

Trey nodded. "You're a great dancer," he said.

"You've got some moves, too," she murmured before lifting her glass in a small toast and then taking a sip of her appletini.

His smile said he'd rather be holding her in a close embrace on the dance floor. She looked out at some of the couples who were apparently taking the DJ at his word about holding their partner tight. A couple of them were grinding so hard that they needed to forgo the dance floor and get a room.

Renee's face flamed. When she glanced at Trey, he, too, was surveying their surroundings.

The guy approaching the table where he and Renee sat wasn't a Trance employee. Trey had already noted that most, if not all, of the nightclub's security detail resembled NFL linebackers on a work release detail. The guy in the ill-fitting gray suit making tracks toward them wasn't a bouncer, but he had his eyes on one thing: Renee Armstrong.

She seemed oblivious as she sipped from her drink and scanned the crowd, all the while swaying to the beat of the silky rhythm reverberating through the club.

Some folks were getting a little too physically intimate for his tastes—apparently, in the years he'd been off the market, he'd morphed into a replica of his sixtysomething-year-old uncle Carlton. He knew he shouldn't be surprised at what he was seeing on the dance floor. This was, after all, Trance, where anything and everything could and did happen.

Renee turned toward Trey just as Gray Suit approached.

"Hey, girl," the man said. "I've been watching you."

Renee lifted an arched brow and placed her drink on the table.

"Excuse me," Trey said, stepping closer and putting his arm around Renee's waist. Marking his territory, he pulled her close. "She has a date."

The man's gaze flicked over Trey. Although the man outweighed Trey by at least seventy-five pounds, something in Trey's aggressive stance seemed to halt the predator.

Renee lifted her right hand and put it on Trey's chest. "That's right," she said.

The man dipped his head, giving Renee a gap-toothed smile. "I'm right over there," he said, nodding toward a VIP booth. "You change your mind, you know where to find me."

Renee just smiled.

The man's gaze hardened as he again surveyed Trey's measure. Then, just like he'd come, he barreled his way across the floor and back to his booth. His boys were seemingly waiting for him there, a group of four who'd apparently sent their best specimen to approach Renee.

"What was that all about?" Renee asked, turning her back on the observers.

But Trey knew that her back gave them plenty to see, so he maneuvered himself around until his own body blocked their view.

"I guess the rules have changed a bit since I've last been in a club," he said.

"I'm not referring to him," Renee said. "Bozos like that are a dime a dozen. I'm talking about your caveman routine, slamming me against you like you have a claim."

Trey shook his head as if to clear it. "Excuse me."

Renee lifted her drink glass and took a tiny sip. "Look, Trey. A guy hitting on a woman in a nightclub is pretty much the norm. It's why people come to places like this."

"Is that why you suggested we come here? So I could watch you get hit on by other men?"

She cocked her head to the right. "Are you picking a fight?"

Trey closed his eyes for a moment and ran a hand over his head. When he opened his eyes, he saw that Renee had been joined by a woman in a low-cut red dress that highlighted her ample cleavage.

Oh, for the love of God, he thought. *Of all the people.*

This wasn't just some random woman or a friend of Renee's. It was someone *he* knew…and had a history with.

Great. Just great.

Of all the places to run into an ex. They'd hooked up a bit right before he'd met his wife. It had been years since he'd seen her, but Jazmin hadn't changed one bit.

"Trey Calloway. Imagine seeing you here," she said in that sultry voice that in the distant past had made him weak in the knees. "I've missed you."

From the corner of his eye he saw Renee narrow hers.

"Hello, Jazmin," he said. Then he made introductions, using only first names.

"Trey and I go way back," Jazmin said to Renee, all while giving Trey the sort of once-over that left no doubt just what that relationship had been like. Then, as if Renee weren't even standing right next to him, she sidled in close, giving him a full display of her assets. She ran a ringed fin-ger up his arm. "The last I heard, you were single again."

"Yes," Trey said, as he took Renee's hand and threaded his fingers through it, a move that wasn't unnoticed by Jazmin. "But things change quickly."

Jazmin's mouth tilted at the corners. "Looks like my timing is all wrong again."

"Nice to meet you," Renee said, her tone and nice-nasty smile saying the exact opposite.

Jazmin's eyes flicked over Renee. If she felt a bit of grudging respect, she hid it well.

"Well…it was good seeing you." Her gaze shifted to Renee for the briefest of moments and then went back in a none-too-subtle way to Trey. "And if you change your mind—" her hand rose to her chest and she deftly produced a business card that she offered him "—here's where you can reach me."

It took everything in Renee to not snatch the card from the viper's hand and rip it to pieces. To Trey's credit, though, he didn't accept it.

"I don't think so, Jazmin. We're done."

The seductress's mouth quirked up and she returned the card to whatever cache she had in her bra. "Your loss, Trey," she said before turning to walk away.

"Well, *that* was interesting," Renee said drolly.

"Now that it's been clearly established that we're both hot, how about we go somewhere else?"

"Let's roll," she said.

After collecting their coats and getting into his truck, they sat in the parking lot of Trance with the vehicle warm-ing in the cold December air.

"You mind telling me what was going on in there?" Renee said.

"Sorry," Trey said, rubbing his eyes. "Unlike you, I'm not used to that sort of place. It's been a while for me."

Renee drew her wrap closer and turned toward him. "Unlike me? What's that supposed to mean?"

He glanced at her. "Well, uh, you know. Your, uh, I guess your job regularly takes you to places like Trance."

Renee's brow furrowed. "My job?"

He shrugged. "Yeah. I mean, I'm cool with it, I guess. Everybody's got to make a living."

She folded her arms across her chest. "I'm not exactly sure what we're talking about here, but just what is it you think I do, Trey?"

"Look, Renee. We're both adults. It's really none of my business."

"What do you think I do for a living, Trey?" she asked, her voice stern.

He met her gaze head-on.

"At first I thought you were a stripper," he said.

Renee sucked in her breath.

"But then, after seeing all the men coming and going from your place, I, well, I thought you were…"

"You thought I was a hooker!"

Trey had the grace to wince. "Actually, *call girl* came to mind."

For a moment, Renee stared at him. All she managed was "Wow. Just wow. And what, exactly, is the difference?"

"Renee, I…"

But before he could get out his next words, she convulsed. Trey thought she was having some sort of attack and reached for his phone to call 9-1-1.

Then he realized she wasn't in the middle of a seizure. She was actually laughing. Doubled over laughing. She looked over at him and fell forward in her seat again, leaning against the passenger door and trying to catch her breath. Every time he thought she was done, she'd sit up, glance at him and start laughing again.

"I take it you're not a call girl," he said drily.

"Oh, oh," she said, trying to stem the laughter and sit up. But another look at him and the giggles persisted.

Trey was glad she was taking it in such good humor. He knew plenty of women—as in every single one of his female cousins—who would have either slapped him or never forgiven him for making that sort of allegation.

Renee was wiping at her eyes with her index finger.

"Trey Calloway, you just made my day."

He looked at her askance. "Most women would have been insulted."

Noises of amusement were still coming from her mouth, but she was able to answer him. "If you hadn't proven my point, I would be."

"What point?"

She turned in the seat, crossing her legs as she did. "Up here, buddy," she said when his gaze lingered on the long length of leg that captured his attention. When his gaze again connected with hers, she asked, "Was it the outfit on Sunday?"

"You looked like you were on your way to a strip club as the star performer."

Her grin widened and she slapped her thigh. "I told Melody it was too over the top."

Like the detail man he was, Trey didn't let her stray from the topic at hand. "What point did I make, and who is Melody?"

Shaking her head, she opened her mouth to speak and then started laughing again.

"Wait, before that," she said. "The men. You said you saw men coming and going from my place."

"Yeah. I guess they're not your customers?"

"Men in expensive cars?"

"Yeah."

That answer brought forth another round of giggles. "Peter and Jeremy are going to love that one."

Fed up, Trey reached for the gearshift.

Her soft hand on his stayed the motion. "I'm sorry."

"Mind letting me in on the humor?" His tone carried little of it.

"Peter and Jeremy are a couple of my close friends from college."

"Please tell me they're gay."

She grinned. "Sorry. At least Peter isn't. And I'm not a stripper," Renee said. "But thanks for the backhanded compliment. I stay in shape by working out at the Y. And I'm definitely not a call girl. Ick to that, by the way."

"So what is it you do?"

She grinned. "I work in retail."

"'Retail'? Like a store?"

She nodded. "A consignment store, to be exact. It's called Return Engagements. I moved down here from Durham to Cedar Springs to open and manage the newest location." She let out a little chuckle. "I say 'down here' like Cedar Springs is hours away from civilization. But really, from our old place to the new house is only forty minutes or so."

"Cedar Springs has a much slower vibe," he said. "So tell me a little more about this, uh, consignment store."

She gave him a look, but let his hesitancy go.

"It's on Main Street. It's a small chain, six stores, all in eastern North Carolina, but the owner, Melody, wants to expand and offer franchises."

"And you specialize in a clientele that…?" He let the question hang, clearly not willing to make another leap of an assumption that he'd regret.

She understood the unspoken question. "I have no idea if Return Engagements customers are strippers or by-the-hour escorts," she said. Looking at him, she chuckled again. "Although I suppose fishnet stockings and stripper platforms could give one pause."

"Ya think?"

"We have monthly Sunday-morning sales-team meetings," she said. "The stores are closed and that's really the only day that works for everyone. The theme for this one was 'Outfitting your pleasure.'"

"Uh, Renee, so far none of what you've said…"

"'Outfitting your pleasure' means the stores aim to have any type of clothing for any occasion in stock and available. We drew slips of paper and each manager had to come to the meeting dressed in the style of whatever was on the slip of paper."

"And you drew 'streetwalker'?"

"I was *supposed* to be a socialite out for a night of partying."

Trey rolled his eyes.

Renee punched him in the arm. "I thought it looked kind of hookerish, too," she admitted.

"What were the other, er, costumes?"

"Suburban mom going Saturday-afternoon shopping. College student on a budget. Traditional grandma going to church or a tea party. Hipster artist, and vintage aficionado. I wanted the vintage look, but got… Well, you saw what I got."

"I'm sorry about what I said," Trey told her.

"Don't worry about it. I will, however, let the sales team know that my interpretation of the theme was exactly as I'd feared."

This time when he put the Navigator in gear, she didn't object.

Trey handled the streets and the vehicle with ease and it didn't take long for them to reach the Cedar Grove subdivision.

"Where's Kelly tonight?" she asked when she realized they were headed home.

"At my aunt's. She and my uncle love having her around. What about Keisha?"

"One of my best friends is babysitting. But neither of them like that word. They call it 'hanging out.'"

When Trey pulled into his driveway, a late-model Jaguar was parked at the curb and Renee's sedan was in her driveway. It hadn't escaped his notice that she'd explained away her clothes and her job, but not her late-night company. Peter and Jeremy. He'd never met either man, but was pretty sure he didn't like either of them.

He couldn't be sure, but he thought the Jag was the same one he'd seen the other night. But he had to remember, despite his "caveman" actions earlier that night, he didn't have any claim on her.

He killed the ignition and turned to her.

"Renee..."

"Trey..." she said at the same time.

He motioned for her to go first.

Renee smiled, the action demure and sexy for its non-sexual indication. "I was going to ask if maybe you'd like to start over. Go out someplace that isn't filled with loud music..."

"And aggressive exes?"

"Speak for yourself, Trey Calloway. I'd never seen that man before in my life."

He grinned. "All right. I like that idea. How about lunch? That way the girls will be in school and sitters won't be an issue. And," he added, "it can be someplace downtown near your, uh, store."

She shook her head. "It's a date. And, Trey Calloway, you can pick me up at Return Engagements so you can see that it really *is* a consignment shop and not a front for a prostitution ring."

He cocked his head a bit. "That's the third time."

She paused in reaching for her bag that she'd placed on the floor. "The third time what?"

"That you've called me by my full name."

She dipped her head, and he was sure he'd caught a blush.

"I just like the way it sounds."

With that admission, she opened her door and slid out of the high seat of the Navigator before he could get out to open the door for her.

It wasn't until he'd watched her safely enter her house and he went into his that he reflected on how extremely glad he was that Renee wasn't a stripper or a call girl. It was bad enough that he'd had the hots for her for the past month. While both professions had certain…merits…the last thing he wanted to do was move. And he'd absolutely have to if that sort of element had established itself right next door to him.

Over the next twenty-four hours, Renee had little time to think about what her next-door neighbor thought of her wardrobe and actual profession.

"I don't want to go back to that school!"

Keisha was throwing a fit, the third one this week. Renee knew she had to get to the bottom of whatever was going on before the problem escalated. Keisha had already missed the school bus and Renee was calculating how much time she had to get Keisha settled down and dropped off at Cedar Springs Primary School before she, too, was late to work.

The eight-year-old was sitting on the edge of her bed in full pout. She'd showered and had put on a pair of jeans and one sock. A turtleneck sweater, her shoes and other sock had been thrown across the room.

Renee called on all the reserves she had as well as the training she'd received from Dr. Hendrickson, the child psychologist Keisha saw twice a week. They would get through this crisis, just like they'd gotten through the others, she reminded herself.

Renee sat on the bed next to Keisha and took a deep breath, calming herself. Blowing up was exactly what Keisha wanted, so that was out of the question. Instead she scooted closer and tugged one of Keisha's hands until she clasped it in both of her hands.

"Keisha, honey, whatever is going on at school, we can work through it together."

"We can't!" the girl wailed and yanked away.

She stomped over toward her dresser and stood there, looking down at her feet.

"Tell me what happened," Renee prodded.

Silence.

Biting back a sigh, Renee got up and went over to Keisha. She stood behind the girl, put both hands on her shoulders and pulled her to her for a semblance of a hug.

When Keisha didn't pull away, Renee counted it as progress.

Slowly she turned the girl in her arms and gave her a proper hug.

"Keisha, I'm not going anywhere. You are mine and I love you."

"I know, " Keisha mumbled against the sweater Renee was wearing over white jeans.

Renee walked Keisha back to the double bed and sat them both at the foot of it.

"What happened?"

"They don't like me."

Well, this was indeed progress, Renee thought. If Keisha was concerned about other kids liking her, it meant she cared in the first place.

"Who is 'they'?"

"The kids in my class."

"Why do you think that?" Renee gently asked.

"They're all like Kelly."

That brought Renee up short. Kelly? Kelly Calloway from next door? Before she could ask for a clarification, Keisha was talking, the words tumbling out at a frenetic pace.

"They all go to dance class and that's all they talk about. What they wore. What they did. This tutu and that tutu. And I hate them! I hate them all!" She then burst into tears.

Renee pulled Keisha into her arms and rocked her.

She'd known that moving in the middle of a school year had the potential to be problematic, and going from the inner city to a quiet street in a suburban city was like moving from New York to Mars. She needed to get to the root of the issue here.

"Would you like to take dance lessons?"

"I don't know," Keisha mumbled in response.

Renee knew from experience that meant yes. She mentally calculated how much dance lessons might cost in addition to the art lessons she wanted to surprise her with for Christmas. She made a note to check with both the YMCA and the Common Ground Recreation Center to see if either offered the lessons at a possible discount.

"Come here," Renee said, tugging Keisha's arm. The girl reluctantly followed.

"Where are we going?"

"To the bathroom. I want to show you something."

Renee pushed open the door to the hall bathroom. The mess inside resembled the aftereffects of a tornado in a small space, but she ignored the wet towels and soap on the floor and continued to the clothes hamper.

She paused with Keisha in front of the big mirror. "Do you see what I see?"

"No."

The obstinate word almost made Renee smile. But she

maintained her serious mien. "I see a beautiful girl who can achieve anything she wants to. I see a smart girl who aced her spelling test and her math test. I see you, Keisha Thompson."

"Armstrong," Keisha corrected.

This time, Renee's smile was broad and it blossomed from her face straight to her heart, where she had so much love for the little girl in front of her. "We're working on that, okay?"

Keisha nodded.

Then something dawned on Renee. "Is that it?" she asked. "Do all the kids at school have the same names as their parents?"

Keisha nodded again. "I'm the only one in my class whose mom isn't her real mom and who doesn't have a dad."

The "real mom" part hurt—as it always did.

And Renee doubted that she was the only single parent of a child at the primary school, but she wouldn't dare get into a debate with Keisha right now.

"I don't even remember my real mom that much," Keisha said.

"You have her picture," Renee reminded her.

"But it's like it's somebody I don't know," Keisha said. "Just a face. And the face in the picture is smiling. She never smiled. At least not at me. I remember that part."

Not for the first time since Renee had become Keisha's foster mother, she cursed the woman who had given birth to a daughter but preferred men and drugs.

Suddenly and notwithstanding the costume for work, Trey Calloway's supposition that she was a hooker or call girl wasn't so funny. It was too close to the truth that had been Keisha's existence before Child Protective Services had rescued her from the apartment that had become a crack and heroin den. Keisha had been rescued before she had been forced to turn tricks to feed her mother's habit. The woman had been willing to barter her daughter for crack cocaine and heroin. The fact that there were sickos out there who would prey on a five-year-old galled Renee to the core.

Keisha had been left alone to fend for herself for weeks on end in her young life. Her mother either out on the streets trying to score enough money for her next rocks or too high to realize that her child needed attention.

To say Keisha had abandonment issues was putting it mildly.

They'd made a lot of progress together in the more than two years they'd been together. Renee had hoped that the demons that had chased Keisha when she was younger had been slain by Renee's unconditional love. But some of the monsters still lurked in the shadows, jumping out when least expected—like at eight o'clock in the morning.

Renee smiled at Keisha and then pointed at their faces in the mirror.

"Then this is the image I want you to remember," Renee said. "You and me. Okay?"

"Okay."

"Now, what about school?"

"I guess I'm late."

"Yep."

Keisha looked around the bathroom, then bent to pick up the towels abandoned in heaps. "And I guess I need to clean up this mess."

"Yep."

"Are you mad at me?"

The hesitant question nearly broke Renee's heart. She took the towels from Keisha's hands, folded them over the rack and drew the girl into her embrace. "I'm never mad at you, Keisha. Never."

It took them another twenty minutes to get out of the

house and head to school. Renee checked in at the office and explained Keisha's tardiness to the school secretary.

She then hugged her again and shooed her off to her class. But before going, Keisha asked another question, one that floored Renee.

"Hey, Mom. Can I get my hair relaxed?"

That was when Renee realized what lay at the core of this latest crisis.

It wasn't dance that was bugging the girl.

Renee now understood more so why Keisha felt out of place in this town and in this school. Renee had seen all of the kids in Keisha's new third-grade class. While the overall class was evenly split between boys and girls, and they were all a mix of races, Keisha was the only one who was dark and whose hair was in cornrows, white and blue beads clacking at the ends. All of the girls in her class at the old school in Durham had some variation of cornrows or braids, natural hairstyles that complemented the varying shades of cream, brown and ebony that were reflected among the pupils. In addition to looking good, the braided styles were easy to maintain. But here in Cedar Springs, they made Keisha look different. And thus, feel different.

"I think I've found a hairstylist here for both of us to try," Renee said. "It's the one that Kelly goes to."

Keisha's eyes widened. "Really?"

"Yes."

The girl grinned and threw her arms around Renee's neck for another hug before dashing into her classroom.

It seemed she had finally uncovered the basis of Keisha's acting out this week. She could only hope that something as easily altered as hair was the extent of the problem.

Nevertheless, Renee was left standing in the corridor, wondering when life had become so complicated for kids.

Chapter 4

Working at home had its advantages. But today was not one of them.

The deal Trey had worked out with his management consulting firm when Kelly was an infant had made sense at the time. He was a single parent with a newborn and his responsibilities then were such that a flexible schedule met both his needs and those of Keaton & Myers Incorporated. Now that Kelly was in first grade and in school most of the day, he more often than not found himself driving out to the headquarters of Keaton & Myers at Six Commerce Plaza for meetings rather than video-conferencing in.

The thought had crossed his mind that if he had time to make a lunch date with Renee Armstrong, he had the time to get his rear into gear and into the office.

Trey knew that Bradley Christian, his chief, and really only, nemesis at work, was busy posturing for the operating committee that was holding an impromptu meeting at the office.

"I'll be there in less than five minutes," he told Bradley, guiding the Navigator through the midday traffic of Cedar Springs. The drive, which should have taken all of ten minutes from his front door to the KMI parking lot, was already stretching into twenty.

Trey resisted the urge to lean on his horn and plow through the traffic. Who were these people and what were they doing out and about like this in the middle of the day?

He, of course, had no way of knowing just what traffic was like during the day in Cedar Springs. He was almost always working from home. And even if he'd worked from the main office, he wouldn't be driving around during the day. In the years he had spent raising Kelly, Trey had turned into something of a social recluse. He knew all about dance lessons, enough about crafts, and was well versed enough in the trappings of beauty salons that he made sure to hustle Kelly into the shop before the after-work rush.

That made him think of Renee Armstrong. He'd given her the name, number and address of his aunt's salon.

A grin split his face as he contemplated what Renee's reaction might be if he walked into the salon while she was in the middle of a beauty treatment. Her hair in those giant pink or yellow rollers or plastered with foil and that stinky goop that they slathered all over it. He liked her long curly hair; it was full-bodied just like the woman herself. He liked that she didn't flat-iron it into one of those slick styles that reminded him of anemic models.

She would probably be mortified if he saw her that way, but Trey had grown up one of the few males in a family full of women. He knew the pains females put themselves through to look good for themselves…and for their men. And until this year, when she'd turned six, he'd dutifully sat in those uncomfortable chairs waiting for Kelly because she used to cry if he left. His baby was growing up, though. The last time at Aunt Tiny's shop Styles, Kelly had suggested that he go to the barbershop while she got her hair done.

He'd laughed at the notion, until he realized it made a lot of sense. He usually spent the time browsing the internet or playing games on his tablet, and sometimes eavesdropping on the female conversation all around him. While waiting for his daughter, he'd heard enough juicy gossip to write one of those bestselling romances that his cousins loved so much.

He'd gone to an author book signing once that Sasha had been covering for the television station. The writer had said ideas were all around and that one of the best writing exercises was to play what-if.

Like, he thought, with more than a bit of ironic humor, what if a call girl really did set up shop on a quiet suburban street? Who would be her love interest? A preacher spotted tipping out of her door one Sunday morning or the cop who came to check out an unrelated complaint.

When Trey again gave his full attention to driving instead of his aspirations as a novelist, his daughter and the woman he wanted to get to know even better, he found himself pulling into the employee lot at Keaton & Myers Incorporated.

He checked the Windsor knot in his tie, brushed a hand over his hair, then reached for his portfolio. Running through the mental checklist of things he needed to do, including points he needed to make in his presentation, he made his way to the conference room.

The only thing Trey hated more than posers like Bradley Christian was a brownnoser who wanted nothing more than to take credit for work he hadn't done.

The good thing about working from home was that he didn't have to deal with the B.S. that went on at Keaton & Myers. What he'd learned in the years he'd essentially been an independent contractor with all the benefits of a full-time employee in the office was that he liked it…a lot. The flexible schedule allowed him to take a few side jobs.

While they had necessitated the out-of-town trips that required him to get a sitter for Kelly, he loved the work of designing marketing and imaging campaigns for up-and-coming creativity outlets. The work posed no conflict with KMI and he'd even generated a couple of new clients for the company.

When Trey strode into the conference room, it was to find Bradley Christian all but snuggled up with the vice president of the company. But when Randall Keaton saw Trey, he patted Bradley on the arm and walked away, straight toward Trey.

It took effort for Trey not to grin when he saw Bradley's perplexed look.

The two men shook hands.

"It's good to see you, Calloway. That was a really fine job you did for the Hathaways."

"Thank you, Mr. Keaton," Trey said. He'd worked his butt off on that consultation and was glad to see it recognized. "It was a team effort."

Keaton rolled his eyes. "Yeah, right. I know all about the team down here. Listen, first, call me Randy, and second, are you free for lunch today? After this meeting, there are a couple of things I'd like to discuss with you."

So much for lunch with Renee. Maybe this was the Lord's way of saying he needed to stay away from that woman. He'd have to text her to cancel.

"Sure thing," he told the company vice president.

As everyone was taking their seats, Trey tapped out a quick message and apology to Renee, then turned his phone on vibrate. His mind now occupied with what Keaton wanted to meet about, he didn't wait for a response from her and tucked the phone inside the portfolio.

When the full Gang of Six—as they were called—from corporate were seated as well as the six other senior account execs like Trey, Randall Keaton got down to business.

"There's a mid-Atlantic acquisition that we're making. It represents a new market for Keaton & Myers, one that has untapped potential. And this office, which is central to all of the areas that will be impacted, is key to the success of the project."

Trey noticed that heads were bobbing along the table and he figured the eager account executives were already tallying up the six-figure bonuses they could potentially earn. All of Trey's extra money was deposited into high-interest-bearing investments. He had Kelly's future in mind with everything he did.

"We'll be naming the executive team in a few days," Keaton said.

"Excuse me, sir," Bradley asked, his hand shooting into the air as if the meeting were being held in a fifth-grade classroom and Keaton was the teacher. "Is there an application or nomination process for that team?"

"No, Christian. There is not."

As if, Trey thought. The only team Bradley Christian was capable of leading would be the suck-up one. Trey wasn't even sure if Bradley detected the note of irritation in Keaton's voice or the way his demeanor ever so subtly changed when addressing him. The older man leaned back as if distancing himself from his too-eager employee.

It took Keaton fifteen minutes to run them all through the acquisition plan and to outline what would be required of each of them. An assistant then circled the table, handing each of the account executives a binder with KMI's logo stenciled on the cover.

"It goes without saying," Keaton said, "that the information you're now receiving is confidential. If you'll open the binder to the first page—" he waited while everyone did so, then continued "—you'll find a confidentiality agreement."

Bradley was the first to whip out a Montblanc fountain

pen and proceeded to scrawl his name across the bottom of the document. He did so with a flourish and then sat back with a satisfied grin, as if being first to commit himself would win him a prize at the fair. The idiot hadn't even read the thing.

"I'd like you to take a moment to read it," Keaton said with deliberation as he all but scowled at Bradley, "and then I'll address your questions."

Looking chastened, Bradley lifted the binder to read what he'd just signed. Shaking his head, Trey read the document. What he found there was troubling. It stipulated pledging confidentiality about the project, which was pro forma in all of their client dealings. But there was also a pledge to not discuss the project with media, friends, family, including immediate relatives or any KMI employee other than those in the meeting.

"Why is this project subject to such unusual scrutiny?" Trey asked. "We maintain confidentiality with every Keaton & Myers client."

Keaton nodded. "Yes, we do. But there's an element of this project that I haven't yet shared with you. If anyone would like to recuse themselves, now is that time. And trust me, no one will think ill of you if you choose to."

For a moment, no one moved.

Then, one by one, as if signing their own death warrants, the other account executives signed the document until only Trey remained.

He'd lived and worked his entire life relying on both his gut and his common sense. And the only thing his gut was doing now was screaming that this was a bad idea. A very bad one.

It might cost him his job, but he wasn't about to commit to something that, for all he knew, could be illegal, immoral or unethical.

Trey closed the binder and put his pen to the side of it.

He shook his head. "I'd rather not sign unless I know what I'm committing myself to," he said.

The executives from KMI headquarters exchanged glances, and Trey could have sworn he saw a small smile lift the corners of Keaton's mouth before it quickly disappeared.

"Very well," Keaton said. He then directed them through the rest of the proposal as if the whole document-signing interlude hadn't happened. More than one confused glance scurried around among the account reps. And Trey wondered why he hadn't been directed to leave since he'd all but refused to sign the document.

Much later, while sitting at lunch with Randall Keaton in the small but luxurious dining room of the Magnolia Inn, Trey learned what was going on.

"It was a test," the older man said after finishing the last of his prime rib.

"A test?"

Keaton nodded. "Probably juvenile of me," he said, "but I wanted to test the mettle of the top earners and performers at KMI."

It hadn't escaped Trey's notice that at least three of the six folks invited to the meeting were his equal when it came to hustle and creativity.

"There's a lot of money to be made with this deal," Keaton said. "But you were the only one who didn't seem fazed by it."

"There's more to life than making money."

Keaton dabbed his mouth with a linen napkin. "So I'm told," the older man said on a dry note. "My father and his best friend founded this company with a vision of putting tools in those hands that would make their businesses successful. Sometimes that means doing the hard thing, like laying off employees…."

Although nothing showed on his face, Trey wondered if

this was the way KMI fired people, with expensive lunches to soften the blow.

"And sometimes it means recognizing when there is an asset worth investing in."

Keaton leaned back as their server cleared their plates and offered them both coffee.

When they were left alone again, Keaton continued. "A couple of people hesitated today with that ridiculous demand to sign that agreement, but you not only questioned it—you stood alone in refusing to do so. Well done, Trey."

Since "thank you" didn't quite seem appropriate under the circumstances, Trey remained silent.

"What I'd like to offer you," Keaton said, "is a leadership role in the company. Not just this project, which would also be yours, but a position on the executive team. You heard the goals for this latest effort, and I've thoroughly reviewed your work over the last few years. I think you're the man who can take Keaton & Myers to new heights."

A promotion had been the furthest thing from his mind when he'd been summoned to the office today. "Thank you for your vote of confidence in me. Earlier today I was thinking that with my daughter in school now, it would be the right time to return to a regular schedule."

Keaton nodded. "I'm glad you mentioned that. It's what I wanted to address next. This would require time visiting the other regional offices on a fairly regular basis, at least once or twice a month. I trust that wouldn't be a problem for you?"

"Not at all."

"Excellent."

Keaton reached into his inner suit-jacket pocket and pulled out a pen and small leather-bound notebook. Trey noted that it was the same type and brand that Bradley Christian used.

"In addition to a car and monthly expense account,"

Keaton said, "this is what I'm prepared to offer you." He jotted a figure on the pad and pushed it Trey's way.

After a glance at the amount, Trey's heart started pounding. The number on the paper would push Trey into an entirely different tax bracket. The job would also require a lot of time away from home, at a time when Kelly was growing so fast.

"I'm not going to ask you to give me an answer today," Keaton said. "We have an executive retreat coming up. It's after the holidays, in mid-January. I'd like you to attend it. It's a three-day affair down in Florida on Amelia Island. That's where we hold the annual winter retreat. In the spring, we go to my place off Hilton Head in South Carolina. We do some brainstorming, play some golf and get to know each other. The wives have their own agenda in Florida. It usually involves shopping, tennis and shopping."

"My wife is…"

Keaton held up a hand. "Yes, I know," he said. "My own Nancy has been gone for two years now. Breast cancer," he added quietly. "I should have said 'the wives and girlfriends.' Feel free to bring a date."

A date? To a corporate retreat where his every move would be eyeballed from every member of the Gang of Six? He ran through the women he knew who could fit the "corporate wife" bill even if only for a weekend. His aunt Henrietta topped the list, along with his cousins Sasha and Baden. Next to his wife, they were three of the classiest ladies he'd ever known.

Then Renee Armstrong came to mind. And he just as quickly discarded that thought. She was gorgeous, but from what he'd seen of her wardrobe so far, there wasn't a single thing in it that would be appropriate for a corporate retreat. Everything he'd seen her in was avant-garde. While Andrea used to complain about what she called the "twinset wives" of KMI, she at least could pull something conservative and expensive out of her closet to wear to company events. Old Man Myers would likely collapse if he got a glimpse of Renee in one of her miniskirts or those sexy-as-hell fishnet hose she wore.

"Oh, what a delight to see you again!"

The feminine exclamation drew both Trey's and Keaton's attention to the front of the dining room. Three women stood there, exchanging the air-kisses and hugs of well-to-do ladies who lunched. Two of them were in chic designer suits, and the third shrugged out of an elegant winter wrap.

Trey's gut tightened.

Renee Armstrong was standing there, looking and acting as if she'd just run into her best and longtime country-club girlfriends.

The three women were now seated. And Renee hadn't noticed him. Curiously, Trey found himself both relieved and annoyed that she hadn't.

"Fine-looking group of women," Keaton said, observing Trey's reaction to the group. "Do you know them?"

Now wasn't the time to lie.

"One is my next-door neighbor," he said without casting another glance back at the table where the trio sat. "The one in blue."

"Hmm," Keaton said, again his gaze lingering to admire the women.

The image of Renee was burned into Trey's brain. She had to have the most eclectic wardrobe of any woman he'd ever met. Whereas her stripper look put him in one frame of mind, everything about her this afternoon spoke of privilege, background and wealth.

Renee Armstrong was a chameleon…or one heck of an actress.

With force, he put his mind back on his own lunch meeting with Keaton.

"I have a question for you," Trey said.

"Shoot."

"You asked me to lunch long before you made the presentation. What would we have been talking about this afternoon had I been one of the folks who signed that agreement?"

Keaton grinned and then winked. "I'd have thought of something."

Randall Keaton apparently had an eye for the ladies, the sort of eye that had the older man approaching the table where the trio sat when their lunch was complete.

Trey groaned. If Trey thought he'd escape the Magnolia Inn's dining room without Renee seeing him, he was sadly mistaken.

He didn't at all like mixing business with whatever the hell it was he had with Renee Armstrong.

Trey tried to make his way toward the lobby where their coats were waiting. But he wasn't to be so lucky. Keaton hailed him.

"Good afternoon, ladies," the CEO said.

The three turned and looked up at him.

"I couldn't help but notice when the three of you came in," he said.

Trey had to admire Keaton's style. For a man his age, the opening wasn't too bad. Trey wondered how Keaton was going to play this. It wouldn't take much to turn the moment into "creepy old man" territory.

"You look incredibly familiar to me," Keaton said, addressing a stunning blonde woman that Trey pegged to be in her late fifties or early sixties. She had eyes so blue that they could be seen from where Trey stood a few feet away.

"That's because Nancy and I were on the Governor's Committee for the Arts, Randall," the woman said. As if sensing that he might be floundering for a name, she offered hers. "Lovie Darling. I believe you knew my late husband, Dr. John Darling."

Randall touched his head in an "of course!" gesture. "That's it," he said. "What a delight to see you again, Lovie. My colleague and I were having lunch and I'm sure he wondered why I was so distracted. Other than the obvious," he added, with his glance encompassing the other two women. "I was trying to place your face."

When he said "colleague," he motioned for Trey to come forward.

With a sigh, Trey walked closer to the group, even though he harbored doubts about where this conversation might lead.

"Let me introduce you," Keaton said. "Lovie Darling, this is Trey Calloway, one of the executives with my company."

Trey heard the gasp that was quickly covered with a little cough and then Renee's gaze met his.

He winked.

"Hello, Mrs. Darling. Renee. Ma'am," he said, acknowledging the third woman at the table.

"You two know each other?" Lovie Darling asked.

Trey watched as Renee recovered, now offering him a professional smile rather than a flirtatious one in answer to his wink. "Next-door neighbors," he said.

The third woman nudged Renee. "You didn't tell me…"

Whatever she was about to say was cut off by a little yelp and then a glare sent her way. Trey bit back a grin, sure a high heel had just come in contact with a shin under the table.

"We miss Nancy terribly," Lovie Darling was saying. "She truly was a powerhouse fund-raiser and I counted her a dear friend."

He missed whatever Keaton said in response because

Renee was mouthing something his way. "What are you doing here?"

Then he remembered. They were supposed to have lunch. Had she gotten his text?

The look on her face, a mix of rage and hurt, said no. With the meeting at the office and then his lunch meeting with Keaton, he hadn't had time for a follow-up call or text message to her.

Did she think he'd stood her up?

"That sounds like a wonderful idea. Trey and I would love to join you," Keaton boomed. "Wouldn't we, Calloway?"

Trey's head whipped back to his boss. "What was that?"

"It's a date, then," Lovie said. "So to speak. Since Trey and Renee are neighbors, they could come together."

"What?" Renee said.

"Where?" Trey asked.

But the two were ignored as Keaton nodded and then leaned low and pressed a kiss on Lovie Darling's cheek. "I look forward to seeing you this evening."

Chapter 5

A black-tie reception at the North Carolina Museum of Art in Raleigh turned out to be what Renee had missed Randall Keaton and Lovie Darling discussing during lunch.

Renee wondered what kind of questions Keisha would have about her seeing Trey Calloway. She had deliberately focused on Keisha alone for the past couple of years. Yet, a few weeks after moving to Cedar Springs, here she was—again—going out with Trey and leaving Keisha in the care of one of her "uncles." Peter Shepherd and Jeremy Knight, her best friends since college, had been pumping her for info about her mystery man, but so far, Renee had been tight-lipped. She needed to sort out her own feelings before she could declare them to anyone—including her best buds.

She'd caught Peter en route home to Raleigh from Fayetteville. He and Keisha had sped off in his Jaguar, headed out to see a movie and eat what would undoubtedly be a frightening amount of junk food and sweets.

Peter and Jeremy were her two best friends in the world

and had been urging her for months to go out. They'd each even offered to set her up with friends. But then the thought of dating had held zero appeal to Renee. Her life was already too fractured without adding a relationship to the mix. But now that she'd met her sexy next-door neighbor, things were beginning to change. Even though Trey had not bothered to return her calls about lunch earlier, only to show up at the Magnolia Inn, where she had a meeting with the owner of the Return Engagements chain and a potential investor.

Had he not been at a lunch meeting of his own, she would have accused him of stalking her.

Renee still wasn't quite sure how she and Trey had been roped into attending this reception in Raleigh. Though she'd heard that Lovie Darling wasn't the typical wealthy country-club type and had a tendency toward matchmaking.

Was that what was going on?

She rejected the idea just as fast as it had popped into her head. She'd never met the woman, and from the introductions that had been made at lunch, Mrs. Darling didn't know Trey, either. Melody Evans, the consignment store's owner, saw the invitation for what it was—entrée into a new market of potential investors and franchisees. She'd pressed three of the most gorgeous cocktail dresses from the Cedar Springs store into Renee's hands and shooed her toward a dressing room.

"This can be our big break," Melody had said, barely containing her enthusiasm.

The only good thing about the night, Renee thought, was that finding something to wear had been easy—and she wasn't going to be looking like a streetwalker. She giggled.

She tucked a stack of business cards from Return Engagements into her clutch bag and thought about the night ahead. This was a business meeting, nothing more.

If she kept telling herself that, maybe she might eventually believe it.

While Trey wondered if the new job at KMI Keaton had offered would mean spur-of-the-moment trips that would require a long-term and flexible babysitter for Kelly, he also thought about the best way to apologize to Renee.

He'd been married long enough to know when an apology was in order, and this was definitely one of those occasions. When he checked his phone after he and Keaton arrived back at the KMI offices, he saw the partially written and unsent text message that he'd started to Renee before his earlier meeting. There were also two voice mails from her. One asked if he would call her and the second, about twenty minutes after the first, was a message saying a business meeting had unexpectedly come up and that she would need a rain check for their lunch date. She had managed to at least communicate via a message while he hadn't. In his defense, there was a lot going on at the office that morning, he thought. But deep down he knew that was hardly an excuse.

Trey considered the options: flowers, candy, a little teddy bear. He knew virtually nothing about Renee and had no idea how she would respond to any of those gestures. When he'd been in the doghouse with Andrea, calla lilies and white-chocolate truffles from Godiva had gone a long way toward repairing whatever boneheaded thing he'd done or said. This thing with Renee—whatever it was or might become—was too new to know how any of that could or would be received.

But he would find out tonight.

When her front doorbell rang, Renee paused to consider the sound. She recognized it as the doorbell, but couldn't think of a single person who would be visiting. Both Jeremy and Peter used the kitchen door, just as she and Keisha did. Tightening the top on the tube of mascara, she dropped it in the makeup bag open on her sink and headed downstairs.

Her shoes, handbag and coat were already waiting for her to slip on and pick up.

In her stocking-covered feet, she went to the front door and opened it to find Trey Calloway standing outside.

He wore a black overcoat and held a pair of leather gloves in one hand. Behind him, a light snow was starting to fall, just a few flakes, the forecasters had predicted. The effect of the handsome man in the early evening with the snow flurries behind him took her breath away.

"Oh!"

"Good evening, Renee."

She stood frozen for a moment, not sure what to do, then regained her senses. "Come in," she said, backing away and inviting him with a wave of her hand. "I'm ready. I just thought…" Her voice trailed off as she glanced back toward the kitchen and the back door she'd expected him to knock on. "Never mind. Let me just put on my shoes."

"You look great," he said.

"Uh, thank you."

Renee didn't know what had come over her. One look at Trey and the power of speech fled while her libido kicked into overdrive. *Tall, dark and drop-dead gorgeous* summed him up. The description might be a cliché, but he fit every category.

She'd seen him on Sunday mornings and knew that under that coat would be a suit of impeccable tailoring and style. And all she really wanted to do was see him out of it. Right now.

When she turned to reach for her clutch, his hand reached for hers.

"Renee, I want to apologize about this afternoon. Our lunch date. I started a text to tell you a meeting had come up with the CEO of the company, but I got distracted. I didn't even get your messages until after I saw you at the Magnolia Inn."

She gazed up to meet his eyes. He clearly had a free pass on standing her up, yet took the high road and owned up to it.

Another of the defenses she'd erected around her heart came crashing down, and she didn't know how to respond—to either him or the heat that suddenly pooled in her mid-section.

"It—it's all right," she said. "Let me, uh, let me get my shoes."

She fled to the sofa and sat on the edge to tie the ankle-strap heels on her feet. When she stood and reached for her coat, Trey was already holding it out for her.

"So, it looks like we're having that lunch date for dinner," Trey said as she settled into his truck.

"Imagine my surprise at hearing your name at the Magnolia Inn," she said.

"Not half as surprised as I was to see you walking in looking like you'd just walked off the runway at Paris Fashion Week."

She smiled. "Thank you. I still cannot believe you thought I was a call girl."

"I'm sorry," Trey said. His pained expression told her he meant it.

Renee studied him. He could have added an excuse to the apology, an explanation designed to flatter or further take the sting out of the insult by turning it into flirting—or foreplay. But Trey Calloway apparently wasn't that type of man. He was nothing at all like the guys she used to date. For starters, he was employed.

It then dawned on Renee that she didn't know exactly what Trey did in that home office of his. They couldn't head to Raleigh in silence, so she broached the subject.

"So, what type of work keeps you sequestered in the house most of the day?"

"Consulting," he said. "I work for a firm that tells other companies how to successfully run their businesses. And I have a side gig."

Renee grinned. "A gigolo?"

She expected him to laugh at the jab. He instead reached for her hand and clasped it in his. Warmth suffused her.

She would have fanned herself had she had possession of her faculties. His touch seemed to short-circuit her brain…and her body.

"I really am sorry," he said as his thumb drew an abstract pattern on the back of her left hand. She found herself mesmerized by the caress. Whether he was conscious of the effect it was having on her, she had no idea.

His hands were neither soft nor calloused. They were the competent and strong hands of a man who was comfortable with himself. Idly, she wondered what her own hand told him about her—other than she was overdue for a fill-in on gel nails.

When his gaze dipped to her mouth for a moment, Renee knew he was thinking the same wanton thoughts that dominated her own mind.

"Renee…" His voice held the sexy timbre of tangled sheets and sweat-sleeked bodies.

"Eyes on the road, buddy."

He chuckled, but complied, putting both hands back on the steering wheel. "You're something of a distraction."

"Flattery might get you…everywhere," she said. "But not while you're driving. So what's your real side gig?" she asked.

"Image and brand consulting," he said.

Now things made sense to Renee. He wasn't just a brother who looked good. He specifically worked at it. She winced inwardly at her Sunday-morning outfit for the Return Engagements sales meeting. She really couldn't blame him. After all, he'd been Mr. Buttoned-Down with a young daughter who also always looked as if she were headed to a photo shoot for an upscale kids' clothing catalog.

She and Keisha probably came off as completely and utterly tasteless. Renee suddenly found herself uncomfortably and acutely aware of how Keisha must have been feeling lately—like the proverbial square peg in a round hole.

"What are you thinking about?" Trey said.

Renee forced her thoughts back to the man sitting next to her in the big SUV that, at the moment, seemed to have shrunk to a compact car. "What makes you think something's on my mind?" she asked rather than answering his too-perceptive question.

"You were looking a thousand miles away in some vacation spot."

She smiled at that image.

"Nothing quite that deep," she assured him. "To be honest, I was thinking about Keisha for a moment, and then wondering and picturing what it might be like to have your type of job, you know, shaping people into new images of themselves."

He gave her a curious look. "You do that already."

When she lifted an arched brow, he expanded on his thought. "You work in retail, selling clothing and accessories, too, I presume, mostly to women who would like a new look or at least a refreshed one."

Renee mulled over what Trey had said for a moment and then nodded. "All right," she conceded. "I can see that. But the scale isn't the same."

Trey shrugged. "That's a falsity that's foisted on people, among others, by marketing brand agents."

Her face must have registered her confusion, because he immediately continued. "Think about the millions of dollars that companies pour into marketing campaigns, for, oh, let's just say women's makeup or bottled water."

"Bottled water is a rip-off," Renee interjected.

"Yet there are millions of people who buy into the pitch that a bottle with a label on it and a refreshing name or photo is going to be nutritionally better and more refreshing than a glass of tap water."

"All taps are not created equally," she laughed.

"True," he said. "But in the case of bottled water, consumers buy into the pitch that the clear liquid coming out of that nonbiodegradable plastic bottle from the ooh-la-la spring is better or cooler than that glass of filtered tap water."

Renee had an eight-year-old, so she was used to conversations that went careening off, turning into odd tangents. "So what does that have to do with me selling used clothes and your consulting work?"

"It's all the same."

"That's not possible," Renee said.

"Yes, it is. With the makeover, be it a corporate one like one of my clients or a fashion makeover like the ones you're responsible for, there is change. Typically for the client's better."

Renee nodded, understanding the analogy. But she silently regarded him.

"What?" Trey asked.

"You're a most unusual man, Trey Calloway," she said without thinking. "A moment ago, I thought you were ready to jump my bones. Now you're giving me a lesson on, what, economics and marketing?"

He smiled and his eyes took on a hooded bedroom quality again. Just that fast, her sexy next-door neighbor was back. "I'm used to juggling several things at once, like the fact that I want you, but we're just getting to know each other."

The reception was an opportunity to mix and mingle with the movers and shakers. Despite the distraction of Trey, who was constantly introduced as alternately her partner or her husband, she worked the room as a capable and engaging representative for Return Engagements. She collected more business cards than she had to give out and counted the evening as a success.

Since her mind was on Trey's parting words as they approached the museum, it was a wonder she could focus on Return Engagements at all throughout the evening.

She couldn't deny there was an attraction sizzling between them. But was it the long-term type or the flash-and-burn type? And more important, did she even care about the difference?

Chapter 6

The next day, Trey wondered what Renee thought of his blatant honesty during their drive to Raleigh. He knew he'd surprised her by openly stating what sizzled between them. They were both consenting adults, so what was stopping either of them?

"Daddy?"

He quickly pulled his thoughts away from Renee and to his daughter, who was sitting on a counter stool, watching him put together the salad for their dinner.

"Yes, princess?"

"If you know someone has done a bad thing, but you don't do anything about it, does that make you bad, too?"

Trey took a break from chopping chicken for the toss-it-all-in salad. This was one of those not-so-hypothetical questions that both his mother and Aunt Henrietta had warned him about. But the women had also assured him that he wouldn't have to worry about that sort of thing until Kelly was in her teens.

"What do you mean?" he asked, buying time to both get his thoughts together and brace himself for whatever bombshell she was about to drop on him.

"Well," Kelly said, tugging on one of her pigtails and looking down at the granite countertop. "If I had this friend who took something that, you know, didn't really belong to her—"

"That's stealing, Kelly," he said, cutting his daughter off. "You know that. And you know stealing is wrong."

"But Keisha said—" She slapped her hand over her mouth and darted guilty eyes up at him. "I mean, this friend didn't really…"

"Kelly, what happened between you and Keisha?"

"Nothing!"

"Kelly Elaine Calloway."

Her bottom lip trembled. "I—I'm not that hungry, Daddy," she said, slipping from the stool and turning to run.

But Trey was faster than the six-year-old. He was around the counter in a mere moment and caught her up in his arms.

"Daddy!"

Ignoring the whine, he walked to the sofa in the family room and plopped down on it, the girl secure in his arms.

She squirmed, but he held fast. "Kelly, remember when we talked about always telling the truth?"

She nodded and bit her bottom lip. He recognized the obstinate gesture, having witnessed it on Andrea when she'd been digging her heels in on a topic. With each passing year, Kelly seemed to resemble her mother even more. The fact that she would grow up without a mother's love tugged at his heart.

"If you remember," he said with gentle nudging, "why don't you tell me what's going on."

"'Cause I'll get in trouble."

Well, that made sense. He wasn't a harsh disciplinarian, but Kelly was still familiar with punishment. The two most severe, which ranked even harsher than no *Dora the Explorer* on television, probably hurt him more than it did her: no dance class or no dolls. Eliminating the dance session meant Kelly didn't go and he had to find either a sitter or an alternative for that time. And a no-dolls punishment meant he had to spend the better part of an hour gathering up the dolls in her bedroom and then locking them in the playroom. Kelly would spend practically the entire time on punishment crying.

Since whatever was going on now involved Keisha, Trey doubted that this infraction would warrant a severe punishment. She was clearly trying to protect her friend.

"And you think the trouble you'll get in is more important than telling me what's wrong?"

Kelly remained silent. He watched as his daughter seemed to consider both the pros and the cons of the situation. He wondered what secret a six-year-old could have that was so weighty.

"Has Keisha done something that puts her in danger of hurting herself or someone else?"

Kelly shook her head.

"Have you?"

Again, she shook her head.

Trey sighed. Well, that was one less thing he had to stress about. His daughter knew that lying was wrong, so even though she was being closemouthed on whatever was going on with her and Keisha, he could trust that Kelly was being truthful on at least those two points.

"All right, Kel," he said. "You think about this tonight, and tomorrow you're going to tell me what's up. Got it?"

She nodded.

He placed a kiss on the top of her head and then scooted her onto the sofa as he got up. "Dinner will be ready in ten minutes and I want you at the table."

"Yes, sir," she said glumly.

As he made his way back to the kitchen to finish the chopped salad and the rest of their meal, Trey thought of his wife again. Andrea would have been so much better at parenting than he was. He also wondered what type of punishment for bad behavior got handed out next door. From what he'd witnessed of her tantrums, if Keisha were his child, she'd always be on punishment.

Kelly Calloway got a reprieve from the tough conversation Trey had planned because of a knock on the side door as they were about to eat breakfast.

Trey glanced at the clock on the wall before muttering, "Who in the world could that be?"

When he opened the door, he was stunned to see Renee and a bedraggled Keisha standing there. The girl's coat was half-zipped up and her hair was a tangled mess of half braids. The girl's mouth was poked out in a gesture that was becoming all too familiar with Trey.

"Trey, I'm so sorry to bother you this morning," Renee said. "We're having an issue here."

Keisha folded her arms and stomped her foot, but didn't say anything.

"I'm late and Keisha has missed her bus," Renee said. "Could you drop her off at school?"

Trey glanced back at Kelly, who had taken a sudden interest in the piece of French toast she'd been pushing around on her plate for the past ten minutes.

"Uh, sure. We'll be leaving in about fifteen minutes." He looked at Keisha, who now peered into the kitchen. "Would you like some French toast?"

"I don't like French toast."

"Keisha!" Renee sighed and then cast pleading eyes up at Trey. "I'm sorry," she said, apologizing for her daughter. "It's been a difficult morning."

"Tell me about it," Trey said, opening the door wider so Keisha could scamper inside out of the cold air. She unzipped her jacket and put it on a chair.

"Thanks," Renee said. "Keisha, be polite," she then shouted into the kitchen.

She smiled up at him and then dashed to her car. Trey watched her start the engine and speed off. She'd been wearing a long leather coat fastened at the waist by a leather belt looped around. He found himself wondering, mightily, what was underneath.

"Daddy, you're letting all the heat out."

He glanced back at the girls and then shut the door.

Kelly was at the counter, still playing with the last of the French-toast pieces on her plate. Keisha sat on the stool next to her, pouting.

He went into the pantry, pulled out a box of Cheerios, got a bowl from the cupboard and a spoon from the drawer. He put the cereal, bowl and utensil in front of Keisha and then got the quart of whole milk out of the refrigerator.

"Eat," he said.

The command was meant for Keisha and she reached for the box without a rebuttal, but Kelly picked up her fork and speared a piece of French toast, as well.

When he was satisfied that both girls were actually going to consume something for breakfast, he nodded. "We are leaving in exactly ten minutes," he said, pointing to the clock. "I want you both bundled up and ready to go."

He left the kitchen, knowing they would presume he was headed upstairs and out of earshot. He went as far as the dining room and stood out of sight on the side of the large china cabinet.

"What happened to your hair?"

"I don't like braids anymore," he heard Keisha say.

"Are you going to school looking like that?"

Trey had to smile. He'd been wondering the same thing but wasn't about to ask the girl.

"I can wear my hat," came her reply.

There was silence from the kitchen then. Trey chanced

a glance around the china cabinet. Both girls were actually eating. Shaking his head, he quit the subterfuge and headed upstairs to get his portfolio. Today was a day he'd be working from the office at Commerce Plaza.

When both girls were buckled in the backseat of the Navigator, he looked at them in the rearview mirror. Both girls had taken an unnatural interest in the views outside their respective windows.

"So," he said. "Which one of you is going to tell me what's going on?"

"She started it!" Keisha said.

"I did not!" Kelly shouted.

They'd turned in their seats now and faced each other, both young faces earnest and intent.

"Keisha?" he asked.

"Why does she get to go first?" Kelly whined.

He wanted to fire back, "Because you had your chance to tell me and refused to do so." Instead, he calmly answered, "Because she's the oldest." Kelly huffed at that and flounced back, folding her arms across her chest, not at all hindered by the bulky winter coat.

"I told her she shouldn't do it," Keisha said.

"Shouldn't do what?" Trey asked as he backed out of the driveway.

Silence came from the backseat.

"Ladies."

It took a moment, but an answer came. But not from the girl he'd expected to respond.

"I wanted to trade my Polly Play doll for Erica's Dora watch."

Trey's gut tightened. That Polly Play doll cost almost as much as one of the American Girl dolls. Those plastic *Dora the Explorer* watches came free in fast-food kids meals.

Kelly had been right that she'd get in trouble. But what surprised him the most was that the voice of reason—and

not the culprit in the situation as he'd so readily assumed—
had been Keisha. He'd been quick to assume that it was
Keisha who had done something wrong. But something
nagged at him. Last night, Kelly had referred to someone
taking something that didn't belong to them.

"Where's the Polly doll?" he asked.

Silence came from the backseat.

"Tell him," Keisha prompted after a few moments passed.

"It's under my bed," Kelly confessed.

He glanced in the rearview mirror. Kelly looked pitiful. Keisha didn't look too happy, either.

"And where is Erica's watch?"

He had to keep his eyes on the road, but he didn't miss
the exchange between the girls.

A moment later, a small hand rose up. He held his right
hand back to take whatever was being proffered.

"I had it in my backpack," Kelly said. "I was going to
give it back to Erica today."

Had Kelly actually stolen the watch? He couldn't believe it and didn't want to, either.

"I didn't steal it, Daddy," the girl said, as if anticipating his question.

"Erica gave it to her on collar tail," Keisha explained.
"But I told her not to. That doll cost a lot of money. Way
more than that cheap watch."

"'Collar tail'?"

Trey stopped at a red light and tried to figure out what
the phrase meant.

"I told Erica that collar tail was a good way to do the
trade."

"What is…?" Trey started, and then the lightbulb went
off. "*Collateral?* Is that what you mean?"

"Yeah," Keisha said. "Collateral for the night."

He bit back a grin. This streetwise little girl had saved
his kid's behind.

"Kelly?"

The girl met his gaze in the mirror. "What did you give Erica as collateral on the deal?"

Kelly's lip quivered and he knew tears would be showing up any moment.

"You're not in trouble, Kel. But I need to know what you gave your friend."

"My new hair bows."

The floodgates opened then. The hair bows had been a gift from Aunt Henrietta and Kelly loved them as much as she loved her doll collection. All this over a kids-meal watch destined to fall apart within a month.

"Don't cry, Kelly," Keisha told his daughter. "He said you're not in trouble."

"But I'm gonna get a punishment," Kelly said between sobs. "I just wanted a Dora watch."

Neither girl was in any condition to go to school. One looked as if she'd just run away from her hairdresser, and the other one was boo-hooing as though she'd just lost her best friend.

Trey glanced at the clock on the dash. Keisha was apparently already late for school, and Kelly would be late in about five minutes. He figured another ten or fifteen minutes wasn't going to academically challenge either one of them. And he was good on time to get to the office.

He pulled the Navigator into the lot at the primary school, cut the engine, then unsnapped his seat belt and turned to the girls.

Before he could say anything, a chirping sounded in the car. Trey looked confused. He reached for his phone, not understanding why it would be sounding suspiciously like a bird.

"Excuse me," Keisha said, bending toward her backpack. A moment later, the girl retrieved a mobile phone.

The backseat crying had ceased and both Trey and Kelly

looked at Keisha, mouths agape in wonder at an eight-year-old with a cell phone.

"Hi, Mom," Keisha said into the phone. She was silent for a moment, then said, "Yes, we just got to school."

Kelly's wide eyes met her father's.

"No," he said, anticipating the question. No child of his was getting a cell phone before a driver's license.

"Yes," Keisha said and then disengaged the call. "Mom said to tell you thank-you."

For a moment, Trey was too stunned to speak. More than once, he'd been accused of being an overindulgent parent. But a mobile phone for an elementary-school student took the cake.

He and Renee definitely had different parenting styles. But that was neither here nor there at the moment.

Contemplating whether he should let this watch trade go as an object lesson or intervene with the other girl's parents, he decided that the teachable moment was the better route. And the one that Kelly would remember in the future. It might even prove more beneficial and lasting to her than the punishment she expected.

"Okay, here's the deal, Kel. When you see Erica today, you're going to tell her that you've changed your mind about the deal and that if it's all right with her, you'll give back her watch and get your hair bows."

"What if she doesn't want to?"

"Then you'll be out of those bows, but at least you'll still have your doll. And when Aunt Henrietta asks about them, you'll need to tell her the truth."

Kelly, already looking dejected, seemed to deflate even more. It tore at Trey's heart to see her so miserable, but he knew he was doing the right thing. "Do you understand?" he asked.

She bit her lip and nodded.

If it came down to it, telling her cherished aunt that she

had given away a gift would stay with Kelly for a long time—and hopefully put the kibosh on future trades, Trey thought. She'd then have a sense of what was valuable and what meant the most to her.

"All right, then," he said and glanced at Keisha, who had remained quiet during the exchange. "Kelly, hand me your fix-it bag, please."

A moment later, a small zippered tote was passed over the seat and to him. "There's nothing wrong with my hair," she said, a tremor in her voice telling him fresh tears could be forthcoming at any moment.

"I know," Trey said, unzipping the bag and pulling out a brush and a few scrunchies. "Keisha, hop up front, please."

In the rearview mirror he saw the two girls look at each other. Then Keisha unbuckled her seat belt.

Trey had no idea what had been going on at the Armstrong house that morning, but he wasn't going to let this child spend all day in school looking as if she'd run her hair through a briar patch. While he wasn't sure what he could do, he figured he could tame it at least a little bit.

Keisha hopped into the front seat and looked at him.

"Creating a new style?" he asked, keeping his voice neutral on whether he liked it or not.

"I was taking my braids out."

"Hmm," Trey said. "I don't think you finished. You want me to give you some ponytails?"

Keisha looked back at Kelly, who nodded.

"Okay," she said, turning so her back faced him. "But I kind of made a mess."

That was an understatement, but Trey kept the thought to himself as he studied the girl's hair for a moment.

"How about a twist?" Kelly offered from the backseat.

Trey nodded. "I was just thinking that instead of ponytails."

A few brush strokes later, he'd fashioned two twists,

one with the still-braided hair and the other with the rest. "Hold this," he directed Keisha while he put the scrunchies back in the bag and scrounged for some bobby pins. He tucked them in his mouth and replaced her hand with his. With some judicious pins, he created a passable hairstyle for her that wouldn't have the teachers wondering if the girl was being neglected at home.

"Okay, you're good to go," he told her.

Keisha patted her hair, getting a feel for what he'd done, then pulled down the passenger-seat visor and surveyed his work in the small mirror there.

She turned toward him and gave him a bright grin. "I like it."

Trey smiled. He tucked the brush back in the bag. "All right, ladies. Grab your backpacks. I'll check you in at the school office."

He engaged the door locks, and with a girl on either side of him, they walked toward the school's entrance. Kelly's small hand was in his left one. He felt something brush his right hand and a moment later, Keisha's hand was in his, as well.

The gesture surprised him, but it also made his heart swell in an unexpected way.

Chapter 7

"Cocoa, coffee or wine?"

The girls were doing homework in the dining room with spelling and storybooks scattered across the table while Trey and Renee talked in the kitchen. The text invitation later that night from Trey were just the words Renee had needed to hear to calm her frazzled nerves.

"The day I've had calls for hard liquor, but the cocoa sounds lovely," Renee said.

"One double shot of hot cocoa coming up," he said.

"Thank you for what you did, taking Keisha to school and taming her hair. I was at my wit's end this morning. She decided to take her braids out before consulting me. But I did make an appointment at your aunt's shop."

"No problem," he said. "I told you I had some skills."

Trey made fast work of getting the cocoa together, then, with the mugs in hand, motioned for her to follow him into the family room. As she settled on the sofa, one leg tucked under the other and the warm mug cupped in her hands, he put another log on the fire. Closing the gate, he picked up his mug, took a sip, then set it on the coffee table.

"There's something I wanted to ask you about."

Renee sighed. She knew what was coming. It was one of the reasons she hadn't pursued a relationship since Keisha had come into her life. "You want to know what's wrong with Keisha."

Trey lifted a brow. "Wrong with her?"

"Keisha has had a hard life," Renee said. "She's just eight, but she's seen and experienced things that most adults haven't."

She could tell she had his undivided attention. She blew out a sigh. She'd come this far; she may as well tell him the whole story.

"Keisha is my foster daughter. She came to me two years ago after being rescued from a drug house. Her birth mother was about to turn Keisha out to do tricks to pay for her drugs. Thank God a neighbor intervened and called police when she heard a ruckus next door. Keisha had locked herself in her bedroom and a man her mother promised her to was trying to bust down the door to get in."

"Oh, my God," Trey said. He placed a comforting hand on Renee's knee.

She needed his contact right now and placed her hand on top of his. "Child Protective Services got her out of there, and she came to me a day later."

"What happened to her mother?"

Renee closed her eyes for a moment and then glanced toward the dining room to make sure the girls weren't nearby. She blew out another breath and then looked at Trey. "She gave up all parental rights, was charged and convicted of child abuse, neglect, contributing to the delinquency of a minor, and a whole slew of drug and prostitution charges. She got sentenced to a long time behind bars."

Trey turned to face her and took the mug out of her hand. Putting it aside, he gathered both her hands in his. "I hear a 'but,' Renee."

She nodded. "I got a call this morning. She died of an overdose in jail."

"When?"

"Yesterday. I'm in the process of adopting Keisha, but I don't know how to tell her. I don't know how she'll react. I don't know if she'll even care or if she'll lash out or…" She shook her head, willing away the tears that seemed just below the surface.

Before Trey could say anything, Renee rushed on. "I know you've seen her acting out. The foot stomping and pouting and carrying-on. And then this morning with the hair. I just found out why she wants the braids out. That I could handle. Frankly, I thought we'd gotten beyond all or at least most of the issues she had. I've given her two years of love and stability and she sees a therapist twice a week. And apparently, it's not enough. I'm not enough."

The tears fell then.

Trey instinctively gathered her in his arms. Tucking her head on his shoulder and letting her cry the tears he suspected she'd kept bottled up for a long time.

Things made sense now. And he'd so badly judged both Renee's parenting skills and Keisha. What he'd thought were lax child-rearing duties were the exact opposite.

He thought of the small hand that had clasped his this morning at the school. From what Renee said, Keisha didn't trust many people. Yet, she'd trusted him. She'd opened up in her own way—by placing her hand in his—and gave him a gift he didn't think he deserved.

"I'm sorry," Renee sniffled into his shirt.

He kissed the top of her head. "You have nothing to apologize for," he said.

Renee wiped her eyes and pushed away a bit. He didn't let her go far. She felt too good in his arms.

"I moved here, to Cedar Springs, to get her to a stable

environment. A place where we could have a house and a yard and she could go to good schools and make new friends. But all I've done is uproot her. She's been miserable at school." Renee shrugged. "At least I got to the bottom of that issue. It's like all the forward progress we've made has been turned upside down by coming here."

"What's wrong at school?"

She told him about the hair issues Keisha had been experiencing at school, what she'd identified as an inferiority complex.

"I wonder if maybe adopting her as a single parent isn't such a good idea. She needs so much, and I worry that I'm not enough for her."

Although she was no longer crying, Trey continued to hold her as they talked. He loved the feel of her and wondered if she liked the comfort of his embrace. She hadn't pulled away, even when his hands played along her arm in a languid caress.

The fire in the hearth and the beautiful woman in his arms intensified the feeling of intimacy. Trey realized that he liked it a lot, and he could get used to ending each day just like this—with Renee at his side, with their girls quietly playing. A moment later, he realized he was straying down a path that was not just premature, but highly unlikely. Kelly threw the occasional tantrum and had a doll habit that he should have nipped in the bud a while ago, but overall, she was a great kid who gave him no trouble. Renee had willingly taken in someone else's child, a girl who was likely to have issues for the rest of her life. Taking on that sort of long-term responsibility took a strong person, a strong woman.

"You're being too tough on yourself, Renee," he said. "What you did was good. You made deliberate choices to make life better for Keisha. Besides, it's barely been a month since you moved here. Making friends will take time. And she's already made one good friend," he added.

Renee smiled. "She and Kelly did seem to hit it off."

He then told her about the doll, the watch and the collateral.

"Oh, Lord," Renee said. "What did Keisha do?"

"Nothing," Trey said. "She was the voice of reason in the whole thing. The big sister, so to speak. If it hadn't been for what Keisha advised, Kelly would have permanently lost her doll. Everybody traded back, though. End of drama."

"I'm glad something good came out of this miserable day."

They were quiet for a moment. Then Trey asked the question that had been on his mind. "Why did you take her in? I mean, why be a foster parent? That's taking on a lot of—" he'd been about to say "trouble," but quickly substituted it with "—a lot of unknown. You don't know anything about the kids who come from the foster system."

She twisted out of his embrace and then faced him again. Trey bit back a sigh at losing the softness of her snuggled against him.

"I know what I need to know, Trey," she told him, her face animated and flushed with conviction. "There are a lot of kids in the foster system. And even more who are waiting to be adopted. Many of them age out of the system before they ever find a family. Everybody wants babies, infants, children they can raise from the ground up, so to speak."

She leaned forward, her gaze locked with his as if willing him to understand. "They all need love and attention and someone to care, unconditionally. Before Keisha, I'd done emergency fostering, taking in kids who needed a stable place for a few weeks. The longest I'd ever had a child was three months. But Keisha's situation was different. Her mother had essentially thrown her away. She was so broken, so in need of care and love. She was a little girl that the world had lost hope on. Something in me responded to that in a way that was…" She shrugged. "The best way I can describe it is 'soul-deep.' She was the child I could have been if not for a loving grandmother who didn't give up on me."

He was quiet for a moment, gazing at her with the same intensity that she'd afforded him. And then he did what he'd wanted to do from the moment she'd walked into the house.

He closed the short distance between them and kissed her.

"Ewww!"

The twin voices of two little girls quickly forced them apart.

"Don't look, Kel," Keisha said. "They're kissing."

"Daddy has a girlfriend!"

Trey groaned. He was in the family room at Aunt Henrietta and Uncle Carlton's, chilling with his cousins, when he heard Kelly's announcement. Sunday dinner was a tradition with his family. Once a month, the Calloways got together to break bread. Trey had hoped to keep his relationship with Renee under wraps for a bit…at least until he figured out where it was going.

"Does he, now?" Aunt Henrietta said, the question deliberately loud enough to carry from the kitchen. "Funny, he didn't mention anything like that to me."

"What's her name, baby?" Aunt Tiny cooed.

"Oh, man, you're in for it now," Sasha said as she nudged Trey, who then dropped the controller from the video game they were playing on the flat-screen.

"We don't need any headlines at eleven," Trey said drily as he bent to retrieve it.

"Game over. You lost," a computerized voice said.

"Ha!" Sasha lifted her hands in victory. "I beat you!"

"I was distracted," Trey said, glancing toward the kitchen. "I need to go do some damage control." He tossed the controller to Eric, who was bent over his mobile phone, furiously texting. "And you better not be posting on Facebook."

"The world doesn't revolve around you and your love life, coz," Eric said without glancing up.

"Tell me about your girl," Sasha said.

"No, Miss Action News. No scoops for you. And hopefully, none for Aunt Henrietta and Aunt Tiny."

That hope was gone, though, when he walked into the kitchen.

"They were kissing," Kelly reported. "Keisha and I saw them."

His aunts both gave him The Look. The look that had quelled the Calloway cousins when they were Kelly's age and still had the power to make the now-grown cousins quake.

"And who is Keisha?"

"She's my sister," Kelly informed them.

"Uh, Kel…" Trey said.

Aunt Tiny swatted him with a dish towel. "Let the child speak."

"She doesn't have a dad and I don't have a mom, so we decided we're going to be sisters."

Two sets of inquiring brown eyes turned up to him.

Trey sighed.

The phone rang. "Saved by the bell," he muttered.

"Not really," Aunt Henrietta said. "Sasha or Eric, get that please."

"Who is this woman?" Aunt Tiny asked. "Do we know her people? Where did you meet her? Why is she single? Are you going to marry her?"

"Good Lord, Tiny," Henrietta said. "Give the man a chance to answer at least one question before you knock him over with a hundred more."

"I see where Sasha got those newshound traits," he said on a dry note.

"Don't you sass me, Trey Calloway."

He leaned forward and kissed her on the cheek. "You know I wouldn't do that, Auntie. Kel, why don't you go ask Eric to show you how to play 'Candy Crush' on his phone?"

"Okay, Daddy."

A moment later, she skipped out of the kitchen and Trey was left with two of his aunts, one who'd been more like a mother to him than his own and the other a woman whose hair salon carried more gossip than *TMZ*.

"You'll meet her soon enough, Aunt Tiny," he said. "She's going to be making an appointment at Styles pretty soon, if not already."

Aunt Henrietta opened the oven and checked on the roast. "Dinner will be ready in about fifteen minutes. And you have had plenty of time to stall," she told Trey. "Spill it."

He did, giving them an abbreviated, sanitized and nosy-aunt version of the Renee and Keisha story. It was enough to satisfy Aunt Tiny, who nodded.

"I have some friends up in Durham who can check on…"

Aunt Henrietta eyed him, then said slowly, "I don't think that'll be necessary, Tiny."

"Weelllll," Tiny said, pulling the word out, "I guess he can see to his own affairs. He is a grown man."

"I'm glad you remembered that," he muttered.

"What was that?"

"Nothing, Auntie."

She swatted him with the towel again as she headed

to the refrigerator. "That's what I thought." But her smile said she was cool with him. Tiny pulled out a bowl of potato salad and headed to the dining room.

When it was just the two of them in the kitchen, Aunt Henrietta leaned against the counter and regarded her nephew.

He tried not to squirm under the scrutiny. Yes, he was a grown man with a child and a professional career. But Aunt Henrietta always made him want to do better, be a better nephew, man and father. He knew he wasn't alone in thinking that way. She and Uncle Carlton set the bar high for all of the Calloways.

"Is this serious?"

She voiced the very question that had been on his mind since he'd started thinking of the four of them as more than just next-door neighbors.

"I think so."

She smiled and nodded, then came over and tapped his chest. "When you know so, you'll know what to do."

Dinner was the usual raucous Sunday affair for the Calloways. Thankfully for Trey, the subject of Renee and Keisha didn't come up again. He was glad for it, too, since Aunt Henrietta's closing words on the topic still lingered with him.

"I have an announcement to make," Sasha said, standing up.

He was glad for her distraction. He could focus on something else for a few minutes.

"What is it?" Uncle Carlton asked as he reached for another roll.

Henrietta took it from him, and he sighed. "You're the one who had the heart attack, Henry, and I'm the one who has to suffer."

"That was more than a year ago," she said. "And you need to save room for dessert."

"You all know I've been with WRAL-TV for almost two years now, working mostly out of Fayetteville. I am pleased to announce that you're looking at the new weekend anchor with Independent Action News. I'll be moving up to Virginia Beach in about a month."

"Where is Virginia Beach?" Kelly wanted to know.

When Trey explained, Kelly frowned. "That's a long way from here," the six-year-old said.

"Not so far that I can't come see you, sweetie."

"Okay."

"This calls for a celebration," Aunt Henrietta said after Sasha explained some more about her new job. "And I have just the treat."

She returned with a large red velvet cake, and conversation soon flowed again around the table.

"Don't forget about the Angel Tree program," Henrietta told her family. "The gifts are due back at the church office on Tuesday."

Trey closed his eyes and tried not to groan. He'd completely forgotten about the name tags they'd all pulled off a tree at the Chapel of the Groves. Between them, the Calloways had claimed a full dozen of the little placards. Henrietta and Carlton, who espoused "to whom much is given, much is required," claimed half of them. Each tag identified a child in need along with a few of the child's Christmas wish-list items. Participants were supposed to buy new clothes and toys for the angel they'd selected from the tree. Trey wasn't even sure what he'd done with the tag he and Kelly picked weeks ago.

With all of the things going on at work, he was going to have to fit in an unscheduled shopping trip.

"Remember, don't wrap them," Aunt Henrietta said.

"That's something that will be nice for the parents to be able to do."

"I got the cutest little outfits for my girl, including a red leather coat and matching boots," Sasha said. "And I found a great deal on a set of storybooks, all the classics, illustrated and with a sound track. She wanted in-line skates, so I got those as well as knee pads, a helmet and backpack."

"Overachiever," Eric said.

She grinned. "It's called 'organized,' Mr. Last Minute."

"Can't I just give my kid a gift card to Walmart?" Eric asked. "I'm sure he'd prefer to go get what he wants."

"Eric…"

He held up a hand. "Just joking, Aunt Henrietta. Just joking. I'll make the deadline."

The phone rang again as Uncle Carlton was helping himself to another thick slice of red velvet cake.

"I'll get it," Sasha said, excusing herself. A few moments later, she hollered over, "It's Baden and Jesse!"

"Ooh!" Kelly exclaimed. "I wanna talk to Baden. She sent me a doll from Hawaii!"

"What do you say?" Trey asked before she could scoot away.

Kelly paused. She then dabbed her mouth with her napkin, placed it to the left of her plate and asked, "May I be excused?"

Trey nodded.

She scrambled down and raced into the family room to join Sasha, who was already animatedly talking with her cousin on the line. Then there was a squeal.

"Oh, my God. Really? Baden, that's wonderful!"

Aunt Henrietta glanced first at her husband and then at Trey. "If I were to make a guess," she said, "based on that outburst, I think Sasha isn't the only one with some good news to share with the family. Sounds like another generation is on the way."

Trey eyed his aunt. If his cousin Baden was pregnant, that was good for her, he thought. But just what was Aunt Henrietta telling him with that look?

Chapter 8

"Daddy," Kelly said on the way home, "since Baden is having a baby, we should get one, too."

He glanced in the rearview mirror. God, was it time for *that* talk already? He'd hoped to have another ten, fifteen, heck, thirty years before he'd have to do that. But before he could formulate a suitable answer, Kelly yawned and said, "We have to go shopping for our angel. Can we do that tomorrow?"

Trey relaxed. Now, there was a question he could handle. "Right after school, we'll go find her some gifts."

"Oh, good," Kelly said. "I think she'd like an American Doll like Addy."

Trey had to laugh. If it got Kelly's mind off of the "Where do babies come from?" track, he'd gladly buy the whole line of dolls for their Angel Tree kid.

Later, as he tucked Kelly into bed for the night, she asked another question that he didn't have an answer for.

"Daddy?"

"Yes, princess?"

"When we go shopping tomorrow, can we get Christmas presents for Keisha and Renee, too?"

That was something he had given absolutely no thought to. His mind flashed back to the afternoon he'd seen Renee in the craft store and his wish that Santa would give her to him for a Christmas present. Now, oddly, he realized that he wanted more than just sex with Renee Armstrong.

Earlier Aunt Henrietta had asked him if he was serious about Renee. And he was in fact feeling things for her. But he wasn't sure if his feelings were forever and vows sort of things.

When you know so, you'll know what to do.

"Well, Daddy, can we?"

"Sure, Kel. We'll get presents for them, too."

"Good," she said. "And I'm gonna ask Santa to bring me a baby sister for Christmas."

He kissed her on the forehead and deliberately dodged her comment. "Good night, Kelly."

There had been so much emotional turmoil in the past few weeks that Renee didn't quite know what to do about the news regarding Keisha's birth mother. She'd spent her lunch break on Monday talking to Dr. Hendrickson. She had reservations about telling Keisha because it was so close to Christmas and there had already been so many changes in their lives.

The child psychologist assured her that children were more resilient than they appeared. But agreed that under the circumstances and given Keisha's recent setbacks, now wasn't the right time.

Keisha never talked about her mother unless prompted by Renee or Dr. Hendrickson. And the two pictures of Janice Thompson that Keisha had were nowhere to be found. Renee knew because she'd looked. She wondered if Keisha had destroyed them, but asking would open a wound she didn't want to expose either of them to. At least not right now.

So she'd wait.

Unfortunately, the other topic on her mind was also complicated.

Trey Calloway.

She didn't believe it was possible to fall in love so fast, but she'd done just that. Fallen in love with a man who'd let it be known he was attracted to her. But she wasn't interested in either a casual hookup or a "neighbors with benefits" situation.

"If you keep frowning like that, you're going to need Botox before you're forty."

She scowled at Peter Shepherd. He'd picked her up after work to take her to the dealership to get her car and they'd stopped to have coffee before he headed home. "I have things on my mind, thank you very much."

"Might those things start with a Trey and end with a Calloway?"

Renee sighed, but she didn't take the bait. "Pete, why aren't you married?"

"Because you broke my heart when we were in college. You wouldn't go out with me and you ruined me for all women."

Renee rolled her eyes.

"It's true," he said, placing a hand over his heart.

"I'm serious, Pete."

"I've never found the woman who could love a guy who plays with toys for a living."

"Peter…"

He reached for her hand. "I'm serious about that, Renee. There's more to me than being a computer nerd. Computer nerds I meet are put off by the other parts of me, and other women either can't get over the fact that I play games all day, or they're only interested in the money those games have made me. I'm not settling. I want the real thing. She's out there somewhere. We just haven't connected yet."

"Yet," she said. "I didn't think 'yet' would ever come for me. Now look at me. I came here to manage a consignment store. Now I'm hobnobbing with the rich and powerful, and in a 'something' with my next-door neighbor."

"The word is *relationship*," he said. "Speaking of which, what are you getting him for Christmas?"

Renee scowled at him and then groaned.

Trey loved seeing Christmas through the eyes of his daughter. The wonder, awe and joy of the holiday season as experienced by a small child was a gift he cherished each year. Kelly was growing up so fast. He knew he wouldn't have many more Christmases with her like the ones of the past couple of years.

It had taken him the better part of an hour to find the Angel Tree tag only to discover it in a decorative bowl on the mantel. The Common Ground charity from church that organized the event had tags made up with the name, age, size and Christmas wishes of children in need. People who took an angel from the tree had to purchase at least one piece of clothing and a toy for their Angel Tree child.

Trey had gotten a pang of dread when he'd reviewed their child's wishes, but he let it go as too much of a coincidence.

After Kelly's choices made a sizable dent in his wallet, Trey shepherded her into a dollar store for wrapping paper, tape and package trimmings. Aunt Henrietta had suggested the items would be good to include for the parents of the Angel Tree kids to wrap presents.

The back of the Navigator was filled with bags. Since they didn't have to wrap anything, Trey suggested they go straight to the church to drop off their gifts.

"Ooh, look, Daddy!" Kelly exclaimed as they approached an intersection.

The attraction was a big candy-cane-striped tent with huge inflatables surrounding it.

"Santa's Village! Santa's Village! Can we go?"

He got an idea then.

"How about if we invite Keisha and Renee to join us?"

"Yes!"

Trey laughed. Christmas was coming and life was good.

Things started off well enough. With Keisha and Kelly bundled up and buckled in the backseat, he stole a kiss from Renee before closing her door and coming around the vehicle to slip behind the wheel.

"I see someone who's made a visit to the hair salon," he said. "Your do looks great, Keisha."

"Thanks," she mumbled.

"Who's ready to see Santa?" he asked.

"I am!" Kelly shouted.

Keisha didn't say a peep. He glanced at Renee, who just shook her head, as if in defeat.

"I know what'll help us all get a bit more in the Christmas spirit."

"What?" Kelly asked.

"Christmas music." He punched one of the buttons on the console and "Jingle Bell Rock" suddenly filled the car. From carols to cartoon sound tracks, he and Kelly sang joyously, tunelessly and with gusto.

"Do they know every Christmas song?" Keisha asked Renee as they all piled out of the truck in the parking lot of the seasonal attraction.

"It seems like it," Renee said. She paused and took Keisha's hand. "It was nice of them to ask us to join them for this. Can you at least act like you appreciate it?"

Keisha glared at Renee. "Like the way I'm supposed to appreciate you not telling me about my real mom?"

Renee jerked as if Keisha had slapped her.

Her worst fear had been realized. Keisha had not only found out some kind of way, but she cared. She cared about her *real* mother.

"H-how did you find out?"

Keisha's face fell and Renee knew she'd just made a mistake.

"So it's true?" the girl asked. "She's really dead?"

Renee glanced around. This was not how or where she'd wanted to break this news to Keisha.

"Everything all right?" Trey called from where he and Kelly waited.

"Uh, go ahead. We'll catch up."

Trey raised a brow, but Renee shook her head. Within a second he was at her side, handing her the keys to the Navigator.

"You can talk in the car if you'd like."

Renee blinked. "Thank you?"

"Is it true?" Keisha demanded.

"Daddy, what's wrong?"

Trey glanced from Kelly to Renee.

"We'll be okay," she assured him. "Why don't you and Kelly save us a place in line?"

He was clearly torn about leaving them. She could see it in his eyes. But this was something that she needed to do alone.

"All right," he said. "We'll be right over there waiting for you," he said, nodding in the direction of the mock village.

Renee opened the back door and motioned for Keisha to get in. The girl didn't move.

"She's really dead."

"Keisha, I'm sorry. I didn't know how to tell you."

She jerked her head toward Trey and Kelly. "Do they know?"

"Trey knows."

"And Dr. Hendrickson?"

Renee nodded.

"I thought something was up with him yesterday. He was looking at me all funny and asking how I was feeling even more than usual."

Renee didn't have a road map for dealing with this. She felt sure that any and every step she might take would propel her onto a land mine. "How *are* you feeling?"

Keisha stared at her blankly for a moment. "I feel like just because you all are the grown-ups, you think you know what's best for me. You think I'm a baby."

"That's not true, Keisha. It was my decision," Renee said, reaching out to touch her. But Keisha snatched her arm away.

Renee thought her heart was breaking. The last thing she ever wanted was to hurt this little girl. And in trying to protect Keisha, she'd still managed to do just that.

"I'm sorry, Keisha. I..." She took a breath. "I got a call from the agency. They'd received notice from the prison that your...that Janice had died."

"She OD'd?"

"Who told you this?" Renee asked.

Keisha kicked at the ground, then mumbled, "Shawnie called me and told me."

"Shawnie Alexander from the old building?"

Keisha nodded.

Getting away from the Shawnie Alexanders of the world was one of the reasons they were now living in Cedar Springs. The girl lived with her grandmother three doors down from where Renee and Keisha had lived. The young delinquent was with her grandmother because her mother was in prison and her father had kicked her out after she'd stolen from his girlfriend.

The pieces fell together then, but Renee needed to know the truth.

"Shawnie's mother was in the same prison as…Janice?"

Keisha nodded again. The girl's head was bowed and her hands jammed in her coat pockets. Renee couldn't tell if she was crying or if she was just being obstinate.

News of a prisoner overdosing while incarcerated would spread quickly in the jail system. And it wouldn't take much longer for the story and the details to reach the neighborhood.

"I'm sorry about your mother," Renee said.

She wanted to take Keisha in her arms and hug away the hurt, but the girl had already rebuffed her once.

"I'm not."

Renee wasn't sure she'd heard correctly. "You're not what?"

Keisha turned and faced her then. The girl's face and eyes were dry.

"I'm not sorry she's dead. She didn't like me. She only liked her pipe and needles."

"Keisha, what happened to the pictures you had of her?"

The girl looked at the ground again, scuffing her foot on the gravel of the parking lot. Renee just waited.

"I ripped them up and threw them in the incinerator at the apartment before we left."

Renee's breath caught. "W-why did you do that?"

"We were leaving," Keisha said as if the reason were obvious. "I wanted to leave all the bad things there so they didn't follow me to our new house."

The tears came out of nowhere. Renee swiped at them and took the few steps to close the space between her and Keisha. She didn't need Dr. Hendrickson to tell her what that symbolic purging meant. She wrapped her arms around Keisha, who neither flinched nor pulled away this time.

"I love you, Keisha."

"I love you, too, Mom."

"Everything okay?" Trey asked when Renee and Keisha joined them in time to enter Santa's Village.

"It will be."

Renee slipped her hand into his and followed the girls to the first of the Christmas displays.

They oohed and aahed at the decorative and imaginative light displays in the village, then waited in line with Kelly so she could talk to Santa. Kelly skipped forward, anxious to let the jolly old elf know exactly what she wanted for Christmas.

"Don't you want to talk to Santa Claus, Keisha?"

"Santa's for babies," she said and stalked over to poke at a gingerbread house decorated with candy.

"Three steps forward, six steps back," Renee muttered as she watched the girl's retreat.

"What happened at the car?"

"I'll tell you back at the house," Renee said. "Look, it's Kelly's turn."

Both Renee and Trey watched as Kelly had a long and animated conversation with Santa. An elf took her picture and held out a candy cane in an attempt to steer her toward the exit so other kids could have a turn on Santa's lap.

"What is she asking for?"

Trey let his eyes leisurely wander Renee's body before meeting her gaze again. Renee's tongue ran slowly across her lips.

Trey's mouth twitched. "That's what *I* want. She told me she wants a baby sister."

Renee's eyes widened.

He grinned. "We could make that happen for her. If we

get started now, that little sister would be here before next Christmas rolls around."

"Trey, I…" She paused. "Please don't tease me."

"Who said I was teasing?"

The arrival of his giddy daughter, candy cane and piece of paper in hand, put a halt to their talk.

"The elf said I was to give this to you," Kelly said, thrusting the paper at Trey.

He glanced at it. "Price list and pickup time for the picture."

"Santa said I'm going to get everything I want for Christmas!"

Trey glanced at Renee and winked. "Did he, now?"

Kelly nodded and slipped her free hand into Renee's. "Can we go to the village store now?"

"Sure, princess," Trey said.

The store was a kids-only establishment where children under twelve could shop for gifts for their siblings and other family members.

Renee called for Keisha, who filled out their foursome. At the village store, which was kid-size, so most adults couldn't even get through the door, Trey gave each girl a crisp twenty-dollar bill and told them to look out for each other in the store.

"We seem to be a pretty expensive date for you," Renee said as she and Trey settled in an adjacent café area with cups of coffee. Other parents who awaited their kids' return from the shopping trip busily tapped on phones and tablets.

"I like high-maintenance women," he said.

That earned him a jab in the arm, but she laughed. "You got that right, buddy."

"What happened back at the car?"

"She knows about…the jail overdose."

"How'd she find out?"

"A girl from the old neighborhood called and told her."
Renee filled him in on the rest of what had transpired.

"You know," he said, "that's what I wanted to ask you
the night you told me about Keisha's birth mother."

She raised an arched brow in question.

"When I said I had something to ask you, you proceeded
to tell me about Keisha's background. All I wanted to know
at the time was why an eight-year-old had a mobile phone."

"Oh," Renee said, "yeah, that. It's not what most people
think. You know, the whims of an overindulgent parent.
That phone is Keisha's security blanket. She knows that
with it, I'm just a phone call away. And so are the police
if she's ever in need of help. I programmed your number
into it, as well," Renee admitted rather sheepishly. "I hope
you don't mind."

Last week or last month, he might have. But not now
and he told her so.

"I take it she's not supposed to be chatting it up with
old friends in Durham?"

"Hardly. And I'm going to have to address that."

"This child-rearing is tough business," he said.

"Tell me about it."

The girls were pretty quiet on the drive back home.
Instead of high-energy Christmas music, Trey turned on
an old-school love-jam station and kept the volume low.

"Kelly, wake up," Trey said when he pulled into the
driveway.

"I'm not asleep," a small voice said from the backseat.

"All right," he said. "Say good-night and head upstairs
for a bath and bed. I'll be up in a bit."

He disengaged the child locks and then opened the back
door. Kelly climbed out of the truck while Keisha got out
on the opposite side. Without a word, Keisha went to her

and Renee's side door, opened it with a key she produced from her pocket and then slipped inside.

Trey watched her and frowned. When he got around to Renee's door, he opened it and stepped inside of it, trapping her in a claim-staking move.

"What's gotten into them?"

"Long day. An emotional one for Keisha."

Trey put his hands on the roof of the truck. "Christmas is next week. How are you and Keisha going to celebrate?"

"A quiet day at home?" She voiced the statement like a question, as if asking him if he had another option in mind.

"How about we spend it together?"

"What are you asking, Trey?"

His gaze melded with hers. When he lowered his head, Renee rose to meet him. This kiss wasn't like the others. This one was filled with long-bottled passion, with the longing that spoke of two hearts that were destined to beat as one.

"I want you," he murmured.

"I know. But we can't. The girls."

A guttural growl was his only response to the obstacle that he knew they faced. Their living arrangements and their daughters made it almost impossible for them to find private time beyond stolen kisses like…

The wind buffeted the door, and Trey chuckled.

"Mother Nature is trying to give me an alternative to a cold shower."

"We both should get out of the cold."

"We could warm each other up right here."

She tapped his chest. "Kelly is waiting for you. And I think Keisha and I are going to be talking for a while." She swung her legs around. Trey caught her, sliding her down his body so she could feel the proof of his arousal.

"Mmm," she purred.

Renee lifted her arms and wrapped them around his

neck. "Good night, Mr. Calloway," she murmured before gently meeting his lips with her own.

Trey waited at the Navigator's door until Renee was inside her house and the kitchen light flickered off. He took a deep breath, trying to calm his frustrated libido, then closed up the car and headed inside his house.

When he spied both the candy cane crushed into myriad pieces and the photo of Kelly with Santa on the floor at the base of the stairs, he immediately knew something was wrong. She'd been giddy about her time with Santa, so seeing the photo on the floor was troubling.

"Kelly!"

He took the stairs two at a time, calling her name. She wasn't in her bedroom and he rushed to the bathroom. It, too, was empty. There was no water in the tub, no indication that she'd even been in there.

"Kelly!"

Panic rushed through him. How could something have happened to her inside the house?

"Kelly, can you hear me?"

He pushed open the door to her playroom and stopped in his tracks. There sat his little girl on the daybed, her coat still on and clutching one of her dolls. She was crying softly, the tears more heartbreaking than if she were sobbing uncontrollably.

Trey ran to her and scooped her up in his arms. "Baby, what's wrong? Are you hurt? What happened?"

He sank to the floor with her in his arms. He saw no blood, no visible wounds and thanked God for that.

"Kel, princess, tell Daddy what's wrong." The girl sniffled, hiccuped, then started crying in earnest. "Kelly, talk to me, baby, please."

He held her tight, rocking her and trying to calm her

enough so he could find out what had happened in the few minutes she'd been in the house.

When her words finally came, they tore from her in great anguished gasps.

"Keisha...said...there...is...no...Santa...Claus."

Chapter 9

"You did what?" Renee all but screeched. "Keisha, how could you?"

Keisha snatched up a hairbrush from her dresser. "She needed to know the truth."

Her words were cold, almost calculating, as she brushed her hair and reached for a fat plastic roller.

Renee was so angry she was practically vibrating. Keisha's early childhood had been far from idyllic, but that was no excuse for ruining Kelly's.

"Sit down, Keisha."

"I'm doing my hair."

"I said, sit down."

Renee had never, ever raised her voice at Keisha, so the order stunned the both of them. But Renee held her ground. Wide-eyed, Keisha put the brush on the dresser and backed up to her bed, her eyes never leaving Renee's. She sat and Renee stood, arms crossed.

"What would possess you to do something so mean-spirited and hurtful? Why did you deliberately ruin Christmas for Kelly?"

"I told her the truth," Keisha said, a defensive and combative tone in her voice that forced Renee to cock her head at her in warning. Keisha looked at the floor then said, "We were in that store and she kept going on and on about how Santa was gonna bring her this and that because she'd been a good girl all year. But there's no such thing as a man in a red suit who flies around and delivers gifts to kids he doesn't even know."

"Keisha, because you don't believe in Santa is no reason to steal that wonder and joy from someone else. Kelly is younger than you are. She looks up to you. You had no right and no authority to do what you did."

"I didn't steal anything from her."

Renee came over and sat next to Keisha, taking the girl's hands in hers. She needed to explain this in a way that would be a lesson. She also wondered how much of this behavior was Keisha's way of coping with her birth mother's death. A passive-aggressive lashing out at Kelly as a substitute for the adults who hadn't told her a truth *she* needed to know.

"What you took from Kelly, Keisha, is a gift that you never received because your...because Janice was so focused on her own issues that she didn't take care of you the way a mom should take care of a little girl. I'm so sorry that you had to live the way you did, but I'm also glad for it."

Keisha reared back. "Why?"

"Because I would have missed out on the gift of having you in my life."

"That's not a gift. A gift is a present that's all wrapped up."

Renee nodded. "That's one kind. But there are also intangible gifts, the ones you can't touch or see but ones that you feel in here," she said, lifting Keisha's hand to her heart. "For little kids, that's what Santa Claus is. They believe in him in their hearts."

"I can tell her I didn't mean it."

Renee's mobile phone rang then. She pulled it from

her jacket pocket, glanced at the display and tucked it away after turning off the ringer. *Trey.* It didn't take much thought to know why he was calling.

"The thing about this particular gift is that once it's out of the bag, there's no taking it back, Keisha. You just have to go forward. But I think an apology to Kelly and to Mr. Calloway is in order as a first step."

Keisha sighed. "Does this mean I'm not getting anything for Christmas?"

Admittedly, the thought had crossed Renee's mind, but that wasn't a solution. "Why don't you start with that apology? We'll let Christmas take care of itself."

Trey didn't know who was more devastated by Keisha's revelation: Kelly or himself.

He had so been looking forward to this Christmas. He'd known, of course, that the Santa gig would be up sooner or later. He'd counted on at least one more year of the innocence of youth, the delight and wonder in Kelly's eyes on Christmas morning.

Instead, tonight he'd talked to her about the spirit of Christmas, of giving to others while enjoying the beauty of the season, like all the light displays and the music. He'd gotten her settled in bed with her favorite dolls and bent to kiss her. Her final soft question nearly broke his heart.

"Daddy, does this mean I'm not going to get any toys even though I was good this year?"

He'd assured her that there would be plenty of gifts and toys under the tree. He'd stayed at her bedside until she'd fallen asleep.

Then he called Renee. Twice.

After both calls went to voice mail, he was of a mind to head next door for a few choice words with Renee about Keisha. When he heard a soft knocking at his side door, he knew who it was. He stalked to the kitchen and yanked the door open.

"What the hell, Renee!"

The rest of his frustrated tirade died on his lips when he saw Keisha standing there, looking as if she were about to face a firing squad, and Renee standing two steps behind her.

"Mr. Calloway, I'm sorry about what I said to Kelly. And I'm sorry I ruined Christmas."

Trey let out a deep breath. In the face of her contrition, all of the angst and anger he'd been feeling dissipated like the breath expelled from his body.

He stepped back. "Come inside out of the cold." He motioned to them with his hand.

Keisha shuffled inside followed by Renee, who mouthed "I'm so sorry" as she passed by him.

Keisha jammed her hands into the pockets of her jacket. "Is Kelly still up?"

"She's already asleep."

"Oh." Keisha glanced at Renee as if for direction in this uncharted territory.

"She was pretty upset, Keisha," Trey said.

"So was Mom," the eight-year-old said, sounding defeated.

"Since Kelly is asleep, you can head back to the house, Keisha. I'm going to talk to Mr. Calloway for a few minutes," Renee said. "I expect to see you in bed when I get back."

"Yes, ma'am."

Keisha then looked at Trey and he recognized the telltale signs on her face. She was trying not to cry.

"I didn't mean to mess things up. Really," she said, her lip quivering. "I—I don't want you to hate me forever."

He heard Renee gasp and knew that whatever apology

may have been coerced out of Keisha, this one was real...
and heartrending.

"Keisha, I don't hate you now or ever. I was just disappointed."

Her face crumpled, and for the second time that night,
Trey found himself hugging a little girl close as she cried.

"We make quite the pair," Renee said a little while later
in Trey's kitchen.

He ran a hand over his face. "The joys of parenting.
Kelly asked me if no Santa meant she wasn't going to get
any toys for Christmas."

"Keisha wondered if her stunt meant Christmas was
canceled at our place. I truly wanted to say, 'Yes,' but with
everything else going on with her, that punishment seemed
extreme."

"You know what I'd like to do for Christmas?"

"What?"

His gaze raked her body and then he reached for her.

Renee swatted his hands away. "Good night, Trey."

"No compensation for the aggrieved party?"

"I'm not listening to you," she said as she opened the
door and headed across to her own house.

Christmas morning dawned cold and clear. Trey and
Kelly were late for breakfast.

"Kelly, come on."

"I'm just putting another bow on this package. I want
it to be perfect."

Trey just shook his head. Yesterday, it had taken the
better part of an hour for Kelly to perfectly wrap her gifts
for Aunt Henrietta and Uncle Carlton. This one, for Renee,
had enough bows and stickers on it to wrap six or seven
gifts. But it was Christmas. His daughter was healthy and
thriving. He was contemplating a new executive position

at work. The great Santa debacle had blown over, and he had a gift for his next-door neighbor that he hoped would be received in the spirit it was to be given.

"I'm leaving, Kelly."

"I'm ready now," she said, appearing from the dining room, which had been converted into her gift-wrapping craft center.

She had two packages in hand, one small and the other medium-size.

It didn't take them long to reach their destination for Christmas-morning breakfast. All they had to do was walk across their driveway to the house next door.

Renee's house had been transformed since the last time he'd been there—the night he'd picked her up for their drive to Raleigh, the evening things had changed for them. Today, it was filled with the scent of fresh-cut evergreens in sprigs and swags and something with cinnamon that was baking in the oven.

"It's so pretty," Kelly said of the holiday decorations. "Can we open presents now?"

"We're going to eat first, Kel," Trey said, smiling down at his daughter.

The plan was to have breakfast and exchange gifts here. And later in the day, the four of them would go to Aunt Henrietta and Uncle Carlton's for a big family dinner. Renee had initially objected to that, saying she didn't want to impose on their family time. Trey had just laughed. "Only if you consider half the neighborhood and all of their employees family. It's more of a giant open house with a never-ending buffet," he had told her.

A no-pressure meet-the-family gathering would be ideal, they'd ultimately decided.

Kelly and Keisha managed to eat about three forkfuls of breakfast casserole and a nibble of cinnamon roll before declaring they were both too full to manage any more.

Trey looked at Renee and they exchanged a humor-filled glance.

"Go ahead," Renee said.

The girls dashed from the table and straight to the living room, where a tree was decorated with handmade ornaments and popcorn garlands.

"Ooh," Kelly exclaimed, kneeling to get a better look at Keisha's Christmas haul. "You got a lot of stuff."

"Mom said Santa Claus must have decided that I was off punishment."

Kelly looked at Keisha for a moment, and then both girls fell over giggling together.

"Look at this," Keisha said, pulling out a box with a large doll in it. "I can't believe I got this for Christmas. She's beautiful."

From the doorway, Trey and Renee watched the girls. Renee stood in front of him, his arms around her waist.

"Thank you," she said.

"For what? You haven't gotten your present yet."

"Yes, I did," Renee said.

He leaned around her shoulder and kissed her.

"All of that," Renee said, nodding toward the Christmas tree, where Keisha was showing Kelly a couple of the new outfits she'd gotten for Christmas.

She felt him stiffen behind her, wary now.

"I know, Trey."

"You know what?"

She turned in his arms, tugged him back toward the table, and they sat. "I know you were the Angel Tree benefactor."

"What makes you...?"

"You can deny it all you want," she said. "But I know the truth. Because Keisha came out of CPS, she's eligible for some of the programs they offer. Among them is the Angel Tree project at Christmas. Her information got transferred here from Durham in time to be able to participate in the program. When I picked up the bags last week at a local church, one of the ladies told me something she wasn't supposed to."

"What's that?" he asked.

"She pulled me aside and told me Keisha was picked by a Calloway. And that family is incredibly generous."

He didn't deny it.

"Kelly plucked that tag off the tree about six weeks ago when my aunt decided Angel Tree would be a family project this year. She liked that the girl's first name started with a *K* like hers. I didn't put it together until the day we went shopping. You're not angry, are you?"

"'Angry'? How could I be angry?"

"Maybe it was the universe's way of saying 'merry Christmas' and 'don't mess this up.'"

"Mess what up?" Renee asked.

"Us," he said. "I know I can be a tad overprotective at times."

"Just a tad?"

He continued as if her smart-aleck interruption hadn't bothered him. "And, as you know, I tend to jump to conclusions about some things."

Renee smirked.

Trey laughed then. "Do you want this Christmas present or not?"

"It depends," she said with a grin. "Are you getting ready to get all mushy on me?"

"Yes."

"Then by all means, proceed," she said.

He rose and held his hand out to her. She placed her hands in his and he led her back to the door where they could see Kelly and Keisha opening the presents they'd made for each other.

"This is what I want for Christmas," he said. "Us. As a family."

Renee whipped around. "Trey, I'm not sure I'm...we're ready for a..."

He stayed her words with a finger at her lips. "This is about potential and overcoming obstacles."

She gave him a curious look. "Is this a proposal that just got derailed?"

"No derailments here," he said, pulling from his pocket a small velvet box. "Kelly and I have been puttering along for a while now, getting by the best way we knew how. I didn't know anything was missing from my life, from our lives, until you and Keisha entered it."

He opened the box and lifted from it a heart-shaped locket. He opened it and inside were photos of Trey and Kelly on one side and Renee and Keisha on the other.

"Will you explore with me where this could lead?"

Renee nodded. He slipped the thin gold chain around her neck and fastened the clasp. His fingers lingered at her neck, caressing her tender skin. "Merry Christmas, Renee."

"Merry Christmas, Trey," she said.

And then he kissed her.

Keisha and Kelly looked up in time to see the embrace.

"Ewww. There they go again!"

"That's right," Trey said, against Renee's mouth. "Expect to see a lot more of it."

* * * * *

The last two
stories in the
Love in the Limelight
series, where four
unstoppable women
find fame, fortune and
ultimately…true love

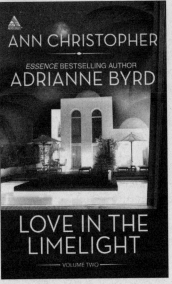

LOVE IN THE LIMELIGHT
— VOLUME TWO —

ANN CHRISTOPHER
&
ADRIANNE BYRD

In *Seduced on the Red Carpet*, supermodel Livia Blake is living a glamorous life…but when she meets sexy single father Hunter Chambers, she is tempted with desire and a life that she has never known.

In *Lovers Premiere*, Sofia Wellesley must cope as Limelight Entertainment prepares to merge with their biggest rival. Which means dealing with her worst enemy, Ram Jordan. So why is her traitorous heart clamoring for the man she hates most in the world?

Available November 2014 wherever books are sold!

www.Harlequin.com

KPLIM21641114

The newest
sensual story in
*The Boudreaux
Family* saga!

TWELVE
Days of
PLEASURE

DEBORAH
FLETCHER
MELLO

When Vanessa Harrison witnesses a crime, sexy FBI agent Kendrick
Boudreaux whisks her away to safety in the Caribbean. In his
protective arms, desire ignites, and soon they're giving in to their
deepest passions. He's determined to turn their days of pleasure into
a lifetime of bliss. Until a shocking revelation threatens their future
together, forcing Kendrick to choose between his career and the
woman he has come to cherish.

THE BOUDREAUX FAMILY

●●

H HARLEQUIN®
™ www.Harlequin.com

*Available November 2014
wherever books are sold!*

KPDFM3771114

Is their long-ago
love worth the risk?

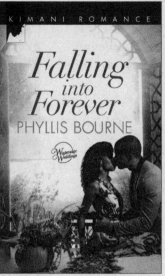

Falling
into
Forever

PHYLLIS
BOURNE

Isaiah Jacobs is back in Wintersage to care for his ailing father.
And when he and Sandra Woolcott meet after years apart, it's all
the former high school sweethearts can do to resist falling for each
other all over again. But they've built such different lives and so many
years have passed. Can they bury the pain of the past and build a
promising future together?